FRACTURED
The Deep in Your Veins Series

Suzanne Wright

The characters and events portrayed in this book are fictitious.
Any similarity to real persons, living or dead, is coincidental and
not intended by the author.

Copyright © 2015 Suzanne Wright

All rights reserved. This book or any portion thereof
may not be reproduced or used in any manner whatsoever
without the express written permission of the publisher
except for the use of brief quotations in a book review.

ISBN-13: 978-1532892066
ISBN-10: 1532892063

For H & S – I had so much going on while writing this book, but you forced me to take the breaks I desperately needed so I didn't stress myself out. Thanks so much for that.

SUZANNE WRIGHT

CHAPTER ONE

(Imani)

Every avid reader knew you didn't fuck with a girl's Kindle. You just didn't. So when the bitch in front of me slammed my purse on the floor and I heard my precious baby crack, things were destined to go to shit.

Initially, I'd ignored Marla's efforts to goad me into a bar fight. If she'd convinced herself that a certain male vampire rejected her because of me, it was her issue to deal with. Besides, it was easy to dismiss someone who clearly had such a low IQ that it would be surprising if she could pass a blood test.

I mean seriously, who would confront a member of the Grand High Vampires' legion—especially when that member was sitting with the other six members of her squad? And *especially* when many others in the bar were part of the legion? It just wasn't done.

Pissed she wasn't getting a reaction, Marla had grabbed my purse and slung it in a huff. As a Pagori vampire, she had some serious strength. The impact had broken my baby, which was why everyone at my table slowly rose to their feet.

"You need to go," Paige hissed at Marla and her nervous-looking cronies. My BFF wasn't easily riled, but if someone pushed her too far…well, things tended to end badly. That was most likely why Cassie and Alora edged closer to her, ready to hold her back.

Our behaviour reflected on the entire legion. Marla wasn't a threat to vampirekind, just a dumb shop assistant who was plagued by jealousy issues and needed her roots done *badly*.

As such, despite that I wanted to lunge at Marla, I dug deep for calm. But as I looked down at my purse and recalled the telling crack, anger pumped through every vein and my fangs descended. That little device had got me through some crappy times; given me the escape I occasionally needed. I'd taken it with me pretty much everywhere; I admittedly had an unhealthy attachment to it. Now it was in pieces, thanks to Marla, and I wasn't good with that. Not at all.

It just went to prove that I was right and you couldn't trust people with perfect teeth.

Marla's eyes narrowed. "What did you say to Butch to turn him against me? He was pretty welcoming last night. Now he's giving me the cold shoulder."

Oh it was like she *wanted* me to hurt her. Butch might not be mine, but I sure didn't like anybody thinking he could be theirs. Since becoming a member of the legion, I'd learned a lot of ways to kill a person. Those ways were swirling around my head, tempting me to act on the fury riding me.

It was clear that my girls were having similar thoughts, especially since Maya's jaguar claws had sliced out, Jude had whipped out her knife, and Ava was eyeing Marla with lethal precision. One tiny signal from me would have them all leaping at these bitches.

"You told him about what happened at the store, didn't you?" continued Marla.

She was referring to when she had accidentally-on-purpose knocked my tub of milk on the floor, causing it to burst open and soak my jeans.

"Yeah, you told him to turn him against me. The legion sticks together, right?" she mocked.

"I said, *you need to go*," repeated Paige, her green eyes blazing.

Marla put a hand on her hip. "Yeah? Well, I wasn't talking to *you*. I was talking to *her*."

One of Marla's cronies grabbed her shoulder. "Come on, let's just leave."

Marla shrugged her off and arched a thinly plucked brow at me. "Nothing to say?"

I sighed. "Not really. I like intelligent conversation."

She smirked, cocky. "You're not denying what I said because it's true."

"You mean that I turned Butch against you? That's your own paranoia at work. You know he's a one-night stand kind of guy. If he rejected you, it has nothing to do with me."

"I don't believe you. Shall I tell you what I do believe? That the reason he has one-night stands is that you quickly turn him against any female he touches. Yeah, *that's* what I believe."

"Well, everyone should believe in something."

"Do you think if you get rid of all the competition, he'll go back to you?" Marla snickered. "How pathetic."

Paige shook her head. "No, blaming Imani is pathetic. I mean, taking into account your peroxide hair, pitch-black roots, blotchy fake tan, and whiny little voice, it shouldn't be a shock that he turned you down."

Marla gasped in horror and slung her drink all over *my BFF*.

Oh the hell no.

I sucker punched her—no warning, no hesitation. Marla's head snapped to the side, her knees buckled, and she lost consciousness before she even hit the floor. Gasps came from the little group at her back. As one, they lunged for me. So my squad and I lunged for them.

It was amazing how quickly a bar fight could escalate. None of us used our vampiric gifts. No, this was a true catfight. There was scratching. Punching. Kicking. Screeching. Slapping. Hair-pulling. And dress-shredding.

All the while, male vampires surrounded us, cheering 'Fight! Fight! Fight! Fight!'

It was a great outlet for my anger and actually kind of fun…until my earring was ripped out. *Motherfucker.* Snarling, I fisted my hand in the bitch's hair and—

A strong arm curled around my waist and started heaving me away. I knew who it was, because I'd know that masculine scent of dark spices and sandalwood anywhere.

"Put me down, Butch!"

He didn't, but I kept a firm grip on the long dark hair in my hands—I wasn't letting go of my prize any time soon. My girls didn't look any more willing to end the fight than I was, which was why it took the combined efforts of the Grand High Pair's personal squad to part us all.

Still, I managed to take a chunk of dark hair with me. Smirking, I showed it to the heifer. She waved a hand my way, and it was like something slammed into my head, *through* my skull...and then I was seriously freaking tired.

"Fuck," cursed Butch.

Then it all went dark.

CHAPTER TWO

(Imani)

I'd woken up in this bed before. Several times before, in fact. But this time, I wasn't naked. That was the only reason I wasn't silently cursing myself.

I slowly turned my head. And there he was. Sharp-boned face. Five o'clock shadow. Sleep-tussled bronze hair. Solid chest and delicious abs. I didn't need to look beneath the covers to know the rest of Robert 'Butch' Richardson was just as spectacularly masculine. Asleep, he looked no more peaceful than he did while awake. There was something untamed about him. A buzz of raw energy seemed to always hum beneath his skin.

The first night we'd slept together had been the night of Ava and Salem's Binding ceremony a year ago; a one-night stand that had turned into a month of several wild and unforgettable one-night stands. I'd hoped it would turn into something more, but Butch had made it clear—though not in an asshole way—that he didn't do 'more.' So I'd cut my losses. I wanted something that had possibilities; that had the potential to go somewhere. Anything with Butch was a dead end.

It wasn't that he had commitment issues. He just didn't connect with people. Furthermore, he didn't *want* to connect with people. Despite having known him for over a year, I didn't *know* him at all. He never revealed anything personal. Never shared anything about his past. Never confided his feelings or thoughts. He was literally a closed book.

I didn't judge him for it. It wasn't wrong that he didn't want to connect with others or that he didn't do 'more.' It just meant he couldn't give me what I wanted. That didn't mean it was easy to walk away. No. But I'd done it. I'd moved on. I'd even found someone else—a human I'd dated right up until a month ago.

Dean was nothing like Butch. He was relaxing, fun, and safe—or, at least, he had been until he betrayed me. Butch was far from a relaxing presence. He had a way of unnerving people. And he definitely wasn't 'safe.' Many called him sociopathic and a natural born killer.

Sam—the female half of the Grand High Pair—had once remarked, *'I can't help but be fascinated by how Butch can stand there plotting someone's death while looking cool and calm, like we're strolling in the park.'*

It was true. Butch's air of downright coolness went to a whole new level. But I liked that about him. I liked his air of self-assuredness. Liked how at ease he was in his own skin. Liked how daring and determined he could be. Hell, I just plain liked him.

I wasn't the only one.

Many females flocked around him. I loathed them all on principle, especially Marla, the Kindle-killer. Butch wasn't a slut, but he was no choir boy either. Honestly, I'd probably find him boring if he was.

Despite how much I liked him, I'd walked out eleven months ago, swearing to myself that I wouldn't return. Yet, here I was again in his bed. Only, I hadn't made my own way here.

I recalled the catfight, recalled struggling against Butch's grip and then…suddenly I was tired. Obviously the female's vampiric gift had been to induce sleep.

It wasn't often that there was trouble here at The Hollow, which was a gated community surrounded by a tropical rainforest and situated on an off-the-map Caribbean island. There were cafés, stores, bars, a nightclub, and a bowling alley—all of which were centered round a man-made beach. The Hollow was also the home of the Grand High Vampires, Sam Parker and Jared Michaels—a mated couple that nobody with an ounce of intelligence dared to fuck with.

They had a legion of over one hundred male vampires. Sam was forming an all-female squad of ten, and she had offered me a place. I'd snapped up the offer, and I hadn't once regretted it. Don't get me wrong, it wasn't an easy position. The training was rigorous and exhausting. Even though our squad wasn't yet fully formed, we were sent on risky assignments; saw things that would haunt the hardest hearts. But in the legion, I felt something I'd never felt before: a sense of belonging. It was cheesy, granted, but it was true.

I was the youngest of five in a family of academics. Two were lawyers, one was a CEO of his own company, and the other was a surgeon. Me? I liked to read and sketch. That was pretty much it. I wasn't academically minded. I'd never had great aspirations or any drive to do something with my life. They'd never understood that; never understood me.

As such, although they had involved me in family events, I'd always felt like an outsider—my nose pressed to the window, watching this perfect little family but never being part of it. Thanksgiving had been a nightmare; a day of them making passive aggressive comments that suggested I was lazy, directionless, and a dreamer. Then when I'd speak up and tell them to stop, they would say I was too sensitive and needed to learn to take a joke.

I'd just never fit. And they'd never let me forget it.

Here, I fit. Here, it was okay to be different. Here, we were *all* different. Each and every one of us had freaky preternatural quirks and gifts.

All three vampire breeds were born with an individual gift. Pagoris, like Butch, were the most powerful; known for their aggressiveness, their enhanced speed and strength, and their potent bloodlust. They also had a red tint to their irises that glowed when they were thirsty, angry, or horny.

Keja eyes had the same quirk, only the tint to their irises was amber rather than red. My breed also had hypnotic beauty, allowing us to lure in our prey very easily—whether they be vampire or human. We were also the only breed that possessed fangs.

Sventés were often considered human-like because their bloodlust wasn't strong, they only had notable agility to boast of, their irises were completely normal, and their vampiric gifts tended to be only defensive. Personally, I didn't think being 'tame' made them weak. To me, it was their strength. It allowed them to blend in easily with their prey without losing control.

It was safe to say I'd lost control last night when—

Butch's eyes opened, and his watchful brooding gaze took me in. I'd heard a lot of people describe his eyes as 'eerie' because they were so dark. I didn't think so. Oh, they could sure look scary when he was facing down an enemy. Other times, like now, they could be so languid and slumberous that my insides melted.

I swallowed. "Why did you bring me here?"

"I wanted you here." The response was almost child-like in its simplicity. It was also rather typical of him. If he wanted to do something, he did it. If he wanted something, he went after it. And he made no excuses.

"That heifer sent me to dreamland, huh?"

"I was concentrating so hard on keeping hold of you that I didn't get my shield around you in time." Butch was a Negator; he could negate or deflect any power directed at him. As part of his gift, he could form a defensive shield.

Me? I had the rare ability to sever blood-bonds. There were two types of blood-blonds: the kind formed between fully mated vampires, and the kind that formed between a person and the vampire who created them. I'd long ago severed the bond between me and my Sire, and for very good reasons.

"Well…" I sat upright, smoothed out my shredded top and adjusted the thin straps. At least my wounds had healed. "I'd better go. We have a meeting soon." Both our squads met with Sam and Jared most evenings.

I went to get up, but his hand landed on my thigh. A hand I knew was seriously talented. Even with my pants separating his skin from mine, it made something low in my stomach clench.

"Starting a bar fight…I wouldn't have expected that of you."

I frowned. "I didn't start it."

"You threw the first punch. I saw you."

He was watching me?

"What did she say to you?" Something dark and dangerous moved behind his eyes.

I forced a dismissive shrug. "Not much."

"Bullshit." He braced himself on one elbow. "You don't start fights. You don't punch people for no reason. And you don't go bat-shit for the fun of it."

"Maybe I do. You don't know me."

His gaze raked over me, lingering a little on my cleavage. "Oh, I know you."

"In the biblical sense," I allowed.

"I know plenty of things about you. I know you disappear into a book every time you're stressed out. I know your biggest fear is again being used to hurt people with your gift—so much that you even have nightmares about it. I know you have an aversion to toads, and you can't lie for shit."

I narrowed my eyes. That was the thing about him. He paid attention. Was perceptive on a level I wouldn't have thought possible. And I could *so* lie, thank you very much.

His eyes dropped to my throat. "And I know you taste like fucking heaven. Everywhere." He skimmed his nose under my jaw, inhaling. Then, in under the time it took to blink, he'd slipped from the bed and pulled on some jeans. It was a struggle to tear my eyes away from his bare, well-defined chest. The guy was deliciously ripped. Moreover, he oozed a dark, raw sex appeal that commanded attention.

"I have coffee-flavoured NSTs. You want one?" He was referring to Nutritive Supplemental Tonics that contained blood and vitamins. The previous ruler, Antonio, had developed them. They quickly got to work on the thirst and they gave a good boost, but only pure blood quenched the thirst. "Or I can fix you something to eat, if you want," offered Butch.

I pursed my lips, eyeing him as I slid into my shoes. "You're being weird." I mean, it wasn't like him to be…courteous. In general, Butch never did anything he didn't *have* to do. Interfering in the bar fight, bringing me here, offering to make me breakfast—none of those things were necessary. The times I'd woken here before, he'd been distant, sending me an 'it was just sex' message. "Is this your way of trying to apologise for what you did last week?"

"What should I be apologising for?" He wasn't being flippant. He seemed genuinely confused.

"Chasing away the guy I was dancing with." He'd stalked right over to us in the club, caused a scene—

"You should be thanking me for that."

I picked up my purse and followed him into the kitchen. "*Thanking* you?"

"You barely even knew the guy," he said, pulling two NSTs out of the fridge. "But you were hurting. Something was bothering you, and you wanted to forget"—I'd wanted to forget there was a blonde trying to rub herself all over Butch at the other side of the club— "so you were going to go home with that asshole. You would have regretted it at dawn."

Actually, he was probably right.

He pointed an NST at me. "If you wanted to be fucked that badly, Imani, you should have come to me." He slammed one bottle on the breakfast bar, twisted the cap off his own, and drained the bottle—his dark gaze never leaving mine.

"Did you really just say that?"

Chucking the empty bottle in the trash, he braced his hands on the breakfast bar. "I did. And here's the thing: I'm done waiting for you."

I tensed, confused by his words and stunned by the raw need that momentarily blazed in his eyes. I hadn't seen that look in a long time. It took a few seconds before I could speak. All that came out was, "What?"

"I had to watch you with that human for seven months. Seven. Long. Fucking. Months. The only thing that stopped me from hurting him was that he made you happy. But then he didn't, and now he's gone. I decided to give you a month to get your head straight before I made a move. That time is now up."

I shook my head. "I told you I was done with being a bed-buddy. I want—"

"More. A relationship. The problem is I'm not good for people. I don't know how to make another person happy. That was why I let you go. And I've regretted it ever fucking since. I didn't think I'd get another chance with you. But I have, and I'm taking it. You want a relationship? Fine. But I won't be easy to deal with, Imani. Know that straight up. I'm aggressive and selfish, not to mention dangerously fucking possessive when it comes to you."

He had to be kidding…but I knew he wasn't. Butch was a direct person. He didn't play games. "You're serious, aren't you?"

"Wouldn't say it if I wasn't." He opened my NST and slid it to me. "Drink."

Feeling a little dazed, I picked up the bottle. "Where is all this coming from?" It felt seriously surreal. "You've never acted even *remotely* possessive." Protective, sure, but that was different.

"Why do you think I almost snapped Leo's spine?"

Leo was a member of the legion who I'd liked right up until he grabbed my ass and mentioned how much he'd like to fuck it. "It was *you* that beat the shit out of him?"

"He touched what wasn't his to touch."

I could only gape. This whole conversation was just…I mean…what the fuck? It had totally blindsided me. Seemed too bizarre to be true. I didn't know how to process it, and I didn't know how to feel about it.

He watched my throat work as I drank the NST. "Tell me what you're thinking."

"I'm thinking I need to go."

His hand shot out and grabbed my wrist. "You know what I like about you, Imani? I don't have to play guessing games with you. You let it all hang out. If you're pissed, you show it. If you're happy, you show it. If you've got something you want to say, you just say it. Right now, you're closing down on me. Tell me what you're thinking."

I threw my empty bottle in the trash. "I find all this hard to believe."

"You think I'm lying to you?"

I shrugged. "My mom always said that guys are like commercials—you can't trust a single word they say."

"I'm not lying, Imani."

"Can you blame me for being doubtful? You made it clear eleven months ago that you didn't want anything more than…"

"You beneath me," he finished. "Back then, I didn't. Things have changed."

"What does that mean exactly?"

"It means that I want everything you are."

(Butch)

I could see that my answer took her off-guard. It also spooked her. That was a smart reaction. Because I wouldn't accept anything less than everything. And because, contrary to what little Imani Prince liked to think, I wasn't a good guy. I was close to the sociopath that I'd long ago been branded. Yes, I was well aware of what people said about me. I didn't care; that would require energy I could use on something else.

I'd been protective of her since the second she was brought to The Hollow. Limbs tight to her body and her hand at her throat, the pretty little doe-eyed female had regarded my entire squad with a wary gaze. She'd done her best to look calm and unafraid so that Paige would agree to leave her side and help the injured vampires around us. But it had been blindingly clear that Imani expected one of the squad to pounce on her.

Then she'd looked right up at me. Even as a human, people were wary of me. *'It's something about your eyes,'* so many had said. I'd heard my eyes be described as eerie, dead, and empty. I used to spook the shit out of my teachers as a kid, which had been pretty entertaining.

Yet, Imani's first words to me had been: *'Your eyes are really dark. I have total eye colour envy right now.'* And I'd sworn I wouldn't let a damn thing happen to this female who looked at me with absolutely no fear. She was the only person who seemed to think I was normal. Or maybe she just didn't care that I wasn't.

I'd watched her closely, looked out for her on assignments. And I'd eventually acted on the unrelenting urge to take and claim; to live out the fantasy of her little body wrapped around me while I pounded in and out of her. She was all wicked curves and smooth muscle, and there wasn't a single inch of her that I hadn't tasted.

There was something transfixing about her; in the way she carried herself with confidence and poise. In some ways, she made me think of a cat. She was graceful. Curious. Independent. So easy-going she often came across as aloof to those who didn't know her. Not to mention that she could fall asleep just about anywhere. And then there was that condescending look she'd mastered. Perversely, when she jutted her chin and gave me that haughty attitude, I wanted nothing more than to bend her over and fuck her raw.

What appealed to me most about her was the quiet strength that stamped her as a survivor. Not just a survivor, a fighter.

She thought I didn't know her. She was wrong. I'd watched her grow and toughen since joining the legion. I'd seen her at her weakest, seen her at her strongest, and seen her at her most dangerous. I both admired and respected Imani Prince.

I'd spent the entire time we'd been sleeping together telling myself I didn't want more. I'd spent the time since then realising that I did. I just didn't have much to give her. But I couldn't stay away. She was an addiction I couldn't shake. A dangerous obsession that wouldn't fade. She was...important.

"Everything I am?" she echoed.

Slowly rounding the breakfast bar, I stalked toward her. Tensing slightly, she turned to face me—head up, back straight, and eyes boldly on mine. So fucking strong. I brushed my thumb over her pulse. "I've missed the taste of you." Sweet and tangy. "Missed being *in* you."

Missed her blood flowing into my mouth while her body tightened around my cock.

"Butch—"

"I'll have that again. Because when I say everything you are, I mean exactly that. Your blood, your mind, your body, your soul—everything." I buried my hand in her silky long hair; it was just a few shades darker than her hazelnut brown eyes. It always smelled like vanilla, and it perfectly complemented her unique scent of strawberries and cream—a scent that seemed to have embedded itself in my lungs, just as her taste seemed embedded on my tongue.

When I'd watched her walk out of my apartment the last time we were together, knowing that she'd never be back, it had felt like a punch to the solar plexus. Back then, I hadn't understood why it hurt. Not until I saw her with Dean.

The jealousy hadn't come as a surprise, considering the possessiveness that I hadn't been able to shake off. But the pain…I hadn't expected that. My stomach had rolled whenever I saw them together. Each time she'd smiled up at him or laughed at something he'd said, an ache built in my chest. That ache had gotten worse the longer they were together.

So many times I'd come close to punching the prick—especially when he shot me one of those smug smirks. He'd seen the way I looked at her, and he'd known he had what I wanted most. And he'd loved that. Got a kick out of it.

The only thing that had held me back was that he was good to Imani. He'd treated her well, and he'd seemed to care for her. That was why his betrayal had come as such a shock to everyone. But some people were just weak against temptation, and some took what they had for granted. Maybe that was why Dean had fucked her over. I didn't know.

The first thing I'd done was beat him to a pulp for hurting her.

The second thing I'd done was decide that I'd somehow get her back. This time, I wouldn't let her go. I'd take this second chance with her, and I'd make it work. Nothing would get in my way—not Imani's doubts, not my issues with relationships, and definitely not Dean.

"Is the prick trying to win you back?" I rumbled.

"He has a name, you know."

"Don't care. He had what I craved every fucking day and night. That makes him a prick."

Flushing, she briefly averted her gaze. "The constant cravings…They're not real. It's the Keja allure that makes you feel that way—it keeps our prey coming back again and again. It's probably what caused your jealousy and possessiveness too."

I gave a slow shake of the head. There were plenty of her breed around The Hollow; I'd learned to withstand the Keja allure a long time ago. "If that was the case…" I put her hand over my cock. It was so painfully hard, I could hammer nails with it. "This would happen every time I was around Paige, too."

Lips flattening, Imani made a feral noise in the back of her throat. She snatched her hand free and folded her arms over her chest.

"If he does contact you, be sure to tell him how things are with you and me."

She sighed, looking sad and weary all of a sudden. "You don't want a relationship, Butch. Not really. If you feel possessive and jealous, it's because of the Keja allure. The cravings will fade, they always do."

Speaking softly, I smoothed her hair between my fingers. "Ah, baby, you're not listening to me. I fucked up before. I let you go. That's not happening again. Get used to it. Learn to like it. We're gonna do 'more,' and we're gonna make it work." There was no other acceptable option for me.

Her spine snapped straight and her chin lifted at the command in my tone. I should have remembered she lost her easy-going temperament when anyone pushed her.

"Is that so?" She backed away, irises flaring slightly. "It's been almost a year, Butch. You didn't want me. Not badly enough to try a relationship. I wasn't mad at you for that. I don't think it's fair to be upset with someone for what they do or don't feel. So I accepted it. I wasn't a bitch to you. I didn't let any of it bleed over onto our working relationship."

No, she hadn't. It was something that I'd appreciated.

"I accepted that I wasn't enough for you that you'd push yourself out of your comfort zone, and I moved on. *Moved on*, Butch. You can't come to me now and expect me to just fall right in line because *you've* decided that, hey, you've changed your mind."

"I can. And I just did. As for you not being enough for me? That's total shit, Imani. I never once thought that. I never once felt that way."

"Yet, you weren't prepared to try a relationship until another guy entered the picture. How typical."

I closed the distance between us. "Typical? Typical would have been for me to try and come between you out of jealousy and because I'm *that* fucking selfish. Don't think I didn't consider it. I did. But I have too much respect for you to fuck with your head like that."

"*This* is fucking with my head."

Because she was too shocked to process it, I realised. I probably should have anticipated that. Forcing myself to take a step back, I said, "If you need some time to wrap your head around everything I've said and accept what I want from you, take it. Three nights, baby." That was the most I could give her. "Three nights. Then I'm coming for you, and we'll continue this conversation and lay everything out. But don't make the mistake of thinking those three nights include freedom. You're mine. That's the way it is, and that's the way it's gonna stay."

CHAPTER THREE

(Imani)

Meetings always took place in the main building of the gated community. It was a huge mansion that had once been solely Antonio's home. Although he'd offered it to Sam and Jared when he stepped down from his position, the pair declined. In their minds, it was too much Antonio's home. They felt it wouldn't feel right to ask him to move.

As such, Antonio built them a beach house and divided the mansion into two sections. Half was his 'living quarters', which he shared with his mate. The other half was work space for Sam and Jared, including an office and several conference rooms. Antonio's opinion was that their space should be in the centre of the community to place significance on their role and status.

Entering the building, I passed Sam and Jared's office. Their personal assistant, Fletcher, paused in his typing and peered at me over his spectacles. "You're a broth of emotions this evening." Like Sam, the Brit had a strong London accent. He was also an Empath. "Frustrated. Anxious. A little dazed."

Well, yeah. Feeling exposed, I fought a blush. "Good evening to you too," I said, pressing the number for the elevator.

"Does this have anything to do with Dean? I hope not. You can do better."

FRACTURED

I'd figured that out when I heard he'd let another vampire drink from him. Biting was very intimate for my kind. His act was a form of cheating. And Dean knew it. "How's Norm?" I asked, referring to Fletcher's adorable boyfriend.

"Annoyed and upset that you missed two movie nights in a row. But he'll forgive you, because he loves you."

I smiled, stepping into the empty elevator. "See you later."

The conference room was only half-full when I entered. Noticing that Butch wasn't yet present, I greeted everyone before taking the seat between Paige and Denny, who had the cutest baby face.

I chatted with the people around me, but my mind was on Butch. I was still having trouble accepting the things he'd said. It all still seemed much too surreal. It had to be the Keja allure messing with his mind and playing his body. Had to be.

'I had to watch you with that human for seven months. Seven. Long. Fucking. Months. The only thing that stopped me from hurting him was that he made you happy.'

The words had rung with a pain I wouldn't have expected. A pain that suggested this was about more than just cravings. A pain he hadn't acted on because he'd wanted me to be happy. But it was also a pain that I'd never once sensed. Wouldn't I have noticed it if it was truly there?

Maybe. Maybe not. Butch was emotionally stoic and very good at projecting an outward calm. I had the feeling that he hid a lot behind that calm, but I didn't know him well enough to be sure.

Still, did I want to try a relationship with him? A part of me did—the same part that wanted to believe he wasn't simply roped in by the Keja allure. It was probably a bad idea, given that he was very distant and detached. But he had a lot of good points; he was loyal, trustworthy, and he always had my back. Even when I'd been with Dean, Butch had never been any less protective or supportive. And if he genuinely had found it hard to watch me with someone else, he'd never taken that pain out on me.

However, I wasn't at all comfortable with giving him everything that I was. Not at all. There was knowing someone, and there was *knowing* someone. I didn't *know* Butch well enough to put my soul in the palm of his hand like that. I trusted him with my life, but not with *everything*. I couldn't give him what he wanted.

Since he wasn't the type to take no for an answer, I doubted he would accept that. He wouldn't behave, tip his hat, and walk away if this was truly important to him. And if he *did* accept that answer and walk away, well I'd know that I still wasn't enough for him. That thought kind of depressed me.

Paige nudged me. "Cheer up, sunshine."

I forced a smile. "I'm just tired."

"Hasn't the induced sleep completely worn off yet?" asked Alora, her expression thoughtful. "It struck you fast. One second, you were struggling like a wildcat. The next thing, you were limp in Butch's arms."

"I tried to take you," said Paige, "but he wouldn't have any of it. He said he'd take you home himself."

Did he now? "He took me to his apartment."

Alora's lips pressed together. "You promised yourself you wouldn't—"

I raised a hand. "Nothing happened." I didn't tell them any of the things he'd said because I knew what their advice would be: 'Stay clear of Butch.'

It wasn't that my squad didn't like him. They just didn't like that he'd let me go. Sweethearts that they were, they wanted me to be with a guy who'd treat me right. As far as they were concerned, Butch had treated me as nothing more than a fuck toy and he didn't deserve me. I'd insisted that it wasn't like that, and I'd tried to explain that connecting with others was simply difficult for him. That hadn't appeased them at all.

They would see me trying a relationship with Butch as a definite route to Heartbreak Avenue. As such, I couldn't rely on them to give me unbiased advice. I also couldn't rely on them not to pull Butch's squad into it. The guys hadn't been happy with Butch's behaviour either, since they were protective of me and the girls. They wouldn't approve of me being with him, and they would be seriously pissed at him for even suggesting that we try a relationship. So, yeah, I was on my own with this one.

A familiar giggle made me look to the door. Ava was skipping inside with her mate, Salem. They were total opposites. The tiny brunette was sweet, bubbly, and high on life. He was a grunting, growling, surly male who didn't seem to smile for anyone other than Ava. Yet, they suited each other perfectly.

That was what I wanted. A mate who took me as I was. Something deep and real. I wasn't sure that Butch could truly give me that, no matter what he said.

Ava gave us a cheery smile. "Evening, people." She took the seat next to Alora. The two females had become quite close, and I suspected it was because they were both often underestimated by people—Ava because she was cute and bubbly; Alora because she had a very hippy-like look and quirky attitude.

Alora's partner, Evan, was Jared's twin brother, a commander within the legion, and also Sam and Jared's appointed Heir. That meant he would replace them when they were ready to step down—probably with Alora at his side, since Evan had no intention of letting her go.

"How are you feeling, Imani?" Ava asked. "It looked like that psychic blow hurt."

"It did for a few seconds." Like a hammer hitting my head.

Ava's sigh was dreamy. "It was so cute the way Butch cradled you against his chest and carried you away." She slanted an annoyed glance at her mate. "Salem picked me up by the back of my top and dragged me out of there. And they say romance is dead." Salem just grunted.

"Here comes your saviour now with Chico and Jude," Cassie whispered, fiddling with her wheat-blonde braid.

I wouldn't look at him. No. I'd keep my gaze firmly ahead, I'd—

I looked. It wasn't strictly my fault. Not when he walked with that sexy, purposeful, confident stride that drew attention. And certainly not when he emanated an intense raw masculinity that could raise the hairs on my arms.

Seriously, how was I supposed to ignore that? I couldn't. Particularly since he stopped at the seat beside mine and just stared at his squad mate. Denny heaved a sigh and stalked off. Butch took the now empty seat without even acknowledging me.

Lips flattening, Jude raised a questioning brow at me. I just shrugged. I liked the Sventé a lot. She was a relatively serene and friendly person...although she'd soon as cut your throat than look at you. Her mate, Chico, was freaked out by her love of knives and Michael Myers vibe, but the Hispanic Pagori adored her anyway.

At that moment, Sam and Jared entered the room. Really, there were no two people better to guard and discipline vampirekind. The British female vamp was a Feeder, which meant she could absorb and manipulate the surrounding energy and shape it into various things like bolts, beams, and balls. Her favourite weapon was her energy whip. Thanks to Antonio having once imparted her with additional power, she also had the ability to merge her body with others. It was a gift she rarely used.

As Antonio had twice imparted Jared with additional power, the Pagori had three gifts: teleportation, electrokinesis, and telepathy. He wasn't able to read minds, but he could hear any thought that was directed at him. He was also absolutely freaking merciless when necessary.

Both were extremely powerful in their own right. Together, they were a force to be…avoided. Especially since Sam was somewhat different from other vampires. Originally, she'd been a Sventé. But since joining the legion, she'd become a hybrid—a combination of Sventé, Keja, and Pagori. I didn't know the story of how that came about. Most didn't.

Evan and two Kejas filed inside the room, closing the door behind them. The first Keja, Sebastian, was a Tracker who hunted felons and scouted for potential legion members; he had been the one to find Paige and I, and to teleport us to The Hollow. The second Keja, Luther, was their Advisor and pretty much Gandalf's doppelganger. Part of what made him such a good Advisor was his gift of precognition. He could forewarn them of upcoming danger and the best ways to confront or avoid it.

Once everyone was seated, Sam said, "Evening, all. I have some news."

Anticipation filled the air. Max leaned forward, his bright blue eyes wide as he said, excitement in every syllable, "Luther had a vision?"

Scratching her head, Sam replied, "No, he didn't."

Disappointed grumbles and whines rang throughout the room, which made Sebastian smile as he adjusted the collar of his Armani shirt; the guy sure knew how to dress.

Damien slouched in his chair. "Everything's been so quiet and peaceful," the African-American complained in his deep, rumbly voice.

Luther raised a single brow. "You used to complain each time I had a vision that sent you on an assignment. Is it not a good thing that vampirekind is currently on its best behaviour?"

"Sure," said Chico, "but we're bored out of our minds here."

Sam looked at the Advisor, her expression pained. "You've had no visions at all, Luther? Really?" Apparently she was just as bored. It wasn't surprising. She was pretty bloodthirsty and seemed to enjoy an adrenalin rush. So much so that she and Jared came on all assignments, just as they had when they were commanders.

The Advisor shook his head. "Sorry, Sam."

Jared's lips twitched at her long suffering sigh. "Tell everyone the news."

"Fine, but before we get to that…" Sinking into her chair, Sam turned to me with an amused smile. "We should probably discuss what happened at the bar last night."

Alora was speaking before I even had the chance to respond. "Marla was mouthing off at Imani. When she didn't react, Marla threw her purse. That broke Imani's Kindle—"

"Ah," said Sam.

"—and stamped on Paige's Berserk Button."

Paige huffed at Alora. "I do *not* have a Berserk Button."

"You totally do," chuckled Maya.

"When Marla wouldn't go away, Paige spouted a pretty creative insult," Alora went on. "So Marla then slung her drink all over Paige. That was when Imani knocked the bitch clean out."

"*And* she took a chunk of hair from one of Marla's groupies," Ava added. "That was why the heifer compelled Imani to sleep."

"Her gift isn't to induce sleep," said Sam. "It's to cause temporary exhaustion. Initially, it causes a person to pass out. They wake up, but the fatigue doesn't pass for a few nights."

Temporary exhaustion? Great.

"So I'm sure you'll be pleased to hear that Marla and her friends are leaving The Hollow as we speak."

I blinked. "Seriously? I'm not getting in shit for this?" I'd started a catfight, after all.

Sam snorted. "Those plonkers confronted my squad. That shows a total lack of respect and I won't tolerate it. They're lucky none of you killed them. Why did you boys break it up?" she complained.

"We weren't going to," said the typically cocky Harvey. "I mean, catfights are always fun to watch. But then someone lifted a glass to smash over Imani's head. Butch jumped in, and we all sort of followed suit."

See, Butch always had my back.

"Tried to smash a glass over her head?" repeated Jude. "I didn't see that part."

Chico snorted. "Of course you didn't. You were too busy slashing one of the vamp's clothes."

Head cocked to the side, Sam asked me, "Why did Marla smash your Kindle?"

Alora was once again speaking before I could respond. "She blamed Imani for Butch rejecting her and—"

I burst out, "Hey, Chatty Cathy." She had no sense of discretion. The redhead just rolled her eyes.

"You didn't tell me that," Butch said only loud enough for me to hear.

"Because it didn't matter," I said just as quietly.

"It matters to me."

"It was *my* business."

"Which makes it mine."

"Honest to God, Butch, you're like a thong—always up my ass."

"Now that that's over and done with," began Jared, "maybe we should share our news with them."

"Fine." Sam turned to us. "I actually can't believe I'm going to say this…A vampire is feeding info about our kind to humans."

"You're shitting me," breathed Damien.

"The internet is regularly monitored for activity that might concern vampires," said Jared. "If a human reports something they weren't supposed to see or knows too much, we work to cover it up. There are a lot of websites and blogs set up by humans who are convinced we exist and have their own theories about us. These sites and blogs are checked to be certain that nothing too factual is out there—some are even hosted by humans claiming to be vampires. I don't know whether they're delusional or just doing it for fun.

"A new blog has started that raised some red flags for two reasons. One, this person claims to be a vampire and, going by the articles he's posted, he's telling the truth. He talks about the different breeds of vampires, our strengths and weaknesses, and—though he hasn't mentioned any names—he even posted information about the Grand High Pair."

Ava gasped. "Oh, fuck, no!"

Sam's smile was a little on the feral side. "The bloke even went as far as to reveal that I'm a hybrid."

Well, hell. "Why would he do this?"

"He claims he was Turned without his consent and hates what he is," said Sam.

As someone who had also been Turned against their will, I could understand why he might feel bitter or resentful. Still, in spite of my anger, I'd never once even considered exposing vampirekind.

"Tell me you've crashed the blog," Reuben fairly growled.

"We're working on it," said Jared. "Personally, I don't think we need to worry. The blog has had a lot of views, but the content isn't being taken even the slightest bit seriously. Lots of disparaging comments were left by humans who think his claims are 'too farfetched' and 'he's living in a fantasy land.'"

"Once Mona and Cedric have the IP address, we'll get him," said Sam, referring to The Hollow's very knowledgeable researchers. "At least it will give us something to do." Many of the males inclined their head, seeming slightly cheered by the idea. "One last thing before we wrap up the meeting. Girls, I was going to wait until your squad was fully formed to do this, but it's taking longer than I hoped it would."

There had been several try-outs where vampires had been invited to partake in tests. But Sam hadn't chosen any of the candidates for the squad. She needed three more.

She looked at the males as she said, "You can all leave if you want." They didn't. Sam snorted before turning back to me and the girls. "You know Luther has visions. Well, as part of his gift, he can help others have a vision. We offer for new squad members to get a glimpse of what's ahead—it often helps prepare them for something. Only *you* would see the vision, not Luther. And you won't be expected to share it with anyone. Be warned, there's a possibility it won't make much sense. Mine sure bloody didn't. But the offer is open if you want to accept it."

Paige twisted her lips. "I'd like a peek into my future."

"Could be interesting," said Maya.

I was about to say the same when Butch's hand clamped around my wrist. I lifted a questioning brow at him.

"Don't," he said, voice low.

I frowned. "Why?"

"Sometimes it's best not to know what's coming."

"Maybe. But I'm curious." And I wasn't good at letting things go if they intrigued me.

"Visions aren't always pretty."

"Yours was bad?"

"No, but I know someone who's vision *was* bad and I've seen how it haunts him. Sometimes the future shows us something we'd rather not see." His hold on my wrist loosened, and his thumb started to circle my pulse. "The vision could be something that's tomorrow or centuries ahead of you. Do you want to spend all your time waiting for it to happen? It'll influence every decision you make in the meantime. As time goes on, you'll start wondering if it's really going to happen; if maybe you changed the future somehow. Do you want to live like that?"

"What about you, Imani? Are you interested in a vision?"

I double-blinked at Sam. "Um…"

Her aquamarine gaze rested on Butch's hold on my wrist. "All right, boys, time to go." She waved a hand toward the door. Being nosy bastards, they didn't leave happily. Evan, Salem, and Chico were rather put-out when their mates insisted they leave.

Butch lingered long enough to speak into my ear. "Say no." Then he was gone.

As the door closed behind him, Luther gave me a pointed look. "Do not let anyone influence your decision. Many visions prove to be helpful. I think of them as warnings. They show us what will happen if we remain on our present course. Others are simply to prepare us for what's ahead."

Sebastian nodded. "He's right, Imani. Butch probably means well, but this has to be your decision."

Sam rubbed her hands together. "Right, who's first?"

Ava raised a hand high. "Me!"

"All right, come on. All of you remember that your vision is for *you* and you alone. No one will ask you to share it."

Intrigued, I watched as Ava took Luther's hand. Her eyes closed, and then nothing. Her expression didn't change, she didn't tense or anything. Just stood there, very still.

Maybe twenty seconds later, Ava's eyes flipped open and she took a long breath. "Whoa, that was freaking weird." She smiled. "Salem is going to *love* this."

Paige went next. Then Cassie, Maya, Jude, and—after a little hesitation—Alora. Paige and Maya were confused by their visions while the others seemed…not happy, but not worried. None shared exactly what they had seen.

Luther then turned to me, hand held out. Butch was gonna be disappointed, but I couldn't miss out on this. Taking a deep breath, I stepped forward. No sooner had I took the offered hand than I was hit by the feeling of being sucked into something.

It was pure black for a few seconds. Then it was light, and I was surrounded by smoke. My eyes itched like hell and, *fuck*, I was hurting. My chest burned like a son of a bitch; something warm and wet was covering my top. I didn't need to look to know that it was my blood. I could smell it. Just as I could scent fire, burning flesh, and the familiar scents of the rainforest that surrounded The Hollow.

Hearing a guttural growl among the shouting, roaring, and screaming, I squinted at the thing coming at me through the smoke. Then my eyes widened. Shit, that—

I was back in the conference room.

Feeling like I'd been shot out of a cannon or something, I blinked repeatedly as I took in large gulps of air. My eyes no longer stung, and I could see that I was surrounded by a group of very concerned faces.

Paige pulled me into her side. "Sweetie, you okay? You don't look so good."

I fought back panic, swallowing hard. "I'm okay."

"No, you are not," said Sebastian, frowning. "Sit down for a moment."

I flopped into one of the seats and gratefully accepted the vanilla-flavoured NST that Paige pulled out of her purse.

Alora brushed my hair away from my face. "Wanna tell us what you saw, honey?"

Finishing the NST, I looked up at Sam. "Dragons. I saw dragons."

CHAPTER FOUR

(Imani)

"**D**ragons?" repeated Jared, incredulous. After my announcement, Sam, Luther, my squad, and I had walked out of the rear of the mansion, passed the beautiful gardens, the pool, the private beach, and to the enclosed training arena. The interior was much like a large horse paddock. Each wall was marked from A – D, which represented north, east, south, and west. It was surrounded by a large seating area which featured a VIP box on the middle tier.

Inside, Jared and the males had already begun the session. Now they were all circling me, their faces in different stages of confusion.

"That's what I saw," I told him.

"Tell him the rest," urged Sam.

"We were in the rainforest. There was smoke all around us. I could hear growling, roaring, snarling, and the crackling of fire. People...people were screaming. I could smell blood and flesh burning. A dragon was coming toward me just as the vision ended."

David, the youngest but most powerful of his squad, said, "You're saying dragon shifters are coming to The Hollow to battle with us?"

"It would seem so," said Luther, who was put-out that he hadn't seen the event in a vision of his own. "I do not suppose you have any idea of when this will happen?"

I worried my lower lip. "Sort of. I can't give you a timeline, but I can tell you that I had something with me that I don't own yet." I'd been wearing a Harley Davidson vest. It was pretty cool, despite being drenched in blood.

"So this isn't going to happen until you actually have it," said Sam. "Well that's better than nothing, because it tells us that the dragons aren't on their way here. As soon as you come into possession of whatever that item is, you call me."

"Why would they come here?" Paige asked.

"Dragon shifters do not like our species very much," said Luther. "It was once believed that dragon blood could cure vampirism. It is not true. Nothing can cure it. But for a long time, vampires captured dragons and drained them of blood in their attempts to create a cure."

Max skimmed a hand over his military haircut. "No wonder they hate us."

"Still, I do not believe they would senselessly attack. If they are planning to come here to fight us, they must have some motivation." Luther sighed. "But, since each preternatural species is insular and private, I do not know enough about dragon shifters to be certain."

I cleared my throat. "I know someone who does."

Jared immediately asked, "Who?"

"The Master Vampire of my nest."

Eyes narrowing, Sam stilled. "I think we should have this conversation in private." Probably because she knew I'd never been open about my past, and she figured there was a very good reason why.

Jared nodded. "We'll discuss this in my office."

"Wait!" said Paige, but Jared teleported Sam and I out of the arena and to their office. The space was seriously cool. White walls, white floor tiles, a stylish oak desk, leather chairs, an ultramodern computer, and huge glass windows. Sam sat at her desk while Jared leaned against the filing cabinets that were built into the wall.

She gestured for me to take the seat across from her. "Tell us about your nest."

"I'm guessing you did a background check before hiring me. How much do you know?"

Sam nodded. "Mona and Cedric tracked you to Lazarus Cray's line." He was a very old, powerful, and widely feared Master Vampire. "Your Sire is Marco, his best assassin. And you're the first vampire Marco ever created."

Just hearing Marco's name made me grind my teeth. "Yes."

"You fled from your Sire and severed your blood-bond using your gift," added Jared. Sam was a seriously lucky girl, because he was honestly the personification of sex. Oddly enough, though, he didn't hold the same appeal for me as Butch did. "What we don't know is why you did that. Did he hurt you?" There was a promise of retribution in those words.

"I met Marco when I was human. We dated for a while. Many Kejas can put humans in a trance before feeding from them, so that the humans have no memories of the event. He put me in that same trance, and then he Turned me. One minute I was human, the next I was in agony and going through the transition with absolutely no idea what was happening to me."

That made the mercury glint to Sam's irises flare—it was the marker of a hybrid. "Unfortunately, that happened far too much until we gave it a death sentence." She flicked her dark hair over her shoulder. "What happened after that?"

"Like all newborn vampires, I was struggling with bloodlust and fighting for control. And he just dumped me on Lazarus."

Jared's face hardened. "He *abandoned* you?"

"Yep." As if it wasn't bad enough that he'd effectively stolen my life from me, he'd then carelessly put me aside. Sires typically monitored their vampires while the person went through the transition, overcame the bloodlust, and their gift surfaced. "I was in shock, I was scared, I was confused, and I was surrounded by people I didn't know. All I wanted was to go home. That was all I kept saying—that I wanted to go home. Lazarus said I couldn't, but that he'd teach me control so that I could exist in the human world if that was what I wanted."

Jared's forehead creased. "If Lazarus was watching over you, he must have seen your gift manifest itself."

"He did."

"But he didn't make you stay?"

"I thought he'd go back on his word when he realised what a good weapon I'd make." After all, I could be used to separate mates against their will. In fact, a vampire had tried forcing me to separate Sam and Jared by using Paige as leverage. "He didn't. Like me, he and his sister were Turned against their will. So maybe he took pity on me. I left, and I severed my bond with Marco. He didn't try to track me."

"Are you sure?" asked Sam. "You're not just one of his vampires.

You're *his first-born*. That's pretty significant."

It was, which was why a lot of acknowledgement and respect came with being a first-born. We, for whatever reason, were the inspiration that led to our makers starting their own line. It was a serious thing to run a line and it involved a lot of responsibilities. To become one was a huge decision. First-borns were the catalyst of that decision, and so they were deeply respected and their Makers tended to have a soft spot for them. As such, it was odd that Marco would just overlook my existence. "I know, but he never came looking for me."

"I was going to ask if he Turned you because he cared about you and wanted to keep you," said Sam, "but if that was true he wouldn't have abandoned you or let you go."

"Marco doesn't care about anyone other than Marco. Given everything, I'm sure you can understand why I ran from him."

"You didn't just cut your ties with Marco, you cut yourself off from the entire nest," Jared pointed out. "That left you very vulnerable; completely without protection. Why would you do that?"

It seemed melodramatic *now* but… "You have to understand that at the time, I still didn't see myself as a vampire. I was convinced I could return to my old life, pretend to be human. Both Lazarus and Annalise warned me not to cut all contact, but I just wanted to be away from that world. I didn't listen to them.

"Once people heard of a vampire that could sever bonds, I was hunted. I had no protection, so I became a drifter. Paige was sent to track me, only she joined me instead of taking me to her Sire. In return, I severed her bond with him so she could be free. That was all she really wanted. To be free."

Sam leaned back in her chair. "Have you had any contact whatsoever with anyone from your nest since leaving?"

"When Lazarus and Annalise watched your ascension via V-Tube, they caught a glimpse of me in the background and also heard you offer me a place in the legion. They contacted me shortly afterwards to pass on their congratulations. Annalise and I now occasionally exchange emails. She's even invited me to the Binding anniversary of two of their vampires, which is taking place in six months' time." Binding formed a powerful psychic connection between two vampires, joined them on a level that far surpassed any marriage or other type of bond.

"You plan on going, even though it will mean facing your Sire again?" asked Sam.

"A year ago, I would have said no. I wouldn't have wanted to be anywhere near him. I'm stronger now. I've cut myself from my nest for long enough. Lazarus, Annalise, and the rest of the nest are, for all intents and purposes, my family."

"They are," agreed Sam. "And maintaining connections outside The Hollow is a good thing. Most of the legion are in regular contact with their nests; life shouldn't always be about work."

"You say Lazarus knows about dragon shifters," said Jared.

I nodded. "Yes. Lazarus is a scholar, and he's knowledgeable about a lot of things. He admires and respects dragon shifters for their strength, power, and viciousness. I heard that Marco had negotiated a peace treaty between Lazarus and the local dragon drove."

"You think Lazarus would be happy to share information with us?" asked Jared.

"I don't see why he wouldn't," I replied.

"Then we'll contact him tonight."

"He never leaves his home, so he won't agree to come here," I told them.

"But I don't doubt that he'll invite you there. I'd like to come along."

Sam exchanged a look with Jared. "I'm not sure I'm comfortable with that, Imani. How do you think Marco will react to seeing you again? I mean, you not only dared to try to escape him, you were able to do it. You cut your connection to him. He has to be, at the very least, seriously offended and a little embarrassed that you escaped his hold without his permission or knowledge."

"What makes it more complex is that you're not just one of Marco's vampires," said Jared. "You're his first-born."

I blew out a long breath. "I don't know how he'll react. I never really understood why he Turned me, or why he then abandoned me. Still, he'll be pissed that I fled because first-borns are supposed to be flattered that we somehow inspired a vampire to begin their own line. We're supposed to stay at their side and serve them faithfully. We're not supposed to run."

Expression pensive, Sam tapped her fingers on the table. "What about the rest of the nest? Won't they look down on you for fleeing instead of sticking around as a good little first-born should?"

"While I stayed with Lazarus, they were all pretty nice to me.

Probably because they felt bad for me, and because Marco is highly respected." Even though he was a complete dick. His high status in vampire society was based on both fear and respect, since he'd been a ruthless assassin for most of his vampire life. As his first-born, all that respect and sense of importance extended to me. "I appreciate your concern, but I have to go back there some time."

A short silence fell. Sam broke it. "All right. You can be part of our entourage, since we'll be expected to take one for support and protection. I'd rather take a small one, or it will seem like we don't believe we can protect ourselves just fine."

Jared nodded. "We'll take six vampires, including Imani. The question is…which ones?"

"We'll discuss it later," said Sam. "Let's get back to the arena. First, Imani, I want to know if you're comfortable with sharing your past with the others. We don't have to go into great detail—we can just give them the bare bones of the story. Or we can tell them to mind their own bloody business, it's your choice."

While I wasn't necessarily comfortable with sharing my past… "They should know about Marco so they know what to expect when we visit Lazarus."

"As long as you're sure?"

I nodded.

"All right, let's go."

Back at the arena, I gave everyone a very brief summary of my past and informed them that we should be visiting Lazarus in the near future. After stating that she would update them on the situation at tomorrow night's conference, Sam then started the session.

Not wanting to think about the upcoming reunion with Marco, I put all my focus into training. When we first started, our goals had been simple but tough. First, we had to learn how to channel all our preternatural energy so that none leaked from us. It was an unnatural energy we began producing when we Turned; making our mind and body evolve. If we didn't know how to hold it inside, we wouldn't be able to use our gift to its full potential. In addition, it meant that Feeders like Sam could leech off our energy.

Within a month, we had completed our first goal. Then we moved onto our second: improve the use of our gifts. We each learned how to use our ability in different ways. Only then were we able to hit our third goal, which was to learn each other's gifts inside out; know every strength and every weakness that came with them. That allowed us to learn how to work together as a squad and how to strengthen each other.

On every assignment, I was paired with Paige. It was a good thing for two reasons. One, Paige was very protective of me, just as I was of her. Two, our gifts worked well together. By sifting into a person's brain with my psychic hand, I could find a vampire's blood-bond and, well, play it like a guitar string. It both hurt and distracted, which gave the tall, lithe Keja the opportunity to pounce.

Her gift was extraordinary, in my opinion. It could be used for both good and bad. Basically, Paige could transfer not only her injuries, but the injuries of others. That meant if someone wounded her, she could transfer that wound to them and it would revisit on them three-fold. The gift thereby allowed her to both heal and cause harm.

Sam had also paired Jude and Cassie together. They matched well. Jude's gift to erase recent memories wasn't offensive, so Cassie's gift of mind control was a big help. Jude was much better at combat than Cassie, so she was good at watching Cassie's back.

Until more females joined the squad, Ava wouldn't have a partner for assignments. In the meantime, she stayed with Salem and the vampire he was paired with. She didn't need their protection, though; not with her awesome gift of muscle memory. Ava could literally memorise and replicate any combat move she saw. The gift not only made her faster and stronger than other Sventés, but it gave her better reflexes. Anyone who underestimated little Ava quickly regretted it.

As always, tonight's training was gruelling and brutal. We were split into two teams: an offensive one, and a defensive one. Paige and I were part of the latter. Sam created a huge mound of Earth with her gift and then ordered the defensive team to defend it from the offensive team.

After a quick lunch break, we were back in the arena for another session. Jared assigned us physical exercises that kept up our stamina and endurance. I threw every ounce of my energy into it and worked myself hard because, yeah, I wanted to forget that I'd just seen myself injured and facing a dragon.

By the time it was done, I was ready to drop—which was no doubt a lot to do with the temporary exhaustion thing, courtesy of Marla's crony. I went straight to my apartment, intending to hit my bed early. That plan was foiled when Paige turned up with vodka-flavoured NSTs.

"Don't think I'm not mad that your fat ass teleported out of the arena without me earlier," said Paige, barging inside.

I shut the door, faking offense. "My ass is not fat."

"Well it ain't fucking skinny."

I laughed. "At least it isn't bony."

She cast me a mock glare, relaxing on my rug. She liked to sit on the floor. "I've been told my ass is cute, thank you very much."

I sat opposite her, lotus style. "Yeah? By who?"

"So, can I just say that Marco is a total asshole?"

"I'm with you so far."

"I don't like the idea of you being in the same building as him."

She probably wanted to lock me away somewhere to stop me from going. "Wouldn't you rather that I had back-up with me when Marco and I see each other again for the first time?"

She sniffed. "I guess."

Wanting to change the subject, I said, "You looked confused after you had your vision."

"I didn't understand it at all." She took a swig of her drink. "And I don't have even an inkling of when it will happen."

"Do you regret having your vision?"

"Part of me does." Paige sipped more of her NST. "I mean, how can I treat it as a warning if I don't fully understand what I saw? Maybe there'll come a time when I do, and then it will help me know what to do. Or, at least, that's what I'm hoping."

We talked a little about inconsequential things. When I yawned for like the tenth time, she barked, "Ha, it serves you right for overworking yourself."

I tossed her a 'whatever' look, not interested in a lecture.

As I walked her to the door, she gave me a hug. "Get a good day's sleep, okay?"

"Okay." I opened the door…and found Butch standing there, hand ready to knock.

(Butch)

Paige perched her hands on her hips and lifted her chin. "I distinctly remember us having a conversation in which I made it perfectly clear that Imani wasn't going to be a booty call for you anymore."

Imani squinted at her friend. "You did?"

Yes, and I'd wondered if Imani knew about it. Apparently not. It was a one-sided conversation. I'd just stared at Paige, waiting impatiently for her to stop ranting about me 'using' Imani. At that point, Imani had already made it clear that she was done with casual sex.

"And yet, you're here," added Paige.

I nodded. "This is true."

"Well, now you're going to leave."

"This is Imani's apartment, so that's for her to decide." I held up my hand when Paige went to speak again. "Stop. I'm not going to talk like she's not standing right there."

Paige blinked, looking both surprised and impressed by that comment. She turned to Imani. "Make the right decision, sweetie. You know what that is." She shot me a narrow-eyed look as she swept past and disappeared down the hallway.

Before Imani had a chance to speak, I pushed my way inside. I liked her apartment. There was something welcoming about it. Maybe it was all the paintings and smart use of colour. Anyone who didn't know Imani would take one look at the large space and think she was a messy, disorganised person. I'd thought the same at first.

Her coffee table was covered in magazines, drawings, pens, remote controls, and other bits and bobs. Books, DVDs, and CDs were scattered everywhere. There was little order in her kitchen. Her bedroom...well, I wasn't sure if she made much use of her wardrobe at all because her clothes always seemed to be piled on the armchair next to it.

As I'd come to know Imani, I'd learned that she wasn't an untidy person with no sense of organisation. It was that she found order in chaos and confusion. She had a system of order; it just differed from that of anyone I knew.

"You're the second person to barge in here tonight," she grumbled, unsurprisingly tired after having overexerted herself. We'd get to that soon.

"I'm not good at respecting people's boundaries." Especially hers, because I wanted nothing at all between us.

"Yeah, if I hadn't already known that it would have been perfectly obvious when you barged in. So, why *did* you?"

"I wanted to see you." I shrugged. "You were upset. I didn't like it." I reached for the object tucked into the back of my jeans. "And I brought you something." She blinked at the object I held out to her. "Take it. I had Fletcher register it to your Amazon account."

Accepting the brand new Kindle, she swallowed hard. "You didn't have to do this. I would've bought a new one when I had the chance."

"Now you don't have to."

"That's really sweet of you." She held the Kindle against her chest. "Thank you."

"You going to tell me what things you didn't say earlier about your nest?"

She rubbed at her forehead. "I'm actually not in the mood to talk about my past. Perhaps I could interest you in a smart-ass comment instead."

I advanced on her. "Imani, I know enough about your prick of a Sire to know he needs to die. Slowly. Painfully. There's more to the story. Tell me what you didn't say earlier."

"So *you* get to be a closed book but *I* have to tell you everything?"

"I just want you to share with me."

"Share? All right, how about I keep the pin and you have the grenade? Sound fair?"

That was one thing about Imani—when she was tired, she could be snippy as hell. Still, I would have pushed her to share if she didn't look so exhausted and vulnerable. "We'll postpone that conversation. You look ready to drop. I'm surprised you're conscious."

Her lips flattened. "Blame that bitch from the bar."

"No, baby, I'm blaming you. You worked yourself too hard during training, even though you knew you were already weak. It was a wonder you didn't pass out. Don't do that again."

"Don't work hard?"

I curled my hand around her chin. "Don't play with me, baby. You know exactly what I mean. If there was some kind of surprise attack tonight, you would be no good to yourself. You'd be off your game, and that could lead to you being hurt. None of that is okay with me."

"I'm fine."

"You're dangerously exhausted."

The amber tint in her irises flared. *"I'm fine."*

"You're lying, and you're shit at it."

She stepped back, breaking my hold on her chin and flashing me that oh-so-haughty look I knew well. "I can *so* lie. And if I want your opinion, I'll give you some forms to fill out, all right?"

"Baby, you need to drop that little attitude."

"Oh, really?"

"Yes, because it makes my fucking cock throb."

She rolled her eyes. "I can't say I know many guys who would—" She quieted as I closed the distance between us and put a finger to her mouth.

I spoke softly. "I don't want to hear about other guys." And I didn't want to be compared to them, because I'd definitely come up short. "I am who I am. Fucked up in a lot of ways. *Too* many ways." She deserved better, but she was stuck with me. "I'd change if I could."

She frowned. "You don't need to change. You're not a bad person."

I wasn't sure I believed that, but I was glad that she did. I splayed my hand around her throat, feeling her pulse beat beneath my thumb. It made my mouth water. "Has anyone fed from you since me?" I didn't like thinking of anyone else's teeth sinking into her skin. We'd exchanged blood many times. I liked having something of her in me, just as I liked knowing there was a part of me inside her.

Her fingers curled around my wrist, but she didn't pull my hand away. She also didn't answer.

"The last person to feed from me was you," I admitted. She didn't look at all convinced. "You thought me a cold bastard who saw you as nothing but a good fuck I'd easily replace?"

She blinked. "I never thought of you as cold."

Well, she'd be the only one.

"And I'm not a good fuck, I'm a *great* fuck. Let's just be clear about that."

My mouth curved. "Yes, you are." She was the best I'd ever had. And I'd have her again. The wait would be torture. It would also be worth it.

"Why do you think you need to change?"

"I know myself, Imani. I know my strengths and I know my faults."

"Everybody has faults."

"But not everybody finds it easy to kill," I pointed out.

"But you don't kill for killing's sake. You kill to protect our kind, to defend your squad, and to serve Sam and Jared. You don't do it because it's a way to get your jollies."

"I'm no model soldier, baby."

"But you're not a monster either."

I lifted a single brow. "Are you sure?"

"Yes. You've saved my ass a number of times."

"That's because it was you. I always protect what belongs to me."

Her eyes narrowed. "I belong to me."

"Wrong." I shook my head. "Very, very wrong. Don't try to fight this. There's no point."

She blew out a frustrated breath. "I find it too hard to accept that you've suddenly gone from wanting sex to wanting everything."

"It wasn't sudden, Imani. It happened over the course of almost a year. It just seems sudden to you because you didn't know until recently."

She was silent for a few moments. "You're asking a lot from me."

I tucked her hair behind her ear. "I know." She'd be dumb not to be wary.

"I can't give it to you."

"You can." And she would.

"I don't know you well enough to give you everything."

"Then we'll fix that. But you might not like everything you hear." But I wouldn't lie to her. We couldn't build something that was based on untruths.

"You're saying you'll share stuff?"

I couldn't blame her for sounding dubious, since I'd dodged every personal question she'd ever asked me in the past. "If that's what you need."

"I have a lot of questions," she warned me. "You don't like questions."

"I like being without you even less. So I'll give you what answers you want, but I won't give them to you all at once."

"Why?"

"You're incredibly curious; you like puzzles. If I drip feed you the things you need to know, you'll be more likely to come back to me again and again."

She scowled, but there was a glint of humour in her eyes. "You don't think that's a little devious?"

"I think it's extremely devious." But I'd do it. Besides, only a dumbass would lay out his dirty laundry in the early stages of a relationship. Only once he was sure that she was happy and as attached to him as possible did he dump it all on her. Otherwise, he'd risk losing her. There was no way I'd risk losing Imani. I'd done it before, and I wasn't keen on doing it again.

"Will you answer me one question now?"

Liking her curiosity, I said, "Ask."

"You said you don't do 'more.' I always wondered if that was because you tried it and it was so bad that you didn't want to try again. Have you ever been in a relationship before?"

"Yes. Twice. Both relationships fucked up because, like I told you, I'm not good for people."

"Or maybe they weren't good for you. Two people can be good but be absolutely shit when together."

"True," I allowed.

"Were they both human relationships?"

I tutted. "That was another question. We agreed on one. But...I'm willing to bargain."

Suspiciousness flickered across her face. "Yeah?"

"I'll answer your question"—I tapped her lower lip—"if you give me a little taste of this mouth."

She swallowed. "I'm not sure that's a good idea."

It was a fucking great idea. I pressed a kiss to the side of her neck, inhaling her tantalising scent. "I just want one little taste of what's mine. A kiss, nothing more."

"Butch—"

"You know how good it will feel."

"You really think you can just walk out after a single kiss, without pushing for more?"

"I give you my word that I won't push." Even though all I wanted was to strip her naked and feast on her. It took extreme effort to shove that thought from my mind. "One taste and I'll stop, I promise."

I could see that she was warring with herself. Eventually, she said, "Answer my question first."

I hid my satisfaction. "Both were human relationships." As curiosity again lit her eyes and she went to speak, I shook my head. "No more questions. We had a deal. Now you have to live up to your end. Of course, I'll answer another question if you're willing to give me more than a kiss."

Her eyes narrowed. "Just one kiss."

"One." I tugged her lower lip with my teeth, her lips parted on a gasp, and I thrust my tongue into her mouth. I groaned at the addictive taste of her. It was just as sweet as her scent, and it was a punch to my senses. I'd missed it. Been without it for too fucking long, and hadn't expected to have it again.

I needed more.

Sliding my hands into her hair, I angled her head; allowing me to go deeper. I took. Feasted. Sank into her. Gorged on what I craved day and night. She had no idea what she did to me. No idea how much I needed this, needed *her*. No idea how far I'd go to keep her.

Once I'd tasted her a year ago, there had been no going back. I'd just realised that too late.

My cock throbbed as her scent changed, ripening with need. Growling low in my throat, I pulled back before I broke my promise, bent her over the arm of the couch, and fucked her until neither of us could walk. She took a steadying breath, licking her lips. I nearly groaned. "Three nights, baby. Then I'm coming and we'll talk it all out."

"You know that no one on this island would give us their blessing, don't you?"

"Can't say I'd blame them." I had a reputation as a hit and run, and I'd let her go once before.

"Your squad is very protective of mine, which means they really won't like it. Do you want to be at odds with them?"

She just wasn't getting it. "Nothing is going to keep me away from you, Imani. Not them. Not you." I brushed a kiss over her forehead. "Sleep well." With that, I left.

CHAPTER FIVE

(Imani)

Settling in the luxury cabana, I sighed happily. I loved the beach at night. Contrary to popular belief, sunlight didn't harm vampires. But we were nocturnal creatures that preferred the cover of darkness for hunting.

After the conference and a grueling training session, I went to the beach with Paige, Ava, and Alora. At the meeting, Sam and Jared had announced two things. Firstly, dealing with the ever-so-chatty blogger wasn't going to be easy. Their attempts to crash the blog weren't working any better than their attempts to electronically track the IP address. Their theory was that he could have an affinity to technology and was using it to hide and protect himself. In any case, they intended to keep working on the problem.

Their second announcement was that Lazarus had issued an invitation for them to visit. He'd also subtly hinted that I join them, to which Sam had consented. It was concluded—after much deliberation—that Ava, Salem, Max, Paige, and Butch would come along.

It made a good entourage. Paige, Butch, and Ava had amazing abilities. Salem had a psychic punch, and Max could cause sensory paralysis.

Jude had complained that she wanted to come along and had suggested that Butch remain behind. Personally, I thought she was just messing with Butch to get a reaction. But I was hoping that just maybe Sam would agree to the switch. I didn't have the emotional patience for him right now. I was still finding it difficult to digest the things he'd told me. However, I hadn't been able to argue with Butch's point that he was the logical choice.

He'd said, "In terms of protection, there's no better person to go with Imani than me; I'm a living fucking shield." That meant he could protect me without having to actually kill or hurt anyone, and he could do it fast and easy. Still, I needed space to think. Butch didn't like giving me space.

He must have sensed that I was ready to object because he'd pinned me with his gaze and said, "If you think I'll stay here while you face your Sire again after all this time, think again. This won't be easy for you, so I'm going to ensure it goes as smoothly as possible."

It was sweet in a Butch-like way.

"Something you want to tell us?" Alora's voice snapped me back to the present. It took a moment for me to realise that she was speaking to Paige.

Having exchanged a baffled look with me, Paige replied, "Nope."

The redhead arched a brow. "You sure?"

"Positive."

"Not even that Stuart and Max had some kind of argument over you last night?"

Paige's head jerked back. "Argument?"

"You haven't heard about it yet?"

Ava held up a hand. "Wait, wait, I thought you and Stuart broke up."

"We did," confirmed Paige. "Months ago. He's a good guy and all, but he just...he doesn't *get* me. And I need that, you know?"

Ava nodded, unusually solemn. "I totally do know. Salem gets me, and he lets me be. Which is important because I'm a fucking nutcase."

"Tell me about this argument," I said to Alora.

"Oh, right. Well, Evan heard from one of his squad members, who heard it from his brother, who heard it from his friend, who—"

"Oh my God, just tell us," Paige burst out.

Alora held up a placating hand. "Now don't get upset. But apparently Stuart, well, talked a little smack about you; said you're made of ice and you're closed off and...and you don't look surprised."

Paige sank into the cream cushion, one arm above her head. "I told you; he doesn't get me. Stuart, well, he likes people to need him. Which is fine. It's not a bad thing if being a rock for people makes you feel good. But I've always relied on myself. I like doing things for myself. *That* makes *me* feel good. I don't want a guy to complete my life. I want him to enrich it. That wasn't enough for Stuart."

I nodded, understanding. "He didn't respect your need for independence." I knew her well enough to know how much she needed that.

"He took it personally," said Paige. "Like I do things for myself to spite him. He doesn't see that I'm just being me. It quickly became clear to me that I'm not right for him. He needs someone different."

I pursed my lips. "So calling you cold as ice…that was his ego talking. It took a beating when you didn't make him the centre of your world." What a little shit.

Paige shrugged one shoulder. "I guess so. I mean it when I say he's not a bad guy. He's just not for me."

Ava put a hand on Alora's arm. "Hang on, what did Max have to do with this?"

Eyes brightening, Alora smiled. "Ah, well, Evan heard that—"

Paige waved a hand. "Alora, seriously, just get to the important part."

"Well apparently, Max told him that badmouthing you was immature, shitty, and disrespectful. Stuart's drunken response was a snort followed by, 'It's not like she'll care; she's stone cold…until she's in bed; then she's all fire.' Max didn't like that. He told Stuart to zip his mouth shut before he said something he'd regret but couldn't take back. Stuart accused him of 'having a little thing' for you."

Ava flashed a megawatt smile. "Ooh, this is getting really good."

Nodding, Alora went on, "Max just shrugged and said, 'Some guys like strong, independent women. Others feel threatened by them.' The implication was clear. Stuart lunged for Max, but the bystanders intervened before anyone could even throw a punch."

"Hmm, maybe Max does have a little thing for you, Paige," said Ava.

My BFF snorted. "Max has a little thing for everyone."

Alora's smile dimmed. "Okay, I can't deny that his dick doesn't seem to be very discriminating. But that's only if the rumours are to be believed. What about you? Do you like him?"

"What's not to like?" said Paige. "He's cute, strong, fun, and he's got a great body."

"I sense a 'but' coming," said Alora.

"*But* I don't want to be with a slut."

"Like I said, they could be just rumours. There are *always* rumours about guys who are that hot."

Ava turned her smile on me. "Speaking of rumours, I heard Butch is kind of wild in bed. All dark and dominant. That true?"

I gave her my best mysterious smile. "A lady never tells."

"So is it true?"

"Are you implying that I'm not a lady?"

"I thought you already knew that."

"Bitch," I chuckled.

Imani, Jared called telepathically. *Come to the beach house. Sam would like to see you.*

Blinking in surprise, I replied, *Sure thing*. "Girls, I'm done for the night. According to Jared"—I tapped my temple— "Sam wants to see me about something." Maybe she had more questions about my nest. That wasn't a pleasant thought.

After saying my goodbyes, I headed for Sam and Jared's home. I'd been inside the beach house a few times before, and I loved it. The place had such a cosy, relaxing feel to it. They must have heard me coming up the steps to the porch, because Jared opened the door before I had a chance to knock.

As we passed the noisy living area, I asked, "Is that Sebastian and Luther I can hear grumbling at each other?"

Jared's lips pressed together. "Yes. They're playing on Sam's PlayStation."

The image made me laugh as I entered the kitchen, where Sam was sitting at a table, drinking an NST. "Imani, come sit."

Accepting her invitation, I pulled out the chair opposite hers. "So, what's up?"

"In the interests of full disclosure, I'm letting you know upfront that we're going to forewarn Butch about your past with Marco," she told me. "He knows that Marco is your Sire, but he doesn't know the arsehole was also once your boyfriend. If he finds out another way, he might go ape-shit. It will be hard enough to stop Butch from killing Marco on this trip."

I shook my head. "If you order him not to hurt Marco, he'll follow that order." Regardless of what Butch said, he was a good soldier.

"He would if this was about anyone other than you," said Sam. "Look, I'm not going to pretend I don't know that Butch is suddenly all up in your space." When I didn't comment, she added, "I heard he went to your apartment last night."

I should have remembered that nothing that happened on this island stayed secret for long. "We just talked."

Sam cast me an impatient look. "You know you're crap at lying, right?"

"I can *so* lie."

Jared snorted a laugh. "Um, no, you can't."

"Well, seven of the eight voices in my head say you're wrong."

He laughed. "Back to the subject of Butch…he looked really concerned for you in the arena. He even asked me to tell you to take a break. I thought about it, but you seemed to need to escape your thoughts for a while."

It was exactly what I'd needed.

"So, why is he back in your space?" Sam asked me.

I couldn't tell her. Not when I hadn't even told my best friend, and not when I wasn't even sure how I felt about it. I didn't want other people's opinions to colour what decision I made. And Sam no doubt intended to tell me that I should stay clear of Butch. "If you're going to warn me that it's in my best interests to stay away from him, you don't need to. He already told me he thinks he's not good for me."

"He probably isn't," said Sam. "I don't mean it in a bitchy way. But we have to be straight here. Butch is…he's not broken, but he's fractured."

I could agree with that.

"He'd be a difficult mate. He's an alpha, which automatically makes him a bloody handful. He has qualities that make him great at his position. He's confident, disciplined, forever alert, and loyal to a fault. He's got a brilliant, strategic mind. And he doesn't let fear hold him back; never flinches at anything.

"But he's also very dominant. And he's so direct, his words often come out cold. That means he'll be overbearing and absentmindedly hurtful in a relationship. He needs a mate who'll be careful not to take things too personally and to give him a lot of room to fuck up. But she'd also have to push back or he'd walk all over her."

She wasn't telling me anything I didn't already know. Not wanting to hear any more reasons a relationship with him would be hard, I said,

"You really think he needs to know that Marco's an ex of mine?"

Sam's eyes narrowed slightly, but she allowed the subject change. "I do. He's never said anything, but I think he found it hard to see you with Dean. He can be jealous when it comes to you. So when he finds out you used to date Marco, he'll want to see him dead even more than he already does. It really is best if he hears the truth from us."

"Let's be honest," began Jared, "if the situation was reversed, what would you do to Butch's Maker?"

My back teeth locked. "The question is: what wouldn't I do?"

A slow smile surfaced on Sam's face. "I like that answer."

Well, it was true.

"I actually doubt Marco will start any shit," said Sam. "The reunion will be awkward, though. Still, we can deal with 'awkward.' And if Marco does act like a tit, you can take him. And I can watch, smiling with glee the entire time."

"She's not kidding, by the way," Jared told me.

I smiled. "I didn't for one second think that she was."

(Butch)

A few hours before dawn, I was sitting across the kitchen table from Sam after receiving a telepathic summons from Jared. "Imani's been here," I noted, picking up her scent.

"We need to talk to you about her," Sam replied simply.

Everything in me froze. I flicked my gaze from Sam to Jared to Sebastian; they all looked equally serious. "What about Imani?"

Sinking into her seat, Sam said, "After she told us about her past, I had a little chat with Mona and Cedric. I wanted to know more about Marco. According to them, he's a cunning, intelligent, smooth-talking predator who's so cold he's dead inside. Still, he doesn't go around Turning unwilling humans." Sam leaned forward. "*But* something made him do that to Imani. Until her, he was happy without the responsibilities of running his own line; he was happy owing loyalty to only his Sire and his nest. She changed that somehow."

"She's his first-born?"

Sam nodded. "She doesn't believe that he cared for her, even though they were a couple while she was human—which is something you're best knowing upfront."

Oh, fucking were they?

"Stop growling and listen. She also doesn't believe that he tried tracking her after she fled. She's right about that. And that's just bloody weird. If nothing else, he should see her as a possession that he lost. He appears to be just ignoring her existence. Does that make sense to you?"

No, it didn't. I knew Sam well enough to know... "You have a theory."

"Imani was a drifter for years. She had a lot of people tracking her, all intent on using her for her gift. She's a slippery little thing, and she's smart and resourceful. But would that really have been enough to evade all those vampires?"

I narrowed my eyes. "You think Marco protected her somehow."

"Tracking is my specialty," said Sebastian, leaning against the kitchen counter. "But it was no easy thing for me to find Paige and Imani. It was as though someone was wiping away their trail."

I frowned. "Why Turn her, abandon her, let her flee, and protect her from afar?"

"Guilt?" offered Sebastian. "Perhaps he felt badly for wronging her."

"By all accounts," said Sam, "Marco isn't the regretful type."

A thought occurred to me. "Is it possible that Paige is working for him? That he appointed her to protect Imani?"

"No," replied Sam. "I think Imani reminds Paige of her sister, but that's another story."

Jared took the seat beside his mate. "Maybe it wasn't Marco that was erasing her trail. Maybe it was Lazarus."

Her brows lifted. "That sounds much more likely."

It did, but there was no knowing anything for sure. There were too many unanswered questions here. "All I want to know is if Imani will be in danger at Lazarus' home. If the answer is yes, she doesn't go."

Sebastian spoke. "If Marco meant her any harm, he would have put a bounty on her head when she fled. He never did. Instead, he let her be—may even have protected her."

Still... "That's not to say that seeing her won't anger him enough to hurt her now. It would be better not to risk it."

Sam cast me an impatient glance. "Butch, she's a member of the fucking legion. She's been trained to handle and protect herself, she knows a dozen ways to end someone, and she'll have back-up. We don't have a valid reason for forcing her not to go."

"Being careful with her life isn't a valid reason?"

"There's being careful, and there's ignoring her ability to look after herself. It would insult and hurt her to refuse her request to come along. You wouldn't expect any of the others to do that in such a situation."

Jared nodded. "It might be good for her to face the asshole that stole her life."

Good for her? "Like Coach pointed out, he'll be pissed at Imani."

"And we'll be there to make sure he doesn't try to act on it," said Sam. "Honestly though, I sincerely doubt he will. He's allegedly very intelligent. That alone should stop him from attacking a member of the legion."

But we couldn't know that for sure. And that lack of certainty didn't sit well with me. If I couldn't be confident that she was safe, I wouldn't function. Maybe I could convince her to stay behind, maybe if I just talked to her—

"Don't, Butch." Sam, apparently having guessed my intentions, shook her head. "It would insult her, and I really don't think you want to do that. Protecting her means also protecting her feelings."

Yes, it did, but I wanted to keep her safe. I didn't want to take any chances with her life. "She's important," I bit out.

Sam's face softened. "I know she's important to you. I don't pretend to know *what* you feel for her, but I know it's strong and intense. That doesn't mean you get to interfere in her decisions. If you had claimed her as yours when you had the chance, she'd have made compromises. I repeat, *compromises*. Not have given you your own way. And although I don't like to interfere in people's personal lives—"

Jared snorted.

"—I will say now that you were a dumb dick not to claim her. She'd have taken you as you are, Butch. That's a special thing. But in return, you'd have had to take her how she is."

I'd take her any way I could get her, and I *would* claim her, but that was between me and Imani. "While we're at Lazarus' home, I'm with her every second. She doesn't leave my side."

"She won't be leaving your side because you're there as her shield in case Marco tries to harm her. You have to promise me right now that you won't lunge at him unprovoked. I know this situation will be bloody hard for you—being around Jared's Maker was a pain in my arse." Which was partly why Sam had killed her. "But it will be even harder for Imani. Put her feelings before your own."

"Fine," I clipped. But I almost hoped that Marco did something to provoke me just so that I'd have the perfect excuse to kill the fucker.

CHAPTER SIX

(Imani)

Prisons could be very beautiful.

After Marco dumped me on Lazarus, this had been my prison for ten whole months. I hadn't exactly begrudged Lazarus for keeping me here until I was in control of my bloodlust, and it wasn't like I'd had any other place to go. Although he'd never harmed me or done anything but make me feel welcome, the feeling of being trapped hadn't been one I'd enjoyed.

Concealed in the shadows of a nearby forest, Max said, "Wow. This place is fucking amazing."

It really was. With its tall walls, high towers, and thick turrets, the medieval dark-stoned fortress was a sight to behold. Lazarus had long ago claimed the castle that was comfortably situated on a moated island. Many had tried to penetrate and steal it; all had died in the process. The castle wasn't just astounding, it was a military piece of art.

"A gilded cage is still a cage," said Ava. She was right.

With the exception of the guards at the arched gates, the castle always looked deserted. Jared had teleported us to the forest as opposed to the bridge, as he had wanted to first get a feel for the place.

Paige asked in a low voice, "Is it hard to be back here?"

I'd thought it might be, but it oddly wasn't. Maybe it was because I wasn't a prisoner this time round. Or maybe it was because I wasn't alone. "I'll be fine."

As Sam and Jared talked quietly, Butch came to my side and said, "Stick close to me. I don't trust Marco around you. I need to know, to *see*, you're safe."

I looked into eyes glittering with protectiveness. Before I could respond, Paige was speaking.

"*I'm* her partner, so just why would she stick with *you*?"

Butch was suddenly face to face with Paige. "I can protect her better than you, and we both know it. So that's what I'm gonna do. Don't get in my way."

I was about to tell them both to stand down when Sam spoke. "Butch, I've said this before, but I'm going to say it again. I know this Marco thing will be awkward as shit, but don't attack him unprovoked. If he acts like a dick, you can growl and snarl and whatever. But don't lose control. Be smart." When Butch didn't argue, Sam nodded her approval. "All right, let's get moving."

She and Jared left the shadows first. The rest of us walked in pairs behind them. The vampires guarding the bridge recognised the mated couple immediately and, appropriately deferential, waved us all through the gates. Jared teleported us straight to the entrance of the castle, startling the guards there. They parted like the red sea, a mixture of awe and fear in their expressions. Yeah, well, everyone knew that Sam and Jared were crazy.

Stepping through the archway, once again surrounded by all that gothic elegance and the scent of lavender, I should have been transported into the past. I should have been hit by the feelings of helplessness, despair, and confusion that had haunted me here when my human life was so callously stolen from me. There was none of that at all…as if those feelings had all belonged to someone else. Maybe they had. I was a different person now. Stronger. Harder. No longer lost and afraid of what I was.

I recognised the vampire rushing toward us as Pierce, who closely served Lazarus. He'd been good to me; a sort of uncle-figure who had taught me a lot about the history of vampirekind and what it meant to be a Keja. The image of elegance, he bowed to Sam and Jared. "You do Lazarus a great honour in visiting his home." I knew Sam would be grinding her teeth—she hated the bowing-thing.

Pierce peered around them, spotted me, and beamed. "Imani!" Moving to me, he took my hand and kissed it. Beside me, Butch stiffened. "You look radiant. Lazarus and Annalise are thrilled that you

FRACTURED

agreed to come. Let me say, on behalf of all our nest, we're very proud of you for earning a place in the legion."

I squeezed his hand. "Thanks, Pierce."

He gave Butch—who was standing intimately close—a brief, assessing look. "Who is this?"

"Butch, a member of the Grand High Pair's personal squad. The male vampires behind me, Max and Salem, are also part of the squad. Paige and Ava are part of mine."

"Ah." Pierce nodded at them. "In that case, it is a pleasure to meet you all. Now, allow me to personally escort you to the Grand Hall. Lazarus is waiting inside." Pierce's smile faltered slightly. "I feel I should warn you, Imani…Marco is here."

"Should we expect trouble?" Sam's tone said there had better be no trouble.

Frowning deeply, Pierce shook his head. "Marco would never harm her."

"He harmed her when he Turned her without her consent," Butch growled.

Pierce flushed. "Aside from that, I mean." He cleared his throat. "Please come this way."

As we followed Pierce through the castle, I noticed that it hadn't changed at all since I was last here. The walls were still adorned with beautiful paintings, portraits of past battles, and intricate tapestries. Artefacts, statues, and armoury still lined the hallways.

Entering the Grand Hall, I sucked in a breath. It was heaving with people. I wondered if the news of my visit had travelled through the nest and everyone was eager to see how Marco reacted to my presence. It was probably the most action they'd had in a while.

At a subtle signal from Jared, the four vampires behind me paired up and began to circulate the room. Of course, I knew what Paige, Max, Ava, and Salem were doing: scoping out the large space and searching for potential threats.

Butch and I remained with Sam and Jared as they moved through the crowd. It was only a matter of moments before there was a gasp and a whispered, *'There's Marco's Imani.'* My back teeth locked. I hated being called that, but it was what many viewed me as—Marco's possession. I delved into my bag of tricks and pulled out my nonchalant air. That was what I'd need to get through tonight.

Butch said quietly, "Remember, stick close to me."

I did, ignoring the stares and whispers. Soon enough, people came to greet me and pepper me with questions. I was polite but vague, doing my best to hide my discomfort. I was glad to see one particular female Keja, though. Eleanor was Turned roughly the same time as me, so we'd experienced a lot of the early struggles together.

With a warm smile, Eleanor kissed my cheek and gave me a one-armed hug. "My God, I can't believe it's you! Annalise did say you were coming, but I never imagined you would return to this place."

"It's good to see you. I love this dress." The sleek, silver garment suited the brunette perfectly.

She tilted her head as she studied me. "You look the same, yet different. I can't explain it. And who are these vampires with you?" Her face went slack as she took in Sam and Jared. "Oh my God, I'm so sorry I didn't greet you immediately. I was just so distracted by the sight of Imani."

Jared held up a hand. "No offence was taken." She looked so relieved, I was surprised she didn't collapse.

"This is Butch, he's a member of the legion," I told her.

Eleanor did a slight curtsey. "It's wonderful to meet you."

Feeling eyes on me, I glanced to my right. "Eleanor, who's that blonde glaring at me like I've pissed in her shoes?"

Leaning close, Eleanor snickered. "That's Tait. Marco's second-born."

"Ah, so because I left him, she gets the first-born treatment."

"Yes. She's been sulking since she heard you were coming. Have you seen him yet?"

"Not yet."

She patted my arm. "Don't worry about him. The reunion might be a little tense, but that's only to be expected."

Catching a 'let's go' look from Sam, I smiled at Eleanor and said, "It was great seeing you. Take care."

Butch and I once again followed Sam and Jared through the large space. Several times we were stopped by awe-struck people who wanted to meet the pair. It was as we neared the rear of the hall that I caught a glimpse of Marco, surrounded by several vampires, his gun-metal grey eyes cold and predatory. As always, he looked both relaxed and coiled to strike at the same time.

"He's leaning against the wall up ahead," I whispered to Butch. "Tall. Blond hair. Dark suit."

Butch barely glanced his way, but I knew that—in that small moment—he would have absorbed every single detail. "He'll know you're here. He's probably been waiting for you to get close."

I nodded. Hell, Marco probably knew *exactly* where I was at that very moment. He never missed anything. And no doubt several people had ran to him with news of my arrival. I sent a telepathic warning to Jared, who would no doubt telepathically share the news with Sam and the others. It was best for everyone to be on their guard.

Pointedly ignoring Marco's presence, I kept my gaze firmly ahead as we passed his little group. None of them paid me any attention, though they briefly nodded at Sam and Jared. Hmm. Maybe Marco didn't actually care that—

"Well, well, well, the prodigal first-born returns." It surprised me that there wasn't a bitter edge to Marco's words.

Slowly turning, I forced a smile for my Sire, ex-boyfriend, and bad memory. His own smile was oddly warm and, if I wasn't mistaken, a little amused. Something was funny? "Marco," I greeted simply, conscious that a heavy silence had fallen and we were the focus of my entire nest's attention.

His eyes raked over me, though not in a sleazy way. "Looking good, sweetheart."

I didn't like his tone...because it was affectionate, and that made no sense. But then, Marco was a very good actor. As a human, I hadn't sensed the coldness behind that seriously good-looking exterior. And I'd paid for that mistake.

He flicked a look at the vampires with me and asked, "Aren't you going to introduce me, Imani?"

"I don't think I need to introduce Sam and Jared. This is Butch. Guys, this is Marco." As he raised an expectant brow, I reluctantly added, "My Sire."

Marco inclined his head their way, not breaking eye contact with me. "Part of the legion now, hmm, Imani? Good for you."

Well, if he could fake courtesy, I could do the same. "Thanks."

He looked at Sam. "You made a good decision when you recruited Imani."

Sam didn't seem to know what to make of him. "I did," she agreed.

Marco's gaze slid back to me. "Come have a talk with me; tell me what you've been doing all these years." It was more of a gentle demand than a request.

For some reason, I got the sudden and inexplicable feeling that he already knew what I'd been doing. But that couldn't be possible. "Maybe later." Or maybe fucking never.

His eyes flared ever so briefly, but it was enough for me to note the anger he was doing an excellent job of hiding. "Surely you can spare your own Sire a little of your time."

"As I said, maybe later."

A blonde slinked her way into his group and leaned into him, placing a possessive hand on his chest as she looked at me. "Who is she, Marco?" The knowing glint in her eyes told me she knew exactly who I was but was trying to communicate that I had little significance.

He didn't look at her as he replied, "Juliet, this is my Imani."

I gritted my teeth at Marco's use of the word 'my'. Butch went stiff as a board. Juliet…she just switched her full attention to Marco, and I got the feeling that I actually was completely insignificant to her. She was fully secure in her place in his life.

"Are you sure you won't stay and talk with me?" There was a silky menace to Marco's words, and I knew he'd be thoroughly pissed if I once again refused.

Just then, Tait appeared and curled into his other side, equally possessive as Juliet. The display was pitiful. Honestly, the way they stroked his chest and nuzzled his neck…all that was missing was someone fanning him with leaves while they fed him grapes.

"I'll leave you and the Playboy Bunnies to it," I said with a smile. Someone snickered. I wasn't sure whether it was that snicker, my refusal to stay with him, the hand Butch then possessively slayed on my back, or the fact that I'd insulted his consorts, but a low growl rumbled out of Marco. Just like that, I had Max, Paige, Ava, and Salem behind me.

Huffing, Juliet soothingly rubbed his chest. "Be calm, Marco. You don't need to be upset on my behalf, but I appreciate you being so protective."

Glaring at me, Tait sneered, "You might be technically Marco's first-born, but *I'm* the one who's been supporting him. *I'm* the one who's always at his side. *I'm* the one who does everything expected of a first-born."

This was supposed to affect me? I shrugged one shoulder. "Good for you, and good for him."

"You think you're so special, don't you? Well, you're *wrong*."

"So hostile." Seriously, her hatred of me was so thick, I could almost touch it. "You don't even know me."

Another sneer. "I don't need to know you. I've heard enough to know you're a complete bitch."

Wait, Marco had stolen my human life and then abandoned me…but *I* was the bad guy? This girl was wacked.

Butch tensed beside me as she took a small step closer. I placed my hand on his thigh to hold him back. I could deal with her, no problem.

"I've been waiting a long time to give you a piece of my mind."

"Can you afford to give me a piece?" I quipped.

Tait flicked a hand at me. "See, a complete bitch."

"It's a tough job, and quite often thankless. But I'm thinking it's still a better job than being a second-born playing at being a first-born."

Her fangs descended. "Such bravado coming from someone who ran away to play human because they couldn't handle their new life. Pitiful."

I rolled my eyes. "If I throw a stick, will you leave?"

"*You're* the one who doesn't belong here. You ran from your nest, you deserted them, and you can't simply reappear and expect to be welcomed. That's the issue here."

"That's not the real issue. But the issue isn't actually even the real issue. It's your issue with the issue that's the true issue, don't you think?"

Eyes blazing, she bared her teeth. "I'm not someone you should toy with."

"Does that mean you're done now?"

"Done? I haven't even started with you."

"That's too bad, because I'm a little preoccupied right now. But you could try consulting my middle finger if you like."

In a millisecond, she was directly in front of me and her hand was wrapped around my throat. She was unnaturally fast for a Keja. She was also gonna freaking pay for that.

My movements swift and smooth, I grabbed her wrist, snapped it back, punched her in the throat, and swept out my foot. Flat on her back, she gaped up at me in what appeared to be utter shock. That made me frown. "What do you think I do for the legion? Take notes?"

Her eyes tightened around the edges, and she tensed as if readying herself to lunge. But then Marco slowly came forward, his expression hard and his mouth set into a harsh line. I braced myself for an attack from him.

Her cheeks crimson, Tait stood upright. "Marco, you don't need to interfere. Really. She and I will duel this out."

Sounded good to me.

Gently, Marco skimmed his fingers over her face. "You don't like your mother, do you, Tait?" The female blinked, her brow creasing. "As a matter of fact, you hate her," he went on. "You've rambled on countless times about what a bitch she is. But let's say that someone else insulted your mother. You wouldn't like that, would you? No. Because we can insult what's ours but we don't like others doing it, do we? And that's the situation I find myself in with Imani. I can be angry with her, but I really don't like anyone else being angry with her. And I really, really don't like anyone wrapping their hand around her throat. So consider yourself lucky that she put you on your ass, because I'd have done much worse if the punishment was mine."

Okay, well that was *definitely* not what I'd expected him to say.

(Butch)

Based on the facts that Sam had given me, there were a dozen things I'd expected to happen at this little reunion.

I'd anticipated that Marco would be pissed with Imani. I'd anticipated that he wouldn't go the night without speaking to her. And I'd anticipated that he would switch on the charisma to hide his anger. What I hadn't anticipated was that Marco's cold eyes would light up like a Christmas tree when they landed on Imani.

The guy might be somewhat sociopathic, but he wasn't as dead inside as people believed. Something in him responded to Imani. His affectionate tone wasn't false. His possessiveness was more than that of a Sire. He was genuinely proud of her for being recruited by Sam and Jared. And he was truly enraged with his second-born. So maybe Sam was right and he'd protected Imani from afar all these years.

Marco jerked his head at Tait, and she scurried from the hall. He then turned to Imani, and his features smoothed out into a much calmer expression. "You okay, sweetheart?"

That 'sweetheart' shit was getting on my nerves.

Imani gave a careless shrug. "No harm done."

"Which is the only reason why she's conscious," he said. I believed him. Tait would have been on Shit Street if she'd wounded Imani.

"You should ensure your vampire understands there will be dire consequences if she touches Imani again," Sam told him, wisps of energy slithering along her skin, which was a clear sign she was pissed. "Imani won't be so gentle with her next time."

"Nor will I," said Marco. His eyes sliced to me. "You're standing very close to my Imani, but you didn't help her. You just stood back while she was attacked."

I inwardly snorted. "Imani doesn't need me to swat at annoying little flies for her. And if you thought differently, you really don't know her at all."

Jaw hardening, Marco took a step toward me, only to come to a complete halt when a tall vampire with a very *old* vibe about him appeared. Marco gave the vampire a deferential nod, so I had to assume it was Lazarus.

"I almost hope Tait misbehaves again just so I can see more of Imani in action," said the new vampire.

Imani smiled brightly at him. "Well if it isn't Zorro. How are you doing?" The guy really did look like Antonio Banderas in that movie, minus the mask.

Eyes gleaming, he replied, "I'm quite well, thank you. It has been too long since you were last here. But I will not scold you for that as I am too pleased to see you." No one could miss the genuine and rather paternal affection that he had for her.

Leading us all away from Marco, he inclined his head at Sam and Jared. "Good evening, I am Lazarus. It is an honour to have you here."

Imani introduced him to me and the rest of our squads, and we all exchanged brief greetings.

"I'm sorry about the reception you received from Tait, Imani." Lazarus sighed. "I had hoped things would go much more smoothly."

Imani shrugged. "It could have been worse."

It could have been fucking better.

"I expect she feels threatened by your presence," said Lazarus. "The reality is that Tait may behave as his first-born, but she wasn't the catalyst that led to him beginning his own line."

Sam nodded. "Seeing Imani is forcing her to face that reality."

"Precisely." Lazarus put a hand on Imani's shoulder. "Despite that you left and severed your bond, Marco never disowned you. He still acknowledges you as not only one of his vampires but as his first-born."

Imani's nose wrinkled. "I don't get that."

Lazarus opened his mouth to speak again, but then a female voice loudly crooned, "My beautiful Imani."

"Annalise," Imani said to the shapely woman who cradled her face like it was made of fine bone China.

"I have missed you so." Annalise gave Sam and Jared a gracious smile. "I'm sure you have been told this several times already, but we are incredibly pleased to have you here." She lowered her voice. "I heard about Tait's behaviour, Imani. I apologise on her behalf. She had no right to touch you."

"Imani handled it quite well," said Lazarus, clearly proud. "Tait was on the floor before anyone had the chance to intervene."

If I was honest, watching Imani take down that bitch so easily had been damn hot.

"Good. Still, Marco should have more control over his vampires." Annalise huffed in his direction. "Have you seen him with his two consorts? The three of them fancy themselves to be a couple."

A chuckle burst out of Imani, and I had to stifle a smile. Annalise talked as though it was some big scandal. Hell, Jared had three consorts before Sam came along. Clearly Annalise was a little old-fashioned.

Imani was wrong, Jared told me telepathically as Imani introduced Annalise to me and the other squad members. *Marco feels something for her. I think he really has been protecting her.*

Nodding at Annalise in greeting, I replied to Jared, *I agree.* I didn't want to be thankful to Marco for anything. But if that shithead had played a part in keeping her alive all these years, I was grateful to him. I still wanted to slit his throat.

We thought he'd be dramatically pissed because she escaped his hold. He's angry, but he's not as angry as what he should be.

That was something else I agreed with.

Sam and I have been discussing it. Obviously he meant telepathically. *Her theory is that Marco's never felt like Imani escaped him. He wasn't just watching over her to protect her, he was keeping tabs on her; he's always known where she was, what she was doing, and who she was doing it with. In that sense, he remained linked to her in his own way.*

I stilled. *Knowledge is power. Being so aware of every aspect of her life made him feel like he had some control over her.*

Exactly. I think he might have even believed Imani would come back to come when she was ready; that she just needed time to adjust and cool down. She stayed away for many years, but when life is eternal, years don't seem very long.

It would explain why he never renounced her. He'd been waiting for her to return and claim the position that was rightfully hers. *He probably sees her time in the legion as her spreading her wings and having some fun before she takes up the mantle.*

Yep. He hasn't took his eyes from her since she walked away. You should be careful.

Everything in me bristled. *I'm not afraid of that fucker.*

I know you're not, and I don't expect you to be. But he's clearly obsessed with her. He's noticed your possessiveness and he doesn't like it. In a duel, you could take him. But I don't think he'd challenge you. I think he'd attack you from afar before you had the chance to defend yourself.

He could try.

And I'd kill him if he did.

CHAPTER SEVEN

(Butch)

Lazarus and Annalise escorted us all to an empty parlour. With its old portraits, antique furniture, and the painted ceiling, it was even grander than the parlours at Antonio's half of the mansion at The Hollow.

No sooner were we all seated than Lazarus turned to me with a troubled expression and said, "I feel I should warn you to be careful of Marco. He is one of my most loyal vampires. He serves me well. But he can act rashly. I will warn him to steer clear of you. But Imani is his first-born and he believes this gives him rights that no one else should have. As such, I would advise you to keep your wits about you. If he comes for you, you will not sense him until it is too late."

Rather than assuring him I could take Marco, I just inclined my head.

"Tell us what you know about dragon shifters, Lazarus," said Sam.

"They are a fascinating species. Strong. Fierce. Dangerous. Ferociously protective of their own. In their dragon form, they are even stronger and their outer coat of armour comes in various colours. Some look rather exotic, others quite medieval.

"They can shift shape as easily as they can walk, but they cannot maintain their dragon form if they are weak. When they die, their bodies return to their human shape. In their dragon form, the majority have the ability to breathe scalding heat, smoke, and fire. But there are some that can breathe air so cold it encases their target in ice."

Imani raised her brows as she said dryly, "Charming."

"They live in droves, each of which is ruled by an Alpha. Unlike many species, they do not war amongst each other and they have no hierarchy of power. They simply exist. I admire that about them."

Jared crossed his legs at his ankles, looking deceptively relaxed. "I heard they don't like vampirekind much."

"That is true," confirmed Lazarus. "Once it was discovered that their blood had healing properties, people were convinced it could somehow cure vampirism. Those driven to find a cure often kidnapped the shifters and kept them prisoner while they used their blood. Some vampires, however—much like myself—found nonviolent ways of obtaining dragon blood. I pay a high price for donations. Dragon shifters have a weakness for gold and jewels."

Sam's brow furrowed. "Why would you want their blood?"

"To use for my trials," he replied. "Annalise and I were Turned without our consent. I have dedicated most of my vampiric life to finding a cure. Unfortunately, my attempts have so far been unsuccessful, but I have not lost hope."

"Do you do these trials on yourself?" asked Jared.

"No. It is not difficult to find volunteers, despite that some of the serums we developed have proven fatal. Many are so miserable with this life that they would rather be dead than be a vampire. The majority of the time, the serums have no effect whatsoever, even with dragon shifter blood."

I cocked my head. "Given how much they hate us, I'm surprised they'd sell their blood to you."

Lazarus looked at me. "As I said, they have a weakness for gold and jewels and pretty things. They like to accumulate valuable possessions. They hire out their services in other ways, too. For instance, they're often used as mercenary groups."

I stilled. "Mercenary groups?"

"A single dragon can wipe out a small town in a matter of minutes. You can imagine what an entire drove could do."

I exchanged looks with each of The Hollow's vampires; by their grim expressions, they were all thinking the same as me: It was possible that someone intended to hire a drove of dragon shifters to destroy The Hollow.

Sam spoke to Lazarus. "You're on good terms with the local

drove?"

Lazarus hesitated. "'Good terms' is not the phrase that I would use. We have a treaty. The drove does not cross into our territory, and we do not cross into theirs."

"We need to meet with the local drove," Jared told him. "Can you set that up?"

"I very much doubt that they would agree to that."

"It's important," said Jared.

Lazarus shook his head. "I'm sorry, they would do me no favours."

Annalise pursed her lips. "They might agree if…"

"If, what?" prodded Sam.

"If Marco were to ask," Annalise finished. "The Alpha is quite cordial with him. There is a mutual respect there."

"After what he did to Imani, I won't ask that prick for anything," snarled Jared, taking the words right out of my mouth.

"I swear, I won't see it as a betrayal if you ask for his assistance," vowed Imani.

My jaw hardened. "Imani, he—"

"This is bigger than me, Butch," she said. "He might not agree to help—he likes to play games too much. But there's no harm in Sam and Jared asking him."

The Grand High Pair fell silent, and I guessed they were discussing the matter telepathically. Their expressions gave nothing away.

Finally, Sam said to Lazarus, "Call Marco in here." The Master Vampire nodded at Annalise, who then left the room.

I gave Sam a 'You have to be fucking kidding me' look, at which point she studied Imani's face carefully.

"You sure you're okay with this?" Sam asked her.

"I'm sure." She looked as positive as she sounded.

Minutes later, Marco entered the room. His eyes immediately sought out Imani, and his face softened. "Hello again, sweetheart."

Fucker. I wanted to slide my arm around her shoulders and make a possessive statement that he couldn't miss, but it would no doubt piss her off. So I did nothing; I kept my expression blank, unwilling to let Marco see just how much his very existence got to me.

"Marco," began Lazarus, "the Grand High Pair needs to meet with the local dragon drove. Can you arrange that?"

"We don't mean the shifters any harm," Jared quickly added. "We just have some questions." When Marco didn't speak, Jared pushed, "Can you do it?"

"The drove tolerates me well enough," said Marco. "But they would not be inclined to meet with you or your mate. You're the most powerful vampires alive; they would feel threatened by your presence. You can't really blame them for that. If the situation were reversed, you would be just as wary."

"We'd be going there in peace," Sam assured him, but Marco shook his head.

"They wouldn't believe that. I can ask your questions for you."

"I don't trust you to tell us the truth."

Marco smiled at Sam's bluntness. "I can't say I'm surprised."

There was a long pause before Sam said, "We have reason to believe that dragons may attack The Hollow."

Lazarus and Annalise gasped.

Shocked she'd told him, I spoke to Jared, *What the fuck?*

Imani's safety matters to him, Jared pointed out. *If he thinks she is in danger, he might be more inclined to help.*

"Attack?" echoed Marco, eyes flaring.

"You know how much destruction their kind can cause," said Sam. "It's imperative that we find a way to stop this from happening."

Marco's eyes slid briefly to Imani before he said to Sam, "The drove would not accept you on their territory." His mouth twisted. "He might, however, allow one of your vampires to go there as a representative."

Knowing exactly where he was going with this, I snapped, "No."

His eyes darkened. "Imani's my first-born. The Alpha would be curious to meet her, and he has enough respect for me to at least consider the meeting." Marco turned back to Sam and Jared. "He'd point blank refuse to admit you two on his territory, however." He shrugged, as if it was all the same to him. "The choice is yours. I suppose it all depends on just how much you need to speak with him."

We needed it badly, but…"No."

Ignoring me, Marco arched a brow at Sam and Jared. "Well?"

After a tense pause, Sam said, "Fine, but don't think you can manipulate this situation so you have some alone time with Imani."

I was about to lose my shit at her decision when Jared's voice came into my head. *I spoke to Imani. She said she's okay with this. Don't worry, you'll be going along.*

"If she goes, she won't go without some back-up from us," Sam stated.

Marco's eyes narrowed. "She has my protection. She doesn't need anyone to accompany her."

"I don't trust you to protect her," said Sam. "And neither does Imani."

Face once again softening as his gaze slid to Imani, Marco said, "Sweetheart, you know I'd never harm you."

"You already did," said Imani. That arrow hit its mark, because Marco's fists clenched.

"She's not going without guards," Jared insisted.

"Two other vampires can come along with Imani." Marco jerked his chin at me. "But I don't want *him* with us."

"Three will go," said Sam. "And one of them *will* be Butch. He's a shield. He can protect her in a blink."

"Fine." But Marco seemed far from 'fine' with it. "I'll contact the Alpha. He'll probably take a few days to give you an answer purely to annoy you."

Sam gave him a curt nod. "Contact us when you hear from him."

Marco looked at Imani. "I'll be seeing you soon, sweetheart."

Then Jared teleported us all out of there.

(Imani)

By the time I got back to my apartment, I was emotionally drained. Seeing some of my nest, particularly Lazarus, Annalise, and Eleanor, had been great. But I was the kind of person who found social situations tiring after a while. Putting on an 'I'm totally aloof to Marco' act had been just as draining—as had facing Marco again, for that matter.

Whether or not he'd truly be of any help, I wasn't sure. Life was one big game to Marco. But if Sam and Jared were right and Marco had helped me to stay alive all these years, just maybe he would also help with this.

Still, the Grand High Pair hadn't seemed very optimistic when they left to talk with Antonio and Luther. The four intended to work out who would want the entire island destroyed so badly that they would hire dragon shifters. Jared had made a good point when he said that the person behind this didn't have to be a vampire; they could be anyone. That made the pool of suspects much wider.

Not wanting to think about it anymore, I indulged in a long, relaxing bath. Well, it *would* have been relaxing if I'd been able to clear my mind. How could I, when I was consciously aware that my three nights were up? Butch would be here soon, and he'd want us to talk.

Honestly, I didn't have the emotional energy to deal with it. But I didn't want to delay it any longer, because I didn't like having things up in the air. Besides, there would be no turning Butch away. He was too freaking stubborn.

Once the water turned cold, I left the tub. Having pulled on a tank top and pair of shorts, I then settled on the sofa with my Kindle and a vanilla-flavoured NST. I was only two chapters into my book when there was a knock at the door. With a steadying breath, I put down my Kindle and headed for the door. As I opened it wide, my libido went totally hyper.

He looked good. Too good. One thing I could say for Butch was that he had style. Always looked neat and presentable. There was never a single wrinkle in his designer clothes, most of which were dark and plain yet still smart and stylish.

In two slow, predatory steps, Butch was inside the apartment, closing the door behind him. His brow creased in concern. "You look wiped again. I could kill that bitch from the bar."

"I'm not as tired as I was last night, so the exhaustion's wearing off."

His fingers combed through my damp hair. "I'd still like to kill her."

Yeah, so would I.

"Your three nights are up, baby." He stroked his knuckles down the column of my throat. "Now we're going to have the conversation we should have had when you woke up in my bed."

I nodded. "Want an NST?"

"You need pure blood if you're going to get your strength back. But we'll get to that later." He took my wrist. "Let's get more comfortable while we talk." In a blink, he moved so that I was straddling him on the sofa.

And I remembered how much he liked me to ride him; how much he liked to tell me how fast and how hard to take him. Remembered how he liked to look into my eyes the entire time.

His hands cupped my hips and pulled me closer, snapping me out of my memories. "I laid it all out for you three nights ago. I told you what I want and need from you. You needed time to process everything; I get that. I gave you time. Now this is where you lay all your shit out for me. I'm relying on you to be as straight with me as you always are."

I sighed. "Honestly, I'm still not sure this is for real. I never thought you'd choose to try a relationship."

"There was never a choice, baby. I have to have you."

"Because of the cravings. That's just sex, Butch, and it's not enough to keep a real relationship going. It's just not."

He pinned my gaze. "Every time the human touched you, every time he made you smile or laugh, it fucking hurt. My lungs would burn and my chest would ache. Every. Time. That doesn't happen when it's only about sex, Imani."

No, it didn't. And I hadn't expected him to say that; I didn't have a response for it.

"Stop." His thumb tugged my lower lip free of my teeth. "You're making me want to bite it, and that's distracting. Now, tell me, are you fighting me so hard because you don't want this…or because you do but you're scared to take a chance on me?"

"I *did* take a chance on you."

"And I fucked it up. I know that. And trust me when I say that no one regrets that more than I do. I tried to let you go. It didn't work. It was never going to work, but I didn't see that until it was too late. I drove you away, and for that I'm sorry. That shit won't happen again."

Searching his gaze, I saw only sincerity there. But it wasn't enough. "I think you believe that. I think you want us to be together and that you want it to be a permanent thing. But I also think there's a good chance that it won't happen that way."

"Explain."

"We have some obstacles to deal with. If we got together, not a single person would support us in that. They'll doubt that you're serious about it for all the same reasons that I did. You have a bad rep. You like your emotional space. You've never shown any interest in relationships."

"I know—"

"Just hear me out. A year ago, when I lasted more than one night with you, people were hopeful. Even though it seemed to be only casual sex, they thought that just maybe you'd pull your head out of your ass. They thought that just maybe you might take a shot at something more. But then the end of the month came, and you made it clear that we wanted different things. Let me again repeat that I'm not judging you for that—I never did. But *they* did. So it won't matter what you say to them; you won't convince them that you're serious. They'll figure that you'll be gone once we hit the one-month mark."

His hands flexed on my hips. "They'll be wrong."

"My point is that during that time, you can bet your ass that they won't be cool about it. They won't even consider giving you the benefit of the doubt. They'll try to convince me to walk away. There'll be a lot of tension. Is that what you want?"

"You're more important to me than them. I don't give a fuck if I have other people's approval or not. I don't need it. Eventually, they'll see that they were wrong and that shit will be over."

"Maybe, but that's not the only obstacle we'll be facing. My reflex to anyone pushing me is to completely disregard every word they're saying, which will rub you the wrong way because you're a naturally pushy person. Am I wrong?"

"No, which means I'll have to work on not barking orders, and you'll have to work on not doing the opposite just to be contrary."

The guy had an answer for everything. "How about the fact that you don't connect with people? You don't share what's going on in your head; you internalise everything, and you hide your emotions so damn well that most people think you don't feel anything. This won't work if you can't be open with me. And I don't want to be in a relationship where I'm having to read between the lines and guess what my partner is thinking. I need you to talk to me, to share with me, to be upfront with me. I'm not saying I want you to change, I don't. I'm just saying I'd need you to work with me to keep this relationship going, and that means communicating."

"I've been upfront about my feelings so far, haven't I?"

Okay, he had a point there. "But could you keep doing that?"

"With you, yeah. Just don't expect me to be like that with everybody else."

"There's something else that's going to be an issue. I hate to say it—really, really hate to say it—but I have jealousy issues. Don't get me wrong, I recognise that this is *my* problem to deal with, and I wouldn't become paranoid or see things that aren't there. But you've slept with a lot of females on this island, and I won't do well with that. I can be a bitch when jealousy is riding me," I warned.

"None of them meant anything to me. Not one." His thumbs stroked my hipbones. "But Dean *did* mean something to you, and it's pretty hard for me to deal with that even though I'm not a jealous person. So I figure we both need to make the other feel secure enough that those issues go away.

"Look, I know this won't be easy, Imani. *I* won't be easy. I can be pushy, selfish, insensitive, aggressive, and I like my own way. I'll fuck up, but I will never purposely hurt you. I want to be the one who makes you smile, who makes you laugh, who makes you feel safe, and who makes you come every night. I'll do my damn best to make sure all of that happens."

I swallowed, unable to miss the total sincerity in his eyes and tone. I'd never thought I'd hear those words from him. Never.

"You're right that we'll have no support from the people around us. That means we gotta be tight, Imani. It means we gotta stand strong against it and have each other's back. I'm up for that challenge. This is not me choosing to *try* a relationship. I'm claiming you as mine. You belong to me and only me, just like I belong to you."

Pausing, he framed my face with his hands. "I'm a big risk. I get that. No one—not even me, baby—can judge you for being hesitant to take that risk. So maybe you should ask yourself if you'd regret it if you *didn't* take that risk. I know what it's like to live with that kind of regret, Imani. Let me tell you; it's shit, and it eats at you. I didn't take a risk on you when I should have. I didn't make the right choice, and that hurt us both. I won't pull that shit again. I want you to be happy. I don't know how the fuck I'll manage to make you happy, but I'll sure as hell try."

It wasn't often I found myself a little lost for words. I couldn't remember a time when my happiness had mattered to anyone. I'd grown up in a household where I was a constant disappointment to the people around me. I'd just never been good enough for them, never had a real place in my own family. It was more like I'd existed around them.

Not once had my parents ever smiled at just the sight of me. Nothing I did had ever impressed them or brought them joy or pride. Not one single thing. They'd wanted me to live my life *their* way, regardless of if that made me happy or not. I wanted to be happy. Sometimes, searching for good things meant taking risks.

I put my hands on his chest. "Want to know why I don't like entering into relationships that don't have possibilities? My grandmother was in her late twenties when she got divorced. She didn't do too well with it, and she was pretty lonely. She told me that she met a guy a few years later; that he cared for her and she cared for him...but she wasn't ready for anything serious. She needed more time before she committed to someone again. So they went their separate ways.

"She never found anyone else. People take it for granted that they'll meet someone later 'when they're ready.' But that doesn't always happen, so they end up settling for somebody because they don't want to be alone. My grandmother didn't want to settle for someone she didn't truly care for. So she grew old alone, she shared all her highs and lows alone, and she died alone. I don't want that for myself. I don't want to live with that kind of regret."

"Is this you agreeing to take a chance on me, baby?"

"Well...yeah."

His mouth curved into a lopsided grin. "Good...that means I don't have to keep you captive until you agree to give me what I want." I got the feeling he wasn't kidding. "And I want everything, Imani. I know I've gotta earn that. I will. I swear that to you, baby."

I nodded. His mouth closed over mine, and his tongue swept inside. Tasted. Dominated. Owned. Butch didn't kiss, he possessed. Demanded everything I had and took it greedily while his hands pulled me closer, letting me feel how hard he was for me.

He broke the kiss with a growl. "All I want to do right now is fuck you. But first, you need to feed."

I did. When Kejas were thirsty, it caused a slight discomfort at the back of our throat. Mine was now more like a rough tickle. As he cupped the back of my head and put my mouth to his throat, my fangs descended.

"Feed, baby. You need it." He groaned as I sank my fangs into his throat. "That's it. Good girl."

His taste—hazelnuts and dark chocolate—settled on my tongue, soothed my throat, and seemed to spread through me like warm honey. I drank and drank, helplessly grinding against the long, hard cock digging into me. Forcing myself to pull back, I licked over the bite and watched as it closed.

Growling, he fisted a hand in my hair and yanked me closer. I expected him to do what he'd done many times before: pull my head aside and bite hard. Hell, I was looking forward to it. He didn't. Instead, he licked at my throat—long, sensual licks that made my toes curl. I had a seriously sensitive neck, and it seemed to have a direct link to my clit. And the bastard knew it.

I threaded my fingers through his hair as his tongue circled my pulse. When he sucked it into his mouth, I gasped...waiting with anticipation for him to bite down. His teeth dug into my skin, but they didn't break it. Then he was licking at my throat again. Lapping my pulse. Nipping it. Grazing it with his teeth. Everything but biting it.

Was he waiting for me to *ask* him to do it? Was that it? I wasn't too proud to ask, especially not when I was wet and aching for him. "Drink from me." He held my rapidly beating pulse between his teeth, but he still didn't bite down. "Do it and—" I broke off as his hand dove into my shorts and panties, cupping me possessively. "Shit."

He spoke into my ear as he slid a finger between my folds. "I'll have my taste when my cock's in you, taking what belongs to me. *Only me*, Imani." He thrust his finger inside. "Ride it."

I rose up and down on his finger, my head falling back as sensations rocketed through me.

The hand in my hair pulled my face to his. "No," he said against my mouth. "I want your eyes." I kept my gaze locked with his as I rode his finger, my nails biting into his shoulders. "That's it. You're getting tighter. You need to come, don't you?"

I did, I needed it right then...but he shook his head.

"Not until I'm in you."

"I can't wait."

"You will." He drove another finger inside me, his eyes daring me to come despite his warning. *Motherfucker.* It wasn't that Butch got off on defiance or even submission. No, he got off on pushing me; on making me take as much as I could take. So when his fingers curved just right and my release got that little bit closer, he withdrew his fingers—not in the least bit bothered by the insults I slung at him.

In Pagori speed, he took me to the bedroom, stripping us both naked along the way. He roughly flung me on the bed and draped himself over me. Then his hand was palming my breast as he sucked my nipple deep into his mouth. Hard. Roughly. Letting me feel the edge of his teeth. "Fuck, baby, this is going to be fast." His tongue curled around my neglected nipple before giving it one long, hard suck. "I've waited too long for this."

Curling my limbs tight around him, I dug my nails into his back. "Then don't wait any longer." I arched into him, rubbing against the head of his cock. "Now."

He slammed home, groaning as my body squeezed and pulsed around him. I'd totally forgot how much he stretched me; forgot how good the burn felt. He didn't pause to let me get used to his size. Just pounded into me at a feral pace, going so deep it hurt. But I loved that, even needed it. No one had ever fucked me the way he did—his movements were always dominant and aggressive, and yet there was a reverence there that I could feel but not fully explain.

"I've missed this," he rumbled against my throat, closing a hand over my breast and squeezing hard. "Missed the feel of you. Tight and hot and perfect. You were made to take my cock, Imani." He thrust harder, faster. His teeth raked over my pulse, teasing and warning me. And when he slid a hand between us to part my folds, exposing my clit to every hard slam of his cock, my release finally crashed into me.

Contracting around him, I screamed. Butch sank his teeth into my throat, drinking deep. At the same time, his spine locked and he exploded deep in me with a growl.

Feeling totally wiped, I melted into the mattress, panting and shaking.

He licked over the bite. "Needed that." He rolled us so that I was sprawled on his chest with his cock still in me. His eyes roamed over my face. "Never thought I'd have you again." The pain of that was in his tone. "This is gonna be a rough ride, baby."

"I know." We each had our issues to deal with, and people weren't going to accept our relationship in a hurry.

"Are you with me?"

"I'm with you."

"That's all I need to know." He tucked my face into his neck. "Sleep."

CHAPTER EIGHT

(Imani)

Our plan to reveal our relationship was pretty simple: we'd tell everyone all at once by walking into the conference room, hand in hand. Then nobody could be pissed that someone found out before them, and we could get the whole 'you two are making a mistake' thing over and done with in one swoop.

However, Fletcher sent a text message to notify us that there would be no conference that evening. As such, Butch and I altered our plan so that we would make our relationship public when we entered the arena to begin our training session.

I wasn't looking forward to it, but I was in a good mood since Butch woke me at dusk by shoving his cock deep in me. It was slow and sensual this time, but still just as phenomenal. Probably just because it was him.

Ready to leave, Butch gave me one last deep kiss as I opened the door. Then I heard a gasp…and realised our plan had just been fucked up. Paige and Alora stood gaping at us. But Paige's expression quickly became a scowl.

Alora pointed from me to Butch. "You…and you?"

As he slid an arm around my shoulders, I replied, "Yeah, we're together now."

"But…you said you were done with the bed buddy thing."

I nodded. "That's true, and—"

"You said you were done with *him*. You said you were done with letting him use you."

"I know, but—"

"How long has this been going on?" Paige snapped. "Is this why he came here the other night? You know what, I can't believe you'd keep something like this from me."

I'd known that would bother her most of all. We'd been through a lot together; she'd trusted me with all her secrets. "Paige, it wasn't like that." There hadn't been much to tell until last night.

She took a step back, her smile bitter. "Oh, I see what it was like."

"I was going to tell you, tell *all* of you, tonight. This is—"

"Bullshit," Paige bit out. "It's. Total. Fucking. Bullshit. You're smarter than this." She pointed at Butch. "And if you cared about anyone but yourself, you'd realise she deserves better. You'd walk away before you hurt her *again*."

I held up a hand. "Paige, just let me talk a second."

"Talk?" She barked a sardonic laugh. "You weren't interested in talking to me about this before. How many times have I confided in you, Imani? How many times have I told you shit that I've never told anyone? Yet, here you are keeping things from me."

"Paige—"

"Not that I need to ask *why* you kept this from me. You knew I wouldn't like it; you knew I'd tell you that you're being dumb, and you didn't want to hear that. You didn't want to hear the truth, because you didn't want to face it. You wanted to live in a fantasy land where Butch actually gives a flying fuck about you."

He puffed out a breath. "Didn't have you pegged as the dramatic type, Paige."

"Excuse me?" she hissed.

"You're protective of Imani, I get it. You don't want her to be with someone like me, I get that too. But this isn't about you. And if you'd push past your protective streak and your hurt feelings and let her fucking speak, you'd hear that you've got this wrong."

"No, Butch, you might be able to bullshit her, but you won't bullshit me. Nu-uh." With that, she stormed off with a majorly annoyed Alora close behind her.

Sighing, I rubbed at my forehead. "I can't say that didn't hurt. But I also can't say I didn't expect it to go like that. It's going to be mere moments before this reaches the others." Alora would tell Evan, who would tell Sam and Jared. Paige would tell the other girls, at which point Jude and Ava would tell their mates. Salem and Chico would then tell the other members of their squad. "Paige is seriously pissed at me."

Butch kissed my temple. "She'll get over it."

"You don't know Paige like I do. That girl can hold a grudge."

"Having second thoughts?"

I frowned. "No. I knew when I made my choice that people would react badly. You were right; we have to be tight and stand against it."

"So you're still with me on that?"

"I'm with you."

He nodded in satisfaction and twined his fingers with mine. "Let's get to the arena and get the rest of this shit over with."

As if by mutual agreement, we took a slow walk out of the building and to the arena. It seemed that neither of us were in any rush to listen to more people slate our decision. I kept my chin up as we walked inside, still hand in hand. To my surprise, none of the girls were there. I didn't know what that meant, but I guessed it was an 'I'm so pissed at you, I can't even look at you right now' message.

Butch's squad was there, however. With the exception of David and Salem, they all scowled at him. The weight of their disapproval and anger set on my shoulders like lead. It also ticked me off big style. Who were they to freaking judge?

None of them spoke. They just stared at Butch expectantly, as if waiting for him to begin explaining himself.

Finally, Chico arched a brow at Butch. "Got something you want to tell us?"

Butch just shrugged, nonchalant. "You already know."

"It's not enough that you fucked her over once before?"

I was about to make it clear that he hadn't fucked me over; that I'd known what I was getting into a year ago and I'd chosen to take a risk, but Reuben was speaking before I could.

"I thought better of you, Butch. I really did."

"Jude is having a shit fit right now," said Chico. "She's also considering slicing off your balls. I had to confiscate her knife."

"It's nothing to do with Jude or any of you," Butch stated, his tone even.

"Wrong," insisted Chico. "This is *Imani* we're talking about. She's not just anyone. She's a member of the legion, she's under our protection."

"If you want to be a hit and run guy," began Harvey, "I figure that's your business. But when the girl you're running over is a member of the legion and under our protection, it becomes our business."

Chico nodded. "We gave you the benefit of the doubt a year ago, because we trusted that you wouldn't get involved with someone you're supposed to protect unless it was serious. We realised we were wrong. So don't think any of us will trust you not to hurt her a second time."

"There are other females on this island for you to use and drop," said Damien.

I narrowed my eyes. "And you're so certain he'll use and drop me?"

Looking at me like I was dumb, Damien snapped, "Well he's done it before, honey."

"Careful," warned Butch. It was a lethal whisper that made Damien swallow hard.

"He doesn't use women to be an asshole, Imani," Denny told me, his voice gentle. "He does it because he's not capable of more. That's why we're worried here."

Nodding, Max turned to Butch. "I'd like to think you've changed. I'd like to think that you'll be different with Imani. But I know you won't, because you walked away from her once before."

"And you know this isn't good or you wouldn't have hidden it," added Reuben.

Butch lifted a single brow. "Since when do I have to announce the details of my personal life to all of you?"

No one had an answer to that.

Wiping a hand over his face, Stuart looked at me. "Imani, you've got to see that Butch isn't who you need. You just got out of a relationship after being let down by someone you trusted. Do you really want to go through that again?"

"Is this like a rebound thing?" Harvey asked me. "You're feeling lonely and vulnerable and just looking for something to fill the void?"

My eyes widened. "No. It's so far from a rebound, it isn't even funny—not that I need to justify myself to you. And I'd just like to point out that some people worried that Salem wouldn't be good for Ava, but no one said shit about it." Though that may have been because Sam threatened that any interference would be met with bodily harm.

Damien, Stuart, and Denny shifted uncomfortably as they glanced guiltily at Salem.

Reuben jabbed a finger in Butch's direction. "If you have any decency in you, you'll end this before you have the chance to hurt her."

Looking bored, Butch ran his gaze along everyone. "You all done now?"

Reuben cursed. "Don't you have any—" He cut off as Sam and Jared entered the arena. "Have you heard about Imani and Butch's special news?" he asked, his tone mocking.

"I don't think that's the business of anyone here other than Imani and Butch," said Sam.

I blinked, surprised.

Chico gaped at her. "You can't tell me you're okay with this, Coach."

David cleared his throat. "Let's just forget about this and start the session. Coach is right; this is their business." Salem grunted in agreement.

After a moment, Reuben inclined his head. "Fine." His annoyed gaze moved to me and Butch. "I think it would be best if you two go. Emotions are running too high in here right now, and we need to have our heads straight while we're training."

My mouth fell open. Had he really just said that?

Face blank, Butch said to him, "I don't recall asking what you think is best. If Coach and Jared want us to leave, we'll do just that." Butch looked at the couple. "But I'll never enter this arena again. I remember Max once making an offhand comment about you two out of jealousy."

The image of awkwardness, Max averted his gaze.

"You told him personal shit has no place in this arena," Butch said to Sam. "Is that true? Or does that only apply to some people?"

She didn't reply, but her next words made her stance perfectly clear. "Take your usual places."

Chico's face hardened. "Coach, seriously—"

"I *am* bloody serious," she fairly snarled. "You can be pissed at Butch and Imani in your own time. Though why you're all taking this personally as if they're together to spite you, I don't know. It's bloody ridiculous. Stop fucking whining and get your shit together."

Jared nodded his agreement. "You get to feel how you feel, but you don't get to use this arena as a place to vent."

Glancing around, Sam frowned. "Where are the girls?" When no one spoke, she hissed, "Jared, call them here *now*."

Looking a little worried on Jude's behalf, Chico again spoke, "Coach—"

"Not another bloody word."

Everyone fell silent as we waited for the rest of my squad to arrive. Paige fairly marched inside. Other than Ava, who cast me a weak smile, the girls pointedly ignored me. Nice.

Flicking her brown hair over her shoulder, Jude sighed. "Look, Sam—"

"If what's about to come out of your mouth has anything to do with Imani and Butch, I don't want to hear it," Sam snapped, the mercury tint to her irises flaring slightly. It clearly took the girls aback. I couldn't blame them for looking wary; I wouldn't like to be on the receiving end of Sam's anger either.

"Considering we might soon find ourselves in a battle with dragon shifters, we need to be at the top of our game," said Jared, face hard. "We don't have time for this shit."

"You're here to train, nothing else," said Sam, slashing her hand through the air. "Now all of you stand over there and listen to what Jared and I have to say."

(Butch)

Abashed, everyone did as they were told. I led Imani to the front and centre of the group—it was a message that we wouldn't be pushed out. If the scowls directed at me were anything to go by, the message was received and it wasn't much liked.

Slowly pacing in front of us, Sam began, "Most of you have been in battle before; you know what to expect, you know how bad it can get, you know the best attack and defence formations, and you know who to partner with if splitting up is necessary." She halted. "But all of that is going to mean jack shit in the upcoming war.

"We won't be up against our own kind. We'll be up against creatures bigger and stronger than us. Worse, they can bloody fly—I don't need to tell you that's gonna be a *big* problem. It means they can fight from above, dodge our gifts with minimal effort, and it would be difficult to stop them from passing us."

"The latter will be the biggest problem," said Jared, feet wide apart. "In a battle against charging vampires, we could hold them off. But these creatures could just fly right over our heads."

Sam resumed pacing. "Jared and I did a lot of thinking, and we've come up with some ideas that might help. You know I can extend my energy shield outwards to protect others. But what if I used it to contain the dragons in one place? It would mean we were inside the shield with them, so we wouldn't be protected from them. But it would also mean they were trapped with us and unable to go any further. It would mean that any damage they did would be unable to spread."

"Can you do that?" Imani asked.

Sam bit the inside of her cheek. "I don't know. I'm hoping that if Reuben boosts my gift, it will be enough for me to expand my shield that far outwards. I'd have to practice a lot."

"You're a hybrid with a shitload of power," said Reuben. His gift allowed him to strengthen or weaken the gifts of others. "Boosting that power should do it."

"But could you control all that power?" Max asked Sam.

"I'll learn, because there's no other acceptable result."

Harvey raised his hand, like a kid in a classroom. "Um, I hate to be a kill-joy, but...well, I'm guessing they'll be flying pretty fast. Could you cover them with the shield fast enough to keep them all contained?"

"Probably not." Sam looked at me. "That's where you come in. You can form a protective wall. You use that as a shield and often stretch it around you. But what if we enlarged that wall? What if we made it so tall and wide that anything that flew at it crashed?"

It could be possible, but... "I've never done anything like that before."

"That doesn't mean you can't," said Jared.

"I can form walls of energy," began Sam, "but the energy I feed from is a crazy mixture of kinetic energy, solar energy, and my own preternatural energy—that makes it vibrant and visible. The dragons would see it."

But my shield didn't glimmer because it was generated by my own individual energy, not a combination of varying energies. That meant the unsuspecting dragons would fly right into it.

"If they're flying fast, they'll crash hard," Jared pointed out. "Even if they don't fall to the ground, they'll be unbalanced and confused long enough for Sam to extend her shield over us all."

"We can try it now." Sam gestured for me to move forward.

Reluctantly leaving Imani's side, I advanced a few steps.

Nodding in satisfaction, Sam said, "Bring up your shield."

It was easy enough to do, since it was something I'd done a thousand times. Raising my hands, I let the preternatural energy that filled me flow out of my palms and form a shield that I could feel but not see.

"Instead of pulling it around you, stretch it outwards."

As I extended my arms, I pushed out more preternatural energy to widen the shield.

"Now try making it higher."

I raised my arms and made the shield increase in height.

Sam smiled. "That's really good. Reuben, do your thing."

With a brief touch to my shoulder, Reuben's ability caused mine to grow in strength.

"Right, this time I want you to extend the shield so far that it forms a wall between you and everyone else." Sam urged Jared to move with her to stand with the group, leaving me alone. "Think about pushing it outwards."

I didn't move my arms at all, just kept them above my head as I let more and more energy slowly trickle out of my palms until it stretched the shield, making it higher and wider. I felt it bump something—I was hoping it had collided with the walls and the roof.

"Now we need to test just how high it is." Sam pivoted on her heel. "Denny, jump."

The animal mimic could jump as fast and high as a copepod. He swallowed. "What if it worked and Butch's shield stretched that high?"

"It'll hurt," Sam said simply. "Maybe not as much as your attitude hurt Imani and Butch, but it'll be close."

Oh, she was totally ruthless.

She waved an impatient hand at Denny. "Well, go on."

Looking like he'd rather do anything other than that, Denny bent his knees and leapt—it was a seriously impressive move. And it made him crash hard into the shield. He landed with a grunt.

Imani looked down at him, her expression aloof. "Hmm, it worked."

"My shield will need to be a lot higher and wider than that to stop a flying drove of dragons," I pointed out.

"It will," Sam agreed. "We'll have to do some training in the rainforest where you'll have more space. It's not going to be something that happens instantly. It'll take work, just like my attempts to expand a dome-like shield will take a lot of practice."

Max spoke, "If it doesn't work?"

Sam's face hardened with resolve. "It has to work."

"Quick question," Ava interjected. "If you're expending a lot of your energy into keeping the shield in place, does that mean you can't use your gift in other ways?"

Sam sighed. "It does. But if I concentrate hard enough, I can form energy balls while I'm inside my shield. It's hard and it takes a lot of concentration, but it can be done. The trouble is, low level energy balls won't do much against a drove of dragons."

"Our number one goal is to bring the dragons to the ground," said Jared. "Then Sam can afford to drop the shield and direct her energy elsewhere. But you've been trained to fight without us. You've been trained not to rely on us as back-up or as leaders. There'll be a hell of a lot of vampires inside that dome—pretty much the entire legion. The dragons will see that fast enough, and they'll try to flee. We need to keep them contained, which is why Sam's shield is vital. I'll cover her while she keeps it in place. The rest of you will surround us."

"You won't be able to pair up in the same way that you usually do," Sam told us. "Some of you have gifts that will make the dragons drop to the ground. The rest of you will be relied on to kill all those that fall. Salem, David, Max, Denny, Harvey, and Cassie will tackle those in the air. Everyone else here will need to concentrate on the fallen. That won't be an easy task, considering the sods can kill you just by breathing in your general direction. You all need to be at your sharpest, fastest, and canniest."

"Which is why your training sessions will focus on making sure that you will be," added Jared. "So let's begin."

No one's attitude toward me or Imani softened but, to the credit of both squads, they were totally professional throughout the session. But the moment it was over, the guys went back to scowling at me. Also, the girls went back to ignoring Imani—except for Ava, who shot her a small smile. I had the feeling that she wasn't upset with Imani, but she was worried that Imani had put herself in a situation where I could hurt her.

Just as Imani and I were about to exit the arena, Sam called us over. She waited until the rest of the squads had left before she spoke. "You two all right?"

Imani shrugged. "Been better. Also been worse."

"Let's have a little chat. No need to go on the defence," she quickly assured me when I stiffened. "I'm not about to pass judgement or give you crap."

I raised a brow. "Even though it's caused tension in the ranks?"

It was Jared who responded. "I don't think their reaction would have been so bad if they weren't worrying so much about the dragon shifter situation. There's also our blogger, who's still posting articles and remaining out of reach. Everyone's feeling helpless."

Sam nodded. "Hearing about you two was just the cherry on the icing of the messed up cake."

"Still no luck finding the blogger?" Imani asked her.

Sam released a frustrated sigh. "No. His gift is still protecting him well. Right now, I'm more worried about your vision and whether the dragons you saw were mercenaries. If not, we've done something to piss off a dragon drove enough that they want The Hollow's vampires destroyed."

"If Marco doesn't come through for us," said Jared, "we might not find the answer to that question in time to prevent the attack. If that happens, all we can do is prepare for war."

Later that night, as Imani and I lay on the sofa watching a movie, her phone beeped. I paused the movie as she grabbed her cell from the table and read the message. Disappointment flashed across her face.

I tensed. "What's wrong?"

Sprawled over my chest, she said, "Nothing's wrong. It's just Fletcher, sharing a dirty joke."

She'd hoped it would be Paige, I realised. "She'll come round." Imani's smile wasn't fooling me. She was hurting, and it pissed me off. Paige hadn't answered any of Imani's calls or replied to any of her texts.

It hadn't occurred to me that the girls would be so harsh on Imani. I'd known they wouldn't approve of the relationship, and so I'd expected them to attempt to talk Imani into ending it, but... "I would never have thought they would freeze you out like this."

"They've jumped to the conclusion that you and I have been an item for a while and I kept it from them."

I threaded my fingers through her hair. "Even if that were true, it wouldn't excuse what they're doing. They're making this about them, and it's not."

"You don't get it because guys don't really confide in each other much. But women are different. We talk and share secrets and give advice. They—most especially Paige—trusted me with their shit and so they're upset that I haven't done the same."

It was more than that. "They're making a statement that they don't like us being together."

"That too." She sighed. "They worry about me, that's all."

It didn't mean it was cool for them to take that worry out on her. "I'm sorry you're hurting, baby." I kissed her softly. "Want to finish watching the movie or are you as bored by it as I am?"

"It is a little dull." Propping her chin on my chest, she said, "Tell me about your nest. I know you don't like questions, but you said you'd be open with me."

And I'd meant it. Besides, a change of subject might be good for her. "My nest was pretty small."

"Was?"

"There aren't many left. We all lived in one apartment building. I was a sentinel for my Sire. His mate was tough like Sam, only she was sane."

Imani snorted a laugh.

"All three of us went to a Binding event for a week. My Sire's firstborn, Tad, was left in charge. While we were gone, he got into some kind of argument with another vampire in a club. They duelled. Tad lost, but his opponent didn't kill him; he wanted Tad to live with the shame of losing in front of the entire club."

"Harsh on the ego."

"Yes. Tad's weakness was his ego." Slipping my hand inside her shirt, I smoothed it up and down her back. "Tad couldn't let it go. He went back to the club, and my nest all went along. Only this time, they went after the guy's mate. By killing her, Tad killed him. The guy's nest retaliated and wiped out everyone in our building."

She bit her lower lip. "I know this is an insensitive thing to say, but Tad should have known he'd never get away with that. He should have been smart."

"You're right, but he wasn't. We came back to a burned-down building." My Sire had been devastated. "They deserved it. There was no arguing with that." If anyone went after Imani to get to me, I'd make sure she was avenged somehow—even if I wasn't strong enough to do the avenging myself. Depending on how old and powerful the vampire was, it usually took a few nights for them to die after their mate was killed.

"I have another question. How did you become a vampire?"

"It's a common story. I was dying on a battlefield, and someone came along and gave me a choice to live as a vampire or die as a human. To be honest, I thought he was full of shit." Vampires looking to create a nest often went to battlefields, where they were most likely to find willing humans. It was amazing what choices people would make when they thought they faced death.

"You were in the army?"

"Yes." And I'd enjoyed it. The discipline, the neatness, the action—all of it had spoken to me on some level.

"How old were you when you were Turned?"

"Guess."

Tilting her head, she studied every line and curve of my face. "Thirty?"

"Close. Thirty-five."

"Tell me about your human life."

My mouth curved. "Very curious tonight, aren't you?"

She shrugged one shoulder. "You never really told me anything about yourself."

"But if I answer all your questions at one time, you might lose interest," I said with a smile.

She slapped my chest. "No, I won't. Tell me."

"What exactly do you want to know?"

"Where were you born?"

"Miami, Florida."

"Human and vampire years together, how old are you?"

I hesitated to answer, wondering if it would bother her. "Seventy-seven."

She winced, but it was fake and her smile was teasing. "You're way too old for me."

"Since you were Turned when you were twenty-five and you've only been a vampire for sixteen years now, you could be right."

Her mouth fell open. "How do you know that?"

"I told you the other night, I know plenty about you."

"Hmm. It would seem you weren't kidding. I think it's only fair, then, that I know more about you. Any siblings?" At my hesitation to answer, she smiled. "It's not a complicated question."

I gently tapped her lip. "It is when you don't know much about your biological family. I was found on the doorstep of a church when I was a baby. But I didn't have a bad life," I quickly added when her face scrunched up in outrage. "My adoptive parents were good people."

Her expression softened a little. "How do you feel about being adopted?"

It was a question I'd been asked many times. "I've never known any different. It was my life; the only life I knew. I was adopted as a baby, so I didn't have to go through the adjustment period that older kids have to deal with."

"You found out about it when you were young?"

"My parents never hid it from me. A therapist told them to tell me I was adopted once a year, each year until I was nine. Then it would be something that stuck with me; something I grew up knowing." I was glad of that, because I never felt like I'd been lied to.

"Was it an awkward subject at your house?"

"No, my parents talked freely about it. They always answered any questions I had. My mom, Annette, said that it's okay if I was upset that I didn't have my biological family in my life; that she suspected it was the sense of loss an adult might feel for a biological child they just can't have. It's a kind of grief, but it doesn't mean my life is any less good. They even thought I should feel proud of being adopted, because it meant I was chosen."

"Did you always know you were left on a church doorstep?"

I nodded. "They tried softening the blow by making out like being left at a special place made *me* special." But that wasn't the case at all. "They didn't want to lie to me."

"Do you think it was better that way?"

"Yeah. It helped me to accept it."

"It can't have been easy to accept."

"It bothered me most when I was younger. I didn't look like my parents; it was a small thing, but I didn't like it. And I didn't like not knowing about my family's medical history." I sighed. "I'd sometimes ask myself who I would have been if my birth mother kept me."

She petted my chest. "Do you know anything about your biological parents?"

FRACTURED

I clenched my hand in her hair. "My biological mother came looking for me once. I was thirteen. She just turned up one day, out of the fucking blue. She saw my picture in the paper with my adoptive parents at some kind of art gallery opening; said she knew it was me because I looked just like my father, but I had her eyes."

"And?"

"And I told her to go away." I'd rejected her the way she rejected me. "My parents saw that as loyalty to them. Honestly, I was just angry. Know why? Her first words were, 'I'm your mom. Your real mom.' And that just pissed me off. Annette was my mom. This woman gave birth to me, sure. But then she left me. She *chose* to do that. She dumped me on a church doorstep, knowing I could end up anywhere. She didn't go through an adoption process, she didn't hand me over to social services...she just dumped me."

Imani's hands balled up into little fists. Fury glimmered in her eyes. "She shouldn't have just turned up like that. You were only thirteen. For all she knew, you didn't even *know* you were adopted. It was insensitive and selfish."

I soothingly massaged Imani's head. "She seemed surprised that I didn't want to talk to her. People seem to automatically assume you want to meet your biological parents. I didn't. I wondered about them— *wondered* what they looked like, what they did, if they were poor or rich, if my father even knew I existed at all, if my mother ever thought about me and if she was ashamed of me—but I was content with the family I had. Maybe I wouldn't have felt so rejected if she had given me up in a different way. Still, maybe I should have heard her out."

Imani's expression was gentle. "You were a teenager and in shock."

"She probably just wanted money anyway." But I'd never know.

"It's okay that you were angry with her. Hell, *I'm* angry with her."

Her protectiveness made me smile. "I had a good family, Imani. They were good people. They always supported me. They loved me in their way. They were encouraging and gave me the best of everything. Being adopted doesn't define me."

Her eyes narrowed. "What do you mean they loved you 'in their way'?"

"They weren't family orientated. Their relationship was more like a business partnership. They liked to socialise, entertain, and hold dinner parties. Even Christmas was like a gathering that's only purpose was to do some social networking. They were good people," I reiterated, "just not family people. Tell me about your family."

Her smile was wan. "Oh, I was a big disappointment to them."

I frowned, growling, "Disappointment?"

"My family are very ambitious, academic people—which is great, good for them. And I'm proud of all their achievements. They work hard and they deserve what they have. But I've just never been like them. I liked learning new things, but I wasn't academic."

"There's nothing wrong with that."

"I used to get so bored in school because I liked to learn through *doing* things, not by copying things from chalkboards and textbooks. My parents and teachers thought I had a poor concentration span. It wasn't that. I was just utterly bored."

"I can imagine." And I knew her well enough to know... "You used to fall asleep in class, didn't you?" Imani could sleep anywhere.

Her smile widened just a little. "Once or twice."

I had a feeling that was a massive understatement. "So your parents were disappointed because you weren't like them?"

"Yes. My parents wanted me to be a lawyer or a doctor. I had no interest in being either one of those things. I don't think it's wrong if someone isn't ambitious or doesn't have a 'calling' or whatever. But they didn't agree."

"They didn't understand you."

"No, they didn't. They didn't get that I was happy just going with the flow and enjoying the present moment. I didn't think too much on the future. Didn't *want* to make grand plans. I just wanted to be...me, I guess. But I wasn't enough for them."

I kissed her. "Then they're assholes and you never needed them."

She yawned, pretty much melting on top of me. I wasn't surprised. It had been an eventful, long-ass night and she'd not long recovered from a bout of induced exhaustion.

I lightly tapped her ass. "Come on, let's get you in bed."

"I'm not tired," she insisted as I carried her inside.

"Bullshit, baby." In the bedroom, I stripped us both and spooned her. "Sleep."

"You're no fun."

"Tomorrow, we'll have all kinds of fun."

She snickered. After another yawn, she whispered, "Thanks for sharing tonight."

I kissed her hair. "Right back at you."

Seconds later, she was asleep, which was pretty typical for Imani. For a while, I just lay there, listening to her breathe and inhaling her scent—so fucking thankful that she was finally all mine, and determined that nothing would change that.

CHAPTER NINE

(Imani)

Sitting at the breakfast bar, I watched Butch putter about the kitchen as he prepared breakfast. We hadn't spent a day or night apart since we made our relationship public three nights ago. Yet, I didn't feel smothered. I liked having him around so much. Liked it when we'd settle on the sofa while he watched the game and I read my Kindle. Liked it when he made us dinner—yep, the guy could cook *seriously* well—or we watched re-runs of *American Horror Story* and *The Walking Dead*.

I also liked it when he made me come so hard I almost passed out.

He didn't invade my space, he fit into it. I did worry that he might miss having his own space. But he seemed content enough with the way things were.

If it wasn't for the dragon situation and the fact that the girls *still* weren't talking to me, all would be perfect in my world. Ava had paid me a visit, wanting us to speak in private. Butch, however, had refused to leave the room since he didn't trust her not to upset me. I hadn't insisted on him leaving because I figured if Ava was going to insult him, he had every right to be there.

Surprisingly, Ava hadn't spouted any insults. She'd admitted that she worried this wouldn't end well, but she also said we made a cute couple. She could see that I was happy; that Butch made me happy. That was good enough for her.

According to Ava, the other girls' anger had cooled a little. At this point, they were mostly just concerned about me. Paige, however—who continued to ignore my calls—was still nursing her grudge. Knowing my BFF well, I was pretty sure she was holding onto her anger to cover her hurt feelings; Paige didn't like to show pain as she saw it as a weakness.

I didn't like knowing I'd hurt this person who had protected me several times over the years—a person who had been sent to kill me but had instead chosen to join me. But there wasn't a lot I could do until she was prepared to hear me out. I'd thought about tracking all of my supposed friends down to say my piece, but I agreed with Butch that I didn't need to explain myself to them or anyone else.

As for his squad…Salem and David had decided to stay out of the matter, though they had made it clear to Butch that they would be pissed if he messed this up. Max seemed to have backed down, since he was no longer standoffish with Butch. Then again, he wasn't exactly warm with him either. The rest of the squad were, in Sam's words, acting like twats…as if they were all simply waiting for him to let me down and walk away.

It was a shit situation, and it meant I spent many hours debating whether to bitch-slap these people who, though their hearts were in the right place, were being too judgemental. Butch didn't seem as infuriated by it, and I figured that was because he was used to people thinking badly of him. He was used to being judged.

That wasn't something I liked at all. He didn't—

"You're in deep thought," said Butch, placing a coffee-flavoured NST in front of me.

Unscrewing the lid, I sipped at the drink. "You can't walk around bare-chested and expect me not to disappear into my fantasies."

He snorted, not buying that. "What were you thinking about, baby?"

"Nothing new. I'm just annoyed that most of the people we call friends won't even give us—this—a chance."

"That's it?"

"That's it."

He didn't seem totally convinced. "I'm trusting that you'll tell me if something about us is bothering you. I can't fix it if I don't know what's wrong."

"Nothing at all is wrong, I swear. I sometimes worry that you might miss having your space, but that's it."

"My space?"

"You're used to being alone." I took another sip of my NST. "Isn't it strange for you to suddenly have me with you all the time?"

His eyes narrowed. "Is this your way of telling me that I'm taking up too much of your space?"

"If it were that, I'd just say it. It's *you* I'm concerned about. I swear I won't be upset or offended if you choose to have some time alone." I wouldn't. I'd totally get it.

Cupping my chin, he breezed his thumb along my lower lip. "I spent almost a year without you, baby. Not real keen on being away from you now. Just give me this, all right?"

I swallowed. "Okay."

"Good girl." He turned, grabbed our plates, placed them on the bar, and took his seat. "Now eat."

As the taste of biscuits and gravy hit my tongue, I groaned. "I have to say, your cooking skills are much appreciated."

He smiled. "I'm glad, but you won't be benefitting from them tonight." I must have looked petulantly disappointed, because he chuckled. "The new Mexican restaurant opens tonight, remember?"

I'd completely forgotten about that. "Then I don't mind missing your skills for one night."

After breakfast, we dressed and headed for the conference room. It was the first meeting we'd had in three nights, since Sam and Jared had wanted us to focus on training and being at our best. Silence fell as we entered. Only Ava, Salem, David, and Max greeted us. Some of the guys frowned at Butch, the others ignored him. As for the rest of my squad...they didn't even glance my way. Butch's hand supportively tightened on mine.

We took the empty seats between Salem and David, and I cast them both a smile—acting like it didn't hurt that my friends were behaving this way. Butch's arm hung over the back of my chair, his hand rested on my shoulder. The move was both possessive and protective, and I very much doubted it went unnoticed.

It wasn't long before Sam, Jared, and Luther entered. Once they had taken their seats, Sam said, "Evening all. We have some news. Marco called an hour ago. The dragon shifter Alpha agreed to speak with Imani." She looked at me. "He's refusing to allow you to step on his territory, though. He's much too wary of the legion, and he's far too protective of his drove to take any chances."

"So where will the meeting take place?" I asked.

"The land that borders both theirs and Lazarus' territory. Marco will be with you as a friendly face. Butch, David, and one of Evan's vampires, Ian, will go with you."

Paige frowned. "Ian?"

"He can teleport," said Sam. "If there's a problem, Ian will get them away from there fast."

David was also a good choice because, one, he had the gift of knocking someone into a coma with a psionic blast and, two, he was Butch's partner during assignments; they were used to working together. It helped that there was no tension between him and Butch. Tension would be a distraction, and we didn't need distractions in a situation like that.

Sam continued, "The rest of you will wait in the castle with me and Jared in case we're needed." She stood. "Right, time for training."

The session was as gruelling and demanding as always. After lunch, Jared set a punishing pace that left me aching afterwards. But by the time Butch and I were showered and changed, my muscles were once again fine.

As I stood in front of the mirror putting on my earrings, Butch came up behind me and settled his hands on my waist. In his designer shirt and pants, he looked like something out of a GQ magazine. "Love this dress, baby."

The little black sleeveless dress was one of the many garments that Fletcher chose for me; he was a great shopping partner. "Thanks. You don't look so bad yourself."

Smiling, he spoke into my ear. "I'm going to spend all night imagining whipping this dress off you."

"There are worse ways to spend an evening."

He chuckled. "Come on, let's go."

The restaurant was heaving, so it was a good thing that Butch had booked us a table in advance. The interior had a hacienda look to it with the colour scheme of terracotta, gold, green, blue, and mandarin. The Mexican pottery suns, paintings, tapestries, and metal art geckos added to the theme.

Waiting to be seated, I heard a laugh that I knew as well as my own. *Paige.* That was when I realised that the girls, with the exception of Ava, were here. Great. I would have liked to put them at the back of my mind so I could enjoy my evening. No such luck.

Feeling Butch's grip on my hand flex, I looked up at him.

"We can go if you want." So he'd noticed the girls, too.

I shook my head. "I've been looking forward to this meal all night."

He studied me for a few moments and then nodded. The waiter then appeared and guided us to a circular table, which fortunately was far away from the girls. After we ordered our food, Butch moved his chair next to mine and gave me his full attention.

Throughout the next hour, we ate, talked, and laughed. He was sure to touch me constantly. Every touch was somehow sweet, sensual, and possessive all at the same time. It had been a while since I'd had this much fun on a date, and I was pretty sure there was a Barbie-like smile on my face.

"Hey, you two," greeted an excitable voice.

My smile dimmed. "Hi, Jen." Butch merely nodded at her.

Jen was one of the females who worked at the shoe store. She was also…familiar with Butch—the last female he'd been with before he and I got together, to be specific. I reminded myself that, like with the others, it had only been a one-night stand; Jen hadn't meant anything to him. That didn't stop me from being pissed the fuck off at the flirtatious, nostalgic smile she flashed him.

I wished I could say that I didn't like her. I actually did. Jen was a nice, bubbly, friendly person. She could just be a little *too* friendly with guys, even if they were spoken for. That didn't discourage her. Maybe she was just so insecure that she needed that constant reinforcement that guys thought she was beautiful, or maybe it was something else—I had no idea.

Sitting on the table adjacent to ours, she angled her body toward Butch. As the night went on, she laughed too loud and did just about everything to get his attention; stroking her hair, arching her neck, playing her fingers over her cleavage, and licking her lips. He shifted so that his back was to her and he was better facing me. That didn't make her stop.

I supposed I'd have to get used to bumping into his past encounters, since it was a small island with more males than females.

Butch nipped my earlobe, no doubt irritated that he didn't have my full attention. "What's wrong?"

"What do you think?" Okay, that came out a little harsh.

His eyes widened. "Jen's getting to you? I thought you'd find it more pathetic than anything else."

"It is pathetic. That doesn't mean it isn't irritating. I blame you."

"How is this my fault?"

"It's not, but I'm still blaming you." I knew it was pointless and petty to get annoyed about being around females from his past, but I couldn't help it. "I did warn you about my jealous streak."

"Baby..." He stroked his thumb over my jaw. "She's not important to me. Never was."

"I know. It's still not a pleasant situation." Hearing Jen's way-too-loud laugh once more, I grit my teeth. "I'll say one thing for her: she's persistent." She was also close to having my fork shoved down her throat.

He just shrugged, as if she was none of his concern. "If she can't clearly see that you're someone to me, she's either blind or stupid."

I was leaning toward 'stupid' because it sounded better while I was feeling bitchy. "You were with her when I was with Dean, weren't you?"

"With her? I wouldn't phrase it that way."

"Does it bother you that people call you a hit and run?" Even before we started this relationship, I was considered special for the simple reason that I'd lasted a month with him, even though it had been a month of casual sex.

He flashed me a crooked smile. "I've been called worse." His arm slid around my neck until I was burrowed into the crook of his elbow. "None of them wanted more than a night of fun, baby. No one got hurt."

"You're wrong, you know. Plenty of girls wanted more from you, including Jen. She's nice." But still at risk of having her hair shaved off with a blunt razor.

He shrugged. "She's not you." He kissed me. "None of them were you, and that was the problem. I didn't want a pale substitute. I wanted you. The real thing. I just didn't think that would ever happen. Especially not when I heard that Dean planned to be Turned."

As a human, Dean could never have been a real mate to me because we could never have Bound. He'd claimed to want to be a vampire so that we could have a real life together. But... "Sometimes I wonder if he played me, hoping I'd Turn him to keep him with me."

Butch tilted his head. "You didn't offer to ask Sam and Jared's permission to Turn him?"

"I made it clear to Dean that I don't plan to Turn anyone. Starting a line is a serious thing and involves responsibilities that I don't want."

His mouth twisted. "How long was it after that conversation that he cheated?"

"A week." Which made it very likely that I had indeed been played. God, *I* was dumb. A part of me was hurt by his behaviour, but it was a teeny, weeny part because I now had something much better.

Butch rested his forehead against mine. "See, he's a prick."

I laughed. "Yeah, he really is."

Chuckling, Butch kissed me again. It was slow and deep and drugging. It was also a possessive display, so maybe he understood that the only way that people would believe this relationship was serious was if he—a usually commitment-shy guy—made such an obvious and public display.

He broke the kiss with a bite to my lip. "When we get back, I want you to go straight to the bedroom and strip for me."

I arched a brow. "Oh, you do?"

"I do."

Sounded like a plan to me. Just then, our waiter reappeared, gathered our plates, and said he'd be back shortly with our dessert. I gave Butch a quick kiss. "I need to use the ladies' room; I'll be back in a minute."

He bit my lip again. "All right."

As I was passing Jen's table, she smiled up at me. Considering she'd been flirting with Butch all evening, I didn't feel the urge to smile back. Instead, I bent and spoke in a low voice. "I know you flirt as easy as you breathe, Jen. And I like you, so I won't hurt you. But you do *not* try to get my man's attention like that again. It's disrespectful to me and it's pointless for you...unless of course you'd like to be off solid food for a year. Understood?"

She looked from me to Butch, who was watching us closely. "You two are serious? I heard the rumours but, well, it's Butch."

Her disbelief was understandable. "They're true."

She patted my hand. "I'll spread the word that he's all yours and not to be flirted with. You're kind of cute together. I'm happy for you."

See, she was a nice person. Just very misguided and not all that bright. I gave a curt nod. "Have a good night."

Her smile was impish. "Considering what you've got in your bed, I think it's safe to say that you will."

Oh, it was.

I hurried to the restrooms and did my business. I was just washing my hands when the door opened and in walked my supposed friends. Groan. They gathered around me, their expressions determined. Apparently there was going to be an intervention. Awesome.

Drying my hands on a paper towel, I sighed. "Make it quick. I don't want my ice cream to melt. But before you tell me you think I'm making a mistake, you should know that I don't care."

Mouth tight, Jude shook her head in disbelief. "Never thought I'd see the night when you chose a guy over your friends."

Was she kidding? "Um, actually, it was *you* who froze *me* out. Was I supposed to chase after you? Beg your forgiveness for making decisions *regarding my own life* without your approval?"

"It's not that we think you shouldn't act without our approval, Imani," said Alora, casting Jude a 'calm down' look. "We just don't like that you kept something so big from us."

"There was nothing to keep from you until the evening before you and Paige showed up on my doorstep." I splayed a hand over my chest. "I'm sorry, should I have text you all straight away to let you know what happened?"

"Imani, honey, there's no way it all came out of the blue like that," Maya insisted, though her tone was soft and not in the slightest bit challenging. She seemed more concerned than anything else.

"You're right. It didn't. I knew what Butch wanted, and I took some time to think about it." I wasn't going to apologise for that.

Jude put her hands on her hips. "But you didn't tell us."

"Nope, I didn't." And I didn't regret that. "It was a big decision, and it needed to be *my* decision. Asking your advice wasn't necessary since I knew exactly what you'd say."

Paige leaned forward. "We'd say what you didn't want to hear. *The truth*. Butch doesn't do relationships, Imani. You, of all people, know that."

Cassie nodded. "She's right, sweetie. You said yourself that he doesn't connect with people and he doesn't want to. Why give him an opportunity to hurt you again?"

I exhaled heavily. "He's not going to hurt me."

"He hurt you once before, remember? Or have you forgotten about that?" sniped Jude.

It was hard to maintain an even tone, but I managed it. "I haven't forgotten. I happen to believe in second chances."

Paige threw her hands up in the air. "You weren't good enough for him a year ago, so why now?"

"People change." Hell, I'd changed plenty in the past year.

"And you believe he's changed?" scoffed Jude. "God, Imani, what's wrong with you?"

"My elbows itch sometimes. Is that weird?"

"Has it crossed your mind that he could be doing this just to keep you from getting back together with Dean?" asked Maya. "I don't mean it in a bitchy way, honey. It's just that, you know, guys do weird stuff like that. There's no denying that Butch can be weird."

"Weird?" echoed Paige. "He's about as deranged as they come. He hides it well, but we all see it."

"You think he's normal, Imani." Alora gave a soft shake of the head, adding, "He's not. He never will be."

I frowned. "No one on this island is normal. Hell, Alora, you talk to freaking animals."

"Imani, you take relationships seriously," said Paige. "You're going to demand things from him that he just can't give you. Then what will happen? You'll be crushed and devastated, and we'll have to pick up the pieces."

I licked my front teeth. "You'll *have* to pick up the pieces? Like that will be a favour to me? Like I wouldn't do the same for any of you?"

Cassie stepped forward, hands up. "We're just concerned for you. Sweetie, you don't think straight when it comes to Butch; you never have."

Maybe not, but… "This here and now isn't about me, it's about all of *you* and your bruised feelings. At least be honest about that."

Paige folded her arms. "Well, since when do we keep shit from each other, huh?"

Oh my God. I ran my gaze along all of them as I said, "Are you going to honestly stand there and say that *you* tell *me* everything that goes on in your life? Really?"

None of them answered, and I took that as a resounding 'No.' I could practically *feel* them backing down. Well, not *all* of them.

Spots of colour stained Paige's cheeks. "You know, I never had you down as naïve, Imani. Clearly I was wrong, because from what I've seen of Butch and Marco, you sure know how to pick 'em."

I sucked in a breath. "That was a low blow. And it's the last I'll let you make."

Shoulders drooping, Paige looked like she wanted to take the words back.

I didn't give her the chance. "I'm happy. Does that not matter to anyone here? Is it only your feelings and opinions that count? I'm very aware that I'm taking a risk. You don't have to like it. You don't have to like Butch. You don't have to support me in this. But you *do* have to get rid of this idea that I need to explain myself to you. Seriously, why is it that you feel I owe you that? Huh? Why? Because I gotta tell ya, girls, if you really feel I owe you a piece of my soul then fuck you all."

The door swung wide open, and Butch took a step inside. His dark gaze swept the room, taking in everything, and his anger seemed to vibrate through the air. It was simple enough for him to conclude what had just happened. In fact, he may have overheard some of it.

His eyes moved to me and he held out his hand. "Come here, baby."

Pushing back my shoulders, I went straight to him. "Does this mean dessert's ready?"

His arm slid around my waist; the move was both possessive and protective. "It means that you were gone too long and I got worried." He sliced the girls a withering glance that would have made me flinch if I was the recipient of it. "You couldn't let her just enjoy her evening? This was really necessary?"

Alora cleared her throat, the image of regret. "We just—"

"They were rhetorical questions," he rumbled. "There's never a good reason to fuck up your friend's evening."

Paige lifted her chin. "We didn't want to mess up her evening. We just wanted to talk to her."

"And look how that turned out." His face went hard, his voice cold as he added, "All of you hear me when I say this because I'm absolutely serious: You don't talk to Imani again until you're ready to apologise—and that won't happen unless I'm there to make sure you don't hurt her any further. If you're lucky, she'll forgive you. But I won't. She's done nothing to deserve this shit, and none of you have a right to dish it out. She owes you nothing." His glare fixed on Paige. "And you…you're the one person I trusted with her. Now? That trust has gone."

I thought she'd go on the defence, but her face fell. "I—"

He shook his head as he said, "You're not the person I thought you

were."
With that, he guided me out of the restrooms.

CHAPTER TEN

(Imani)

The Alpha dragon shifter was seriously good-looking. Unkempt russet hair, tall toned body, and electric blue eyes that saw way too much. He didn't hold a candle to Butch but, still, I wouldn't kick him out of bed—or, at least, I wouldn't if my bed wasn't already occupied.

Two equally good-looking males flanked him, but they weren't the only ones around. I could sense people standing amongst the trees that fringed the large field. Really, considering the history that existed between our two species, I couldn't blame the Alpha for being so cautious.

For long moments, no one said a word as we sized each other up. The Alpha took in Butch's protective body language, and his eyes smiled. Yep, he saw way too much. Then he nodded at the male on my left and greeted simply, "Marco." The Alpha's eyes shifted to me, now glinting with curiosity. "You must be his first-born."

"I must be."

Marco spoke. "Imani, this is Andres. Andres, Imani."

Andres inclined his head ever so slightly at me. I gave him a brief nod.

"Ask your questions," said Andres. Apparently there would be no chit-chat. Good.

"Actually," I began, "I don't have any questions. I'm here to pass on a message from the Grand High Pair."

His lips flattened. "What message is that?"

I lifted my chin. "Whichever dragon drove is planning to obliterate The Hollow should seriously reconsider it."

The air seemed to chill and the three dragons went unnaturally still. Finally, Andres asked, "What makes you think any such plan exists?"

"Someone had a premonition; they saw the dragons warring with us at The Hollow."

"Really?" He sounded bored and unconcerned. Granted, I wasn't expecting fear from him. But, at the very least, I'd expected him to take this seriously.

"I respect that your kind is powerful," I told him. "But you have one weakness."

He didn't like that comment. "We do?"

"Your numbers are low in comparison to ours. The vampires at The Hollow are there because they're very powerful. If dragons come, they will die. Personally, I think enough dragons have died at the hands of vampires." I didn't hide my regret about the latter, and the emotion seemed to appease him slightly.

"The vampire who had this premonition...they lied."

Of course, Butch tensed. Before he could leap to my defence, I asked Andres, "Why would you say that?"

"If an attack was being planned on The Hollow, I would have heard about it."

"You're sure?"

His eyes narrowed. Oh, he didn't like being questioned.

"The vision was real. Your kind will soon attack mine."

The certainty in my voice seemed to reach him. "How soon?"

"Soon enough." Even if I did have an exact date, I wouldn't have given it to him. That could have led to a self-fulfilled prophesy.

His lips twitched. Why my evasiveness amused him, I couldn't say.

Frustrated, I said, "Let's say that, hypothetically, dragon shifters were planning to attack The Hollow. Why might they do that?"

Eyes gleaming, he said, "Hypothetically?"

"Sure."

"There are only two possible motives. One, your Grand High Vamps made a serious enemy of a drove. Or two, they were hired to attack The Hollow. If the first had occurred, I would know."

Which left... "Mercenaries."

"Yes. They will work for anyone, if the price is right."

Shit. "Maybe you could pass on our message. We truly don't want to war with your kind. But if there is an attack on our home, we will stand against it. There will be deaths on both sides. I don't think you want that any more than we do."

Andres studied me for a moment before shifting his attention to Marco. "We'll no doubt speak again soon." As one, he and his dragons turned—giving us their backs to communicate their lack of fear. Whatever.

At my signal, Ian teleported all five of us to the castle entrance, where Sam, Jared, and the two squads waited on high alert.

Sam moved straight to me, but it was Ian she spoke to. "Take Marco inside; this is Hollow business."

Marco's spine snapped straight. "You brought me into this. That makes it my business."

Sam snorted. "Not on your life, Marco."

Ian teleported him out of there before Marco had the chance to object again. Within seconds, the teleporter was back.

Jared arched a brow at me. "Well?"

After I repeated the short conversation I'd had with Andres, Butch said, "My gut says that he's telling the truth and hasn't heard of a plan to attack our kind. And, since I think Imani's right and he doesn't want a war, I'd say he's likely to pass on our message. I just don't know if anyone will heed him."

Sam sighed. "And that's the problem."

"Now that that's over and done with, we can get back," said Jared.

"Before we leave, I'd like to just wish Eleanor a happy birthday," I said. We'd all been invited to the party that was currently in full swing, but I didn't think it would be a good idea to attend. The guests would most likely be drunk out of their minds by the end of it, which meant they wouldn't be thinking straight. That could lead to either Tait challenging me or Marco blindsiding Butch. Neither of those scenarios appealed to me.

"Not alone," stated Butch.

"I agree," said Jared. So, at his order, I was accompanied by him, Sam, Butch, David, Ava, and Salem through the castle and out to the massive courtyard.

David frowned. "They're having a *rock* concert?"

I smiled. "It would seem so."

(Butch)

Spotting Lazarus and Annalise in a VIP box, Imani mouthed, "Where's Eleanor?"

They both pointed to the front row, near the stage. Imani shot them a smile of thanks, and then we all pushed our way through the crazy throng of dancers. Eleanor gave her a huge hug and seemed disappointed that Imani wasn't staying, but whatever explanation Imani said into her ear had the other female nodding in understanding.

After she gave Eleanor one last hug, we all began to retreat through the tight crowd. I cursed when someone knocked into me, causing me to stumble and—in the process—separate from Imani. With a growl, I shoved my way through them, easily catching up to her since she'd come to a halt. "Keep moving, we—"

A violent tremor wracked her body. "Butch..."

I spoke into her ear. "Baby, what's wrong?"

Turning, she blinked up at me. "I don't know. Something..."

"What?"

"Something pricked me in the arm." She swayed, eyes glazing over in a truly creepy way.

I examined the arm she held out just in time to watch a tiny red mark fade away.

"I don't feel good." Her knees buckled.

"Shit." I lifted her, cradling her against my chest. "Hold on, baby." I carried her to where Sam, Jared, and the others were waiting. They all stiffened at the sight of Imani in my arms.

"What's wrong?" demanded Sam.

"No fucking idea," I rumbled.

Lazarus and Annalise appeared at my side. "Oh my God, what happened?" asked Annalise, face creased in concern.

"I don't know," I replied. "She said she felt a prick in her arm. Now her eyes are misty, she can't stay on her feet, and the occasional tremor runs through her." I watched Lazarus take an almost unconscious step back, head shaking slightly in denial. "What do you know?" I growled.

"We must get her inside." In vampire speed, Lazarus led us all to a parlour. "Please lay her on the sofa so I can examine her."

I was hesitant to release her but I did as he asked. I stayed at her side and kept my hand on her hair, needing to touch her.

"Imani, where exactly did you feel the prick?" he asked, an urgency in his tone that was freaking me the fuck out. She shuddered, but she didn't answer him. He waved his hand in front of her eyes, but they were unfocused and her pupils didn't respond.

"She felt it in her left upper arm," I told him. "When I looked, there was a small red mark fading away."

His eyes flew to mine. "How small? Like an injection site?"

Come to think of it… "Yeah."

Annalise gasped, hand flying to her chest. "Lazarus, you don't think…"

"Think what?" snapped Sam.

Lazarus' expression crumpled as a tremor again assailed Imani from head to toe. "Yes, Annalise, I do."

My frustration mounting, I advanced on him, invading his personal space as I jabbed a finger at him. "You need to explain what the fuck is going on."

As if he didn't have the strength to support himself, he sank into a plush chair. "You remember I told you about my many attempts to create a cure for vampirism?"

"You said they haven't been successful."

"My last serum came very close," Lazarus told me, but there was no excitement in his voice. "We tried it on four people. Unfortunately, the serum didn't work in the way that we'd hoped."

Something about his tone made the hairs on my nape rise. "What do you mean?"

"It is designed to reverse the transition we all endured as we changed from human to vampire. As such, they have to re-experience the pain and bloodlust they suffered during that transition before they are once again human."

My fists clenched, and I barely resisted the urge—no, the need—to punch something. "You think Imani's been injected with that serum?"

Lazarus swallowed. "It is possible."

"She's going to be human again?" asked Ava.

"Not necessarily," replied Lazarus, regret staining his eyes.

The vague answer made me growl. "What happened to the four volunteers?"

"The result differed from person to person. But in all cases, the transition didn't *fully* reverse."

Leaning into Salem, Ava bit her lip. "What happened to them?"

"The first was Pierce's cousin," said Lazarus. "Mid-way through the transition, he weakened until his strength became that of a human. He no longer craved blood. His gift faded. But he also aged at a dramatic rate until his body was that of a hundred year old man. He died of heart failure."

A chill scuttled up my spine. "Fuck." I scrubbed a hand over my face. My breath coming in short, soft pants, I asked, "What about the other three?"

"One developed a stronger craving for blood while at the same time aging even faster than Pierce's cousin. She died when her organs shut down. The second vampire didn't age at all, but he became so weak and frail that he fell into a coma and died."

I took Imani's hand, trying to calm the panic that was riding me hard. "What about the last volunteer?"

He looked pained. "As with the others, the reversal partly worked. But whereas they died mid-transition, he didn't. However, his mental state remained that of a partly formed vampire. Consumed by bloodlust, he was more animal than man in his way of thinking. Saw everything as prey. We had to kill him."

Shell-shocked, Sam gaped. "You're saying that there's a chance that Imani could find herself either dead or stuck mid-transition, consumed by bloodlust?"

"Yes," sighed Lazarus. "I'm sure you remember what that's like."

I couldn't recall every moment of the transition, but I remembered the bloodlust, the pain, the confusion, the high sex drive, and the pressing urge to hunt.

Salem asked the question haunting me, a question I couldn't bring myself to voice. "So either way, she's going to die?"

"It is likely."

The words hit my chest like a fucking sledgehammer, causing the breath to explode out of me. No. There was no way I'd let that happen. *No. Fucking. Way.*

Lazarus sighed again. "I feel responsible."

Right at that moment, I was holding him responsible. "You should," I spat. "You knew the serum didn't work, knew what it could do, but you didn't get rid of it!"

His eyes squeezed shut as his face pinched in pain. "I did not for one moment think it would ever be misused this way."

Jared raised a hand. "Butch, I understand you need someone to blame—"

"Imani isn't like the others! She didn't volunteer to take part in any trial!" I turned to Sam and pointed at the floor as I demanded, "Get Paige in here. She can fix it."

Teeth biting down on her lower lip, Sam looked at Imani's arm. "There's no point, Butch, Paige can't do it."

"*She can.*" If Paige was able to remove the taint of the Reaper's Call, she could fix this.

But Sam shook her head. "Paige heals by taking an injury and passing it to someone else. Imani doesn't have any wounds. The prick from the needle healed. Without a wound…"

Fuck. I swallowed hard, and the movement hurt. "So how do we get rid of it? Don't say we can't. There are thousands upon thousands of vampires out there. At least one must have an ability that will somehow combat this."

"I'll have Mona and Cedric look into it," said Sam.

"Look into it?" I clipped. That was it?

"I know you want something done right here, right now. So do I, believe me. But at this moment in time, we have no bloody clue how to fix this. We *will* find a way."

I looked down at Imani; she'd now passed out. "We need to take her back to The Hollow."

Fists clenched, Salem spoke. "What I want to know is, who the fuck did this?"

"I would like to know the same." Annalise's voice was as hard and dark as her expression.

"It had to have been Marco, Juliet, or Tait," I said. "No one else here would have a motivation to kill her." And that was exactly what the person who was responsible intended when they gave her the serum. And that was exactly why they would die. But they wouldn't die easily. Or slowly. They'd pay in the worst way—I'd make sure of it.

Jared turned to me. "You were behind her outside in the crowd. What did you see?"

"We got separated. It was only for a second. When I got back to her, she told me something had pricked her arm."

Just then, the parlour door opened. Marco, his consorts, and a few other vampires strolled inside. My already pounding heartbeat accelerated and my fingers retracted so they were almost claw-like. I tensed, ready to lunge and kill. I didn't know which one of the fuckers was responsible and nor did I care. If they all had to die just so the culprit would be punished, so be it.

Salem came to my side and said quietly, "Don't. Stay with Imani. Guard her while she's vulnerable."

I was pretty sure Salem had chosen those very words because he suspected they just might penetrate the rage hazing my thoughts. He was right. I took a deep breath, searching for some element of calm.

Marco didn't notice my struggle as his gaze went straight to a trembling Imani. "I heard she was carried inside. What's wrong with her?"

I bared my teeth. "You know." The words were almost animalistic.

Ava took a threatening step forward, only to have her way barred by her mate's arm. "And so do your bunnies."

Ignoring us both, Marco looked at Lazarus. *"What's wrong with Imani?"*

It was Annalise who responded, her eyes on Tait. "Someone injected her with the latest serum."

Marco sucked in a breath. "No."

Energy crackled in the air as Sam also honed in on Tait, her irises glowing. "Was it you?"

The bitch blinked. "Me? *No.* I've been with Marco and Juliet all night. Ask anyone."

I snarled at Marco. "I think it was *you.* You're her Sire, and she escaped you. I think you're so obsessed with her that you'd see her dead before you'd see her with another guy."

Marco's eyes blazed with anger. He spoke through his teeth. "I'd never harm Imani." He looked at Lazarus. "I would never do this. Never. When I find out who did, I'll obliterate them."

"No, *I'll* do that," I growled.

His jaw clenched. "We'll see who finds them first." His harsh expression softened as it went to Imani. "She needs to be in bed."

"She will be," said Sam. "Butch, we're leaving. Get Imani."

I scooped up Imani, holding her close.

"You can't take her away from here," objected Marco, but Lazarus blocked his path before he could advance on us.

At that moment, Ian and the rest of the two squads appeared, no doubt summoned telepathically by Jared. Within seconds, they had Marco, Tait, and Juliet restrained. Strangely, Marco didn't struggle. His attention was solely on Imani.

"Take them straight to the containment cells," ordered Jared, to which Tait and Juliet gasped. "Be sure to put them in separate cells."

A panicked Paige asked me, "What's wrong with her?"

I ignored her, moving to Jared who then teleported me, Imani, and Sam straight to the infirmary at The Hollow.

Though I was reluctant to part with Imani and didn't really see what Mary Jane—who was a nurse in her human life and liked to act as one at The Hollow—could do for her, I laid Imani on the bed and let Mary Jane fuss over her.

Jared then telepathically contacted Antonio, Luther, and Sebastian. They arrived at the infirmary quickly, and he told them about Imani's condition. Luther pretty much beat himself up for not foreseeing any of this, despite Antonio's assurances that he couldn't expect to see everything.

Meanwhile, I sat on the chair beside Imani's bed, her hand in mine as I stroked her pulse with my thumb. It wasn't easy to keep my touch light when fury was still pumping through me. I'd only just got her back, and now I had people telling me I could possibly lose her. No. It wasn't going to happen. "You'll live," I told her, voice gruff. "You have to."

Pacing and clearly frantic with worry, Sam said, "I admit I wanted a bit of action. I *didn't* want Imani hurt and in chance of fucking dying."

Sebastian spoke to Sam and Jared. "Do you think it will be necessary to put Imani in a containment cell?"

"I doubt it will come to that if she has Butch with her at all times," replied Jared. "But if she becomes too wild, it's a possibility."

It would happen over my dead fucking body.

"I'll do what I can to ensure that never happens," Sam promised me. "I've been in a cell. It's absolutely shit."

"Chico may be able to help," said Antonio.

My brow furrowed. "Chico?"

"Obviously he cannot heal her," allowed Antonio. "But if she gets out of control, Chico's darts can put her unconscious."

That was better than locking her up.

"She's going to have a serious case of bloodlust, Butch, which means she'll need more than just your blood," Jared warned me. I growled, and he raised his hands. "Hey, I get it. I'm too possessive of Sam to share any part of her. But I'd suck it up if it was about her health. You'll need to do the same. Some of the most powerful vampires in the world live at The Hollow. Feeding from them might just get Imani through this alive."

He was right. "She can't die." My words were like gravel. "She can't."

Expression fierce, Sam said, "She won't. We won't let it happen."

Imani's hand shook within my grasp as another tremor ran through her. Releasing her hand, I stroked her hair soothingly. "Did you contact Mona and Cedric?"

"Yes. They're looking into whether there are any vampires who might be able to help with something like this," said Jared.

Antonio patted Imani's leg. "I wonder if Lena can be of any assistance."

Lena was the mate of Antonio's Sire and had the gift of genekinesis. That meant she could manipulate a human or animal's DNA. When Reuben used his gift of amplifying power to strengthen hers, it enabled her to work on vampires. She had helped Sam when she went through the transformation from Svénte to hybrid.

"Maybe she could halt the transition," suggested Antonio.

Sam pursed her lips. "I'll contact her and ask. I don't know enough about the workings of Lena's gift to know whether this is something she can help with. Maybe—"

The door flew open and nearly all of mine and Imani's squads rushed inside. The girls surrounded the bed, all in varying levels of distress. But no one came too close, eying me warily. I never showed my anger. Never lost my shit. I could look cool and collected even while I was raging inside. But right then, with Imani unconscious beside me, I no doubt looked as rabid as I felt.

Pale and jerky, Paige kept her eyes on Imani as she said, "Tell me she's okay."

Well *obviously* she wasn't fucking okay. Was the woman blind? I clamped my mouth shut to stop any of the harsh words running through my head from escaping. I didn't want to take my anger out on her, but I *really* didn't want all these people who had been assholes to Imani in here. They had no right, as far as I was concerned. They hadn't given their support when she'd needed it, and there was no way I'd give them a free pass because she was now hurt.

"Why don't you all go outside and we'll talk in a minute," proposed Sam, but they didn't.

Instead, Paige moved to Imani's bedside and went to take the hand

I'd just released. She froze when I growled a warning.

"Leave," I bit out, snatching Imani's hand before she could.

Her eyes narrowed at my arctic tone. "I know I'm not your favourite person right now. I understand why. But she's hurt and I want—"

I leaned forward slightly. "I don't give a shit what you want. If you remember, I told you that you weren't to see Imani again until you'd come to apologise. As you can see, this isn't the time."

Paige sighed. "I know I messed up, but—"

Max put a restraining hand on her arm. "Don't do it. His protective streak has hit critical levels and he's barely holding his anger in. He doesn't trust you, so trying to get near Imani while she's vulnerable…it's not smart."

No, it wasn't.

Paige hissed at him. "She's *my best friend* and—"

"After the way you've treated her recently, I would never have thought so," I clipped. She flinched as if I'd struck her. Shit, it was time to get out of there. "Call me when you've spoken to Lena," I told Sam, lifting Imani into my arms. If she was going to go through the pain of the transition, she could at least do it in her apartment where she was comfortable and had privacy.

Sam nodded. "We'll visit at dusk and see how she's doing."

Imani stirred in my arms, whining something unintelligible. I spoke low into her ear, "Shh, baby, it's me. You're okay, I've got you." With a sigh, she settled, tucking her face into the crook of my neck.

"Jared will teleport you to her apartment." Sam gave me a pointed look. "We'll find a way to fix this, Butch."

I nodded, because there was no other acceptable option. Imani had to live.

CHAPTER ELEVEN

(Imani)

I cried out in utter agony. Everywhere hurt. Every bone. Every muscle. Every ligament. Every tooth.

My eyes stung so badly I couldn't open them. My chest was so tight it hurt to breathe. And my scalp was so sensitive it prickled each time even a single strand of my hair moved. Hell, it even felt like every vein in my body was throbbing with pain.

It hurt to curl up. It hurt to lie straight. It hurt to lie on my back, my front, *and* my sides.

God, what was happening to me?

Why was it happening to me?

Where was I?

I had to be dying. There was no other explanation. There was no way anyone could live through this pain. A pain that almost seemed familiar...like this had happened before.

I knew instinctively that only one thing would feel good. Feeding.

Nothing else would dim the pain, and nothing else seemed important. Just blood. Right now, I needed some badly. I was shaking with the need. Shaking and sobbing and begging. But I couldn't get up. I didn't have the energy or muscle control for that.

A shudder rippled down my spine, making me cry out again.

"Shh, baby, I got you."

I knew that voice. Knew that scent. A body lay flush against mine as a hand drew my head close. I could hear a pulse beating, could hear the rush of blood through veins. I bit hard, moaning as blood filled my mouth. The taste soothed my throat and eased the cramps in my stomach.

More. I needed more.

I jumped awake with a gasp as pain pounded into my head, lungs, and abdomen. It took my breath away, caused my entire body to tighten in shock. The movement made me wince through my teeth and cry out. It still hurt to move even just a little.

How was I still alive? Maybe I was dead. Maybe this was hell. It certainly seemed like hell. My stomach was cramping and burning like it was on fire. My skin felt hypersensitive and raw, as if I'd been scratching in an effort to jump out of it or something.

I tried to open my eyes, but the light sent pain lancing through them. What the fuck was happening to me?

Another gasp flew out of me as I was assailed by a full-body spasm that seemed to go on and on. I tried to shout for help, but only a tiny whimper came out. I wasn't sure if I even *could* speak. My tongue felt thick, and my teeth and jaw ached as if I'd been chewing on a brick. Worse, my throat felt shredded, like I'd been screaming for hours and hours—maybe I had.

I was helpless. Too weak to get up. And in too much pain to do a single thing about any of it. I buried my face in the pillow, muffling my sobs.

Blood. I needed blood again. It was the only thing that would make the pain ease.

Fingers brushed my hair as a body lay against mine, careful not to get too close—as if conscious of just how raw my skin felt. "Feed, baby."

There was that voice again. I did as it told me.

I shredded the bed sheets with a guttural growl. I was sweating. Aching. Thirsty. *So* thirsty that it drowned out the pain and confusion.

I needed to hunt. Find prey. There was prey here. I could smell it, could see it through burning, half-open eyes. But I couldn't catch it.

With a hiss, I launched at it again, wanting that pulse beating in my mouth. I hit something hard and fell back, tasting blood—my blood. But it wasn't *my* blood that I wanted. It wouldn't quench the thirst that was hammering at me so hard there was no room for rational thought.

"Imani, stop!"

Licking my split lip, I lunged again. Crashed into something solid. Heard something crack as pain exploded in my cheekbone.

"Imani, fucking stop *now!*"

I sprung again. Smashed into an invisible wall once more. Again, my blood flowed into my mouth. I spat it out.

"Imani, baby, you need to calm down!"

Two sets of footsteps pounded into the room and skidded to a halt. "Jared told me you needed a donor."

"Shit, why is her face all messed up?"

"She keeps leaping at my shield. Stay behind it."

I didn't understand the words. Didn't care. All I knew was I needed to hunt. Needed to feed.

Snarling, I coiled to strike. Before I could lunge, pain pricked me in several places. I batted away the darts, needing to…to…God, I was tired.

"Feed her now while she's too weak to fight."

A familiar scent washed over me as strong arms curled around me from behind and tipped me onto my side on the bed, trapping my arms at my sides. I didn't have the energy to fight and free myself. I didn't—

My nostrils flared. *Blood.* I sank my teeth into the bleeding wrist that was thrust in front of my mouth. It tasted strange. Fizzy with energy. Syrupy. But good. *So* good.

I drank. And drank. And drank.

I woke with a blazing ache between my legs. My hips bucked and I groaned, feeling empty and restless. I was so wet; could smell the need that pulsed in my veins and drummed through my body.

The cool air chafed my naked, oversensitive skin and my painfully tight nipples. Whimpering, I squirmed and rubbed my thighs together; needing some relief. It didn't help. The fire inside me just blazed hotter and hotter, giving me no reprieve.

My womb clenched hard. I hissed and writhed again, squeezing my thighs so tightly together it sent shooting pains through my muscles. I tried to touch myself, to take away the burning ache, but I couldn't move my hands. They were tied together and secured to something above my head.

I sobbed in frustration, arching my back. I couldn't take any more of this. I had to—

"Again, baby? Fuck, you're gonna be sore."

I didn't know what that meant, didn't care. Two fingers probed and slipped inside me, and I almost wept with relief. My muscles clamped around them, trying to keep them where they were. "Please." My voice was hoarse, and it hurt my throat to speak.

My hands were freed and then a large, hot body draped over mine. The skin-to-skin contact didn't hurt; it calmed me somehow. "Open your eyes for me."

I tried. Light stabbed my eyes, and I winced. "Hurts."

"Okay, baby, keep them closed for now." A kiss was pressed to each of my eyelids just as something prodded my opening.

I arched, wanting more. And then a hard and thick cock pushed inside me. I groaned in both bliss and relief. It felt *so good*. Stretched me just right and soothed the ache. My body tightened around him as he fed me an inch at a time. "Too slow." Too gentle. I needed it hard. I needed the fiery ache to go away. I tilted my hips, taking him deeper.

"Be still."

I couldn't. "More. Faster." I raked my nails down his back.

He growled. Then he was hammering into me, and my teeth bit into his shoulder.

I had the worst hangover, like, *ever*.

Groggy, I licked my dry lips, frowning at the bitter taste in my mouth. My throat was painfully dry, my head felt heavy, my stomach was churning, and there were sharp, shooting pains behind my eyes.

Apparently I'd set out to get drunk like it was my job. I was surprised I couldn't smell alcohol seeping from every pore. I hadn't felt this dizzy since...hell, it hurt to try to remember. I didn't even want to know what I looked like—it couldn't be half as bad as I felt.

I tried to lift my head. A throbbing, head-splitting pain reverberated around my skull. I groaned.

Never again. I was never drinking again.

"Hey, baby, how are you feeling?" The low soft voice belonged to Butch. I'd never heard him sound gentle before.

Slowly, I turned on my side to face him, and a wave of nausea came over me; I closed my mouth tight, fighting the urge to balk.

He slid closer and curled his arm around me. His eyes seemed to be drinking me in, like he hadn't seen me in years. "Not so good, huh?"

Not good at all. In fact—on top of everything else—I felt strangely uneasy. Something was wrong, but I couldn't pinpoint what. "I feel weird." My voice was coarse and scratchy.

He brushed a thumb over my jaw. "Weird how, baby?"

"Just weird." I couldn't explain it beyond that. "Who were my drinking buddies last—?" Images flashed in my pounding head. Snapshots of memory. So much pain. God, the thirst, the need to fuck and—

"Imani, you're gonna be okay," soothed Butch.

Hangover, my ass. "Something's very wrong, isn't it?" Anxious, I went to sit up. My head spun.

"Calm down." Butch gripped my shoulder, keeping me in place. "What's the last thing you remember about the night we spoke with Andres?"

I blinked. My memory was pretty foggy, but... "There was a concert."

He nodded. "That's right. Good. What happened?"

"I went to say goodbye to Eleanor." Things got a little hazy after that.

His eyes searched mine. "That's all you remember?"

The anxiety in his expression made my heart begin to pound. "Tell me whatever it is that I've forgotten."

He inhaled deeply. "You were injected with something at the concert."

I tensed, doing my best to ignore the sensation of my stomach spinning. "Injected? Injected with what?"

He paused. "A serum that's supposed to be a vampiric cure."

My brows flew up. "Are you saying I'm not a vampire?" That couldn't be right. I still *felt* like one...sort of.

"I don't know, baby," admitted Butch. "Your scent hasn't changed, but it doesn't seem to have a vampiric quality to it anymore. You still have the Keja allure, although it's not the same as before."

"What do you mean?"

"The allure doesn't *look* vampiric or even feel it, but it has the same hypnotic effect." He cupped my chin. "Try lowering your fangs."

I tried, but…"They're gone." The words came out in a strangled whisper.

"So is the amber tint to your irises. You're obviously weak, but since you're the first person to get through the entire transition alive, I don't know if that's normal."

There were a whole lot of things wrong with that sentence. "So I've gone through the transition, but I'm still part vampire?"

"I really don't know." And that was clearly worrying him. "Midway through the transition, Lena came to see you. She took a look at your DNA. She couldn't read it because it was, in her words, 'too fluid.'"

"Too fluid? What does that mean?"

"No idea. She tried to stop the transition but, even with Reuben's help to amplify her gift, she wasn't able to help you. Sam and Jared are bringing her to see you some time tonight. Probably in the next hour." Butch threaded his fingers through mine and kissed my palm. "Think of drinking blood. Does it sound good or make you feel queasy?"

I swallowed. The movement hurt enough to make me wince. "The thought of having *anything* makes me feel queasy."

"Okay, we'll review that again later. Does your gift work?"

"I'll try." I reached for it, moved a psychic hand through his mind just as effortlessly as always. "It works." But that didn't seem to relieve him. I used my thumb to brush away the crease between his brows. "You're really worried."

"If you're a little human, that could mean a lot of things."

He was right. I could be weaker now. I could age. I might not heal as quickly. None of those things were good. "You said I'm the only one to get through the entire transition alive. Does that mean others have been injected?"

He told me about the serum, the volunteers, and how each of them died.

Somehow I managed to speak through gritted teeth. "Who did this to me?"

"You know who it's most likely to be."

"Marco or one of his bunnies."

Butch nodded. "All of them are being held in the containment cells. Soon—" A knock sounded at the door, and he sighed. "That'll be Sam, Jared, and Lena to see you." He got out of bed and pulled on a T-shirt and jeans. Then he grabbed another of his T-shirts. "Put this on, baby. I don't want them seeing you naked."

Slowly, I forced myself to sit upright, wincing at the spike of pain in my head. My stomach protested moving, but I managed not to balk. Butch helped me slip on the tee. "Thanks."

He pulled the covers over my legs and tucked them around my waist before pressing a kiss to my temple. "Missed you." He left the room before I could respond, returning moments later with Sam, Jared, Lena, and Antonio.

"Hey," I greeted, tucking my hair behind my ear. I couldn't help feeling a little self-conscious, knowing I had to look like utter crap.

The picture of concern, Antonio asked, "How are you feeling?"

Honestly... "Like a bag of shit."

Jared's lips twitched. "At least you're back to your old self."

"How long was I *not* myself?"

"Three nights." Butch sat beside me and took my hand in his. "Three very long nights."

"You worried the shit out of me, Imani," Sam snapped. Like it was my fault. "I've spent all that time panicking that you wouldn't live through it."

"The question is," said Antonio, "are you any different for living through it?"

"She still has her gift," Butch told them. "She's too queasy to consume anything, so we won't know if she still craves blood until the nausea wears off."

Sam studied me carefully. "Even without the amber irises, you still have a preternatural look about you. But it wouldn't be obvious to our kind that you're a vampire, even with the Keja pull." She turned to Lena. "Do you think you'll be able to read her DNA now?"

"I'd like to try." Lena gingerly sat on the edge of the bed, her smile gentle. "The first time I came to see you, it was impossible for me to tell what was happening to you. Do you know how my gift works?"

I nodded. "You see DNA strands and can alter them."

"Not DNA strands exactly. To me, the DNA looks like numbers and equations. As such, I can see what adds up, what doesn't add up, a person's weak points, and a person's strong points."

"That's sort of awesome."

Her smile widened. "It is, isn't it?" She sobered as she continued. "I was unable to read your DNA on my last visit because the numbers were moving at a rapid rate; the equations were changing so swiftly, I didn't even have time to calculate them. This meant I had no idea if the transition was working or failing. Now that the transition is over, I'd like to take another look. Would that be fine with you?"

"Sure."

Lena gave me a winning smile. "Wonderful. Just be still for me." She didn't move or touch me; just looked at me, her gaze focused and intent, yet not meeting my eyes. Finally, she blinked and straightened. Jared handed her an NST, which she took gratefully.

My stomach churned at the smell, and I tasted bile in my throat. Butch gently rubbed my back until the nausea subsided. Thankfully, Lena drank the NST quickly and Jared took away the bottle.

"Tell us," said Butch.

Lena cocked her head. "I must say, I'm still a little befuddled by your DNA, Imani."

That wasn't good news. "You can't read it?"

"I can read some of it, but it is difficult. What I can tell you, Imani, is that your DNA is no longer in flux. Your body's state is now frozen, just like that of a vampire."

"So I won't age?"

"No. You are once again immortal."

Well, that was both good and bad. Aging would be a problem, since I intended to spend eternity with Butch. But if I was weaker than before and couldn't regain that strength, that would be a major problem. I was a member of the legion. I couldn't afford to be weak. "And the transition won't reverse?"

She shook her head. "You will neither go back to what you were before *nor* alter any further."

Rubbing my back again, Butch asked Lena, "What else can you tell us?"

She crossed one leg over the other. "The serum failed. Imani isn't even *half*-human. Her DNA is more vampire than human, but...some of the equations are now incredibly long and complex. They also contain unfamiliar symbols." And that very clearly concerned her.

His brow furrowed. "What does that mean for Imani?"

"I do not know as I am unable to read the equations. Her DNA is not something I have seen before."

"Do you have any idea *why* my DNA suddenly has these complicated equations?"

"It could indicate that the serum caused side effects," she suggested. "It could indicate that your vampiric system adapted in an attempt to fight the serum. Or it could even be that the serum and your system 'clashed' in a way that caused your DNA to change in certain areas. In fact, it could be all three. I can only speculate as I have never come across anything like this before."

Sighing, Sam gave me a weak smile. "I'm just glad you're alive."

Jared nodded before turning to Lena. "Any suspicions on what might come next for Imani?"

There was a brief, pensive silence before she replied, "Honestly, Jared, I have no idea."

He sighed, his gaze moving back to me. "We'll just have to take this one night at a time. Luther's blaming himself for not foreseeing the danger to you. We've told him to stop beating himself up about it, but it's not placating him."

"Please tell him that I don't blame him at all," I said, feeling bad for the Advisor. The person to blame for this was in one of the containment cells. "Butch told me you have Tait, Juliet, and Marco in custody. Are they talking?"

Sam raked a hand through her hair. "Only a little. I'm sorry to say this, Imani, but we have no bloody clue who did this to you. Each of them denied it, so we brought in Ryder." He had the ability to sift through a person's mind, accessing their memories. "He went to Juliet first, and she slammed him with a psychic blast that's put him in a temporary coma."

I gaped. *"What?"*

"Turns out that it's not actually an offensive gift. It's *de*fensive. If her mind senses an intrusion, it reflexively strikes out."

Damn, that had to have hurt him pretty bad.

"That left us with the option of torturing them until someone confessed," said Jared. "But Butch made us promise not to start that without him. Sam and I thought that leaving the three of them to stew for a few nights, thirsty and tired and agitated, might make them more likely to talk. We'll soon see."

"I can get Marco to talk," rumbled Butch.

"Torture won't work on Marco," I said. "His gift is to block pain."

Butch didn't seem deterred by that. "There are different kinds of pain, baby. Facing the person who has you—someone he very mistakenly thinks belongs to him—will provoke him."

Sam pushed back her shoulders. "All right, let's go interview our suspects."

CHAPTER TWELVE

(Butch)

I'd expected the bunny to be pacing with nerves, thirst, and anger. But Tait was settled in a chair in her cell, admiring her long nails, as if she didn't have a care in the world. I was glad Imani wasn't with us, because this scene would have pissed her off something fierce. Sam, Jared, and I remained silent, waiting Tait out. It didn't take long for her to break.

"Since none of you are looking at me with murder in your eyes, I am assuming that Imani is alive. Shame," she sighed. Her attention snapped to me as I snarled. A hint of wariness appeared in her eyes, but it didn't mollify me.

"I have to say," began Sam, "trying to kill her with a serum instead of challenging her to a duel—now that was cowardly."

Tait sniffed. "I did not inject her with the serum, though I would like to shake the hand of the person who did. Still, I suppose it is good news that she made it through the transition alive; it means I will not be executed for a murder I didn't commit."

"She might be alive, but that doesn't mean you won't be punished for the attempt on her life."

"I had nothing to do with that."

"Why do you despise Imani so much?" asked Jared.

"She deserted Marco, our Sire. That is unforgiveable."

"But you like doing the first-born duties," said Sam. "You like directly serving Marco in all things."

Jared looked at Sam. "Yeah, but it has to chafe that he still acknowledges someone else as his first-born, right? I mean, Tait does all the work. Imani doesn't even send him birthday cards."

Sam slowly nodded. "Ah, I never thought of it like that." She turned back to Tait. "You know what surprises me? That he hasn't renounced Imani. Why do you think that is? Personally, I think the psycho loves her, in his way."

Tait's fists clenched. She obviously didn't like that idea any more than I did.

"At the very least, he's obsessed with her, right?" Sam went on.

Lifting her chin, Tait scoffed, "He feels guilty for Turning her against her will; that is all."

Jared spoke then. "Just how pissed off were you that she went to the castle after all this time? Some would say she didn't belong there. Some would say you made a good point that she was a bad little first-born. Some might even say it was only natural that, feeling defensive on behalf of your Sire, you would feel the need to challenge her."

"I think so," said Tait.

Well I fucking didn't. "But that's not why you attacked her, is it? You wanted her to hurt you. You knew she could. Maybe you weren't expecting her to put you on your ass so easily, but you knew she'd hurt you. You thought it would make Marco pissed at her; you thought it would make him so angry with her that he'd finally renounce her."

Jared grinned. "Didn't work so well, did it?"

"In fact," added Sam, "it was *you* he was pissed at, wasn't it, Tait? That had to sting. And it must have been pretty embarrassing as well."

"Maybe you decided that if he wasn't going to get rid of her, you'd do it yourself," I mused.

Tait scraped her nails on the table. "It wasn't me."

Jared lifted a brow. "Who else could it have been? Marco? Juliet?"

She leaned forward. "I don't know. I don't care. But I sure hope that whoever it was tries it again."

I growled, and she jerked back so fast she almost unbalanced her chair.

Sam smiled. "Such a black-hearted honey pie, aren't you?"

Jared snorted. "I think we're done here. For now." He turned and led us down the long hallway of cells. "I'm not sure what to think about her," he said when we were too far away for her to overhear.

"I think she'd definitely like to see Imani dead," began Sam, "but that's not to say that she's responsible for the attempt on her life."

"I'd like to see Tait dead just for attacking Imani in the castle," I shared.

"Yeah, it does sound like a fun idea," agreed Sam.

We fell silent then as we continued through the passages. The three suspects were being kept far apart to prevent them from communicating and to make them feel further isolated.

When we halted outside another cell, Sam said, "Someone likes yoga."

"You should try it," Juliet told Sam, doing some weird stretch. "It might help with your aggressive nature."

"So might punching you square in the face." Sam tilted her head. "Tell me, Juliet…Just how much do you hate Imani?"

"I do not know her well enough to hate her," replied Juliet. It sounded like a perfectly honest response.

Sam regarded her carefully. "You work in Lazarus' lab, don't you?"

"If you are asking if I have access to the serum, no I do not."

"Who does have access to it?"

Juliet's expression blanked. "A handful of my nest."

The evasive answer pissed me off. "You're very loyal to your nest. It's admirable. But loyalty can be a fault if it's taken too far. You're showing loyalty to someone who betrayed you all by attacking a member of the legion and bringing you all under the scrutiny of the Grand High Pair. Now your precious Sire is facing an execution because, let's face it, he's the most likely suspect."

Performing another weird stretch, Juliet sighed. "Three vampires have easy access to the serum. But I do not believe any of them targeted Imani. Somebody else got to it."

"Who are those three people, Juliet?" asked Jared.

"Lazarus, Eleanor, and Eleanor's partner, Davis."

I folded my arms across my chest. "Who do you think attacked Imani?"

Juliet shrugged. "I have no idea. But I know you have the wrong people incarcerated. I may not have warm feelings for Imani, but I have no reason or wish to end her existence. Tait despises her, but such a sly manoeuvre is not her style."

Jared pursed his lips. "What about Marco?"

Juliet's gaze briefly cut my way. "If the target had been Imani's consort, I would have believed the culprit was Marco. He is very cunning and indeed vindictive enough to commit such an act. But he would not cause Imani any pain."

"He already did that by Turning her," I snapped. "Does no one get that?"

"But he did not do that out of a wish to harm her," said Juliet. "He did it to keep her."

"I don't agree," I told her. "I think he wanted to hurt Imani for being with me. I think that to him she's nothing but a toy that he didn't like losing. He wanted to punish her."

"You are wrong. He would never end her life."

"You act like he's protective of her but the truth is he wasn't with her when she needed his support," Jared pointed out.

She paused in her stretch. "What are you talking about?"

"He abandoned her after he Turned her," said Jared. "Why would he do that if she was important to him?"

Juliet blinked, looking sincerely surprised by the question. "Because Lazarus sent him away, of course. Lazarus only allows his vampires to Turn those who come to this life willingly. Marco broke that rule. The penalty is usually death, but Lazarus is fond of Marco. He ordered him to stay away from the castle and away from Imani."

Jared snickered. "Maybe that's the story that Marco fed you—"

"Ask anyone in the castle," said Juliet. "They will tell you that he did not willingly leave her. After she left, Lazarus allowed Marco to return to the castle, but he forbade him from contacting her. You see, Lazarus let Marco live, but he *had* to punish him. He needed to be *seen* to punish him so that others would not consider repeating the crime. Marco's punishment was to be kept away from Imani."

If that's true, why would Lazarus lie about it to Imani? Jared asked me.

No fucking clue.

"That didn't stop Marco from watching over her," continued Juliet, confirming what we had already suspected. "He hired vampires to erase her trail and keep her safe from hunters."

Sam snorted. "He was keeping tabs on her. Be honest."

Juliet sat on the floor, lotus style. "Yes, he was also keeping himself updated on her whereabouts. But it was her safety that concerned him most. I do not think he has ever given up hope that she would return." She closed her eyes, her features settling into a calm mask. "Now, if you will excuse me, it is time for my meditation." We'd been dismissed.

I don't think there's anything more she can tell us anyway, said Jared as he gestured for Sam and I to follow him.

"Unlike Tait, she's very ambivalent toward Imani's existence," said Sam. "I get the feeling she wouldn't care if Imani lived or died. She's just not on Juliet's radar."

I nodded. "If she's lying, she's good at it."

Jared led us past more cells, turning this way and that. Eventually he stopped in front of another cell.

Marco was standing near the glass. He studied us all carefully. Then he smiled. "She's alive, isn't she? Good."

Sam lifted a single brow. "Is it?"

Jaw hard, Marco said, "You can't think I did this."

Rolling her eyes, Sam waved a bored hand. "You'd never hurt Imani, yeah, yeah. But you already did."

"I brought her into this life without her consent, yes," he allowed.

"Why, Marco? What was it about Imani that made you want to start your own line?"

"Bring her here and I'll tell you."

I growled at that. He smirked.

Sam's nose wrinkled. "Nah, I'll give that a miss."

Marco jerked his chin in my direction. "Get him out of here, and summon Imani."

Fuck that.

"I can't quite work out why you think you're in a position to make demands." Sam turned to her mate. "Can you?"

Jared sighed. "No, I'm stumped here."

"Why do you want to see her?" Sam asked Marco.

"She's mine," he replied simply.

Sam made the sound of a buzzer. "Wrong." Very fucking wrong.

"She *is* mine, and I want to see with my own eyes that she's alive."

"She doesn't think she's yours, does she? She severed all ties with you long ago."

"You watched over her though, Marco, didn't you?" said Jared. "You've spent all these years keeping her safe from people who would hunt and use her for their own gain. And how does she repay you? By shacking up with another guy." Jared put a hand to his chest. "Personally, I'd be pissed. Aren't you?"

When Marco didn't respond, I said, "You wanted revenge. You wanted to punish Imani for being with me. You wanted to hurt us both. Her death would have achieved that."

Marco looked at me, upper lip curled back. "I'd happily see you dead. But Imani will always be safe with me."

Sam snorted. "Considering you're a bloody psycho, forgive me for not believing that."

"You're being blinded by your anger," insisted Marco. "Think. Why would I use serum to kill someone when I can do that with my bare hands? Why would I go through the trouble of keeping Imani safe all these years just to later kill her?"

"If it wasn't you, who was it?" I asked.

"If I knew that, they'd be dead by now."

My gut tells me it's not him, Jared said. Sam gave her mate an odd look, so I guessed that he'd said the same to her. *I don't think Marco would hurt her. Yes, Turning her against her will hurt her, but I don't think he sees it that way.*

Honestly, I was beginning to think that just maybe the guy wouldn't physically harm her, but that wasn't to say that he hadn't injected her with the serum. *Maybe he didn't want to kill her. Maybe he was hoping the serum would work and he was trying to repay her by giving her back her human life or something.*

"Whether you're guilty of this or not, you deserve to die," I said. "You stole her human life from her."

"Perhaps, but you really shouldn't kill me," said Marco, smiling. *Freak.* "I have information you'll want to hear."

"Is that so?" Sam snorted. "I think you'll say anything that you believe will keep you alive."

"You could be right. But you could be wrong." He cocked his head. "Would you like to know what the little insignia is on the blog that's leaking info about our kind?"

Jared stiffened. "How do you know about the blog?"

Marco's smile widened. "You're not the only one who keeps a lookout for such things."

"There is no insignia," said Sam.

"You didn't notice the 'O' that had a 'T' running through it?"

There is a small symbol on the blog, but I didn't think it meant anything, Jared told me.

"What do you know about it?" Sam asked Marco.

He took a step back. "Can't say I'm tempted to help you. I don't like you much. But there is someone I'd like to speak to."

No prizes for guessing who he was talking about. "Fuck that."

He ignored me. "Bring my Imani to me. If she wants to hear about the insignia, I'll tell her."

"You'll toy with her," I corrected.

Again, he ignored me. "It's a fair deal. You let me live, and I'll tell Imani what the insignia means."

"If we let you live," began Jared, "it would be inside this cell."

"At least I'd be alive. Bring her to me. Or don't. The choice is yours."

Before I could tell him to go fuck himself with a jagged blade, I found myself standing in Sam and Jared's office.

I immediately began to pace. "He doesn't know anything. The bastard's just buying time and playing games. He'd say anything to see Imani. He's obsessed with her." Not that I was in a position to judge.

"I agree," said Sam.

I heard a 'But', and I didn't like it. "But…?"

She sighed. "But this has to be Imani's decision."

"No," I bit out.

"Butch, think about it—"

"He's bullshitting us, Coach. We can't ask her to let him play a fucking game with her. He's hurt her enough."

"I know, but I will not make decisions for her. It would insult and disrespect her. You know that, which is why you're not going to pressure her into making the decision you want her to make."

Inwardly, I snorted. Sam didn't know me well if she thought that. I was as overprotective of Imani as I'd warned her I'd be. During the transition, she'd been in so much pain, so crazed, and so close to death, that there had been several moments when I'd been sure I would lose her—and it had been fucking excruciating. Whenever I thought about it too much, anxiety chafed the edges of my consciousness until I wanted to punch something.

It had been so fucking hard to watch her in such gut-wrenching pain; to feel so helpless because there wasn't a damn thing I could do to take it away. The only way I'd been able to help was to feed her. Sam, Jared, and Antonio—being the most powerful on the island—had also acted as regular donors. I'd be eternally grateful for that.

Although a whole lot of people had stopped by to see Imani during the transition, I hadn't allowed any inside; aware that she wouldn't have wanted everyone to see her that way. The only vampires I'd let inside that hadn't been donors were Chico and Lena.

Of course, Fletcher being incredibly dramatic, had staged a protest outside her apartment; marching with huge 'We want to see Imani' boards. One deathly look from me had sent him scampering.

Taking a calming breath, I unclenched my fists. "You saw her, Coach. She's not at full strength yet. And we have no fucking idea what 'full strength' will even be now for Imani."

"I know, and I hate that as much as you do. But there are different kinds of strength. Imani will *never* be weak. She can do this. Marco can't hurt her when there's an impenetrable glass wall between them."

"There are different kinds of hurt," I said, paraphrasing her. "We could just torture the info out of him." I was up for that.

She shook her head. "Imani told us that his gift is to shut off pain, remember?"

I cursed. "Coach, I can't condone this. The sick fuck will sense that she's vulnerable, and he'll leap on it."

"Probably," said Sam, grim. "But it still has to be her decision."

"And if she decides to do this and he fucks with her, we pull her out of there," Jared vowed.

There was no 'if' about it. Imani would do this, Marco would mess with her, and she'd been through enough the past few nights. Still, I nodded, because I knew it was the best deal I'd get. I just hoped Imani declined.

(Imani)

I was just making my way back from the bathroom—and I was *not* about to admit to anyone that the simple act took a fair amount of energy out of me—when the front door opened. Seconds later, Butch strolled inside the bedroom with Sam and Jared close behind.

As Butch's anger crashed into me, I tensed. "Did you find out which one of them did this to me?"

"They're still maintaining their innocence," said Butch before smacking a kiss on my mouth. "Tait says she'd happily see you dead but claims it wasn't her. Juliet says she doesn't care enough about your existence to bother trying to end it. And Marco swears you'll always be safe with him." Butch gave a snort of derision. "There's something else that Juliet said. She claims Marco didn't abandon you; that Lazarus sent him away from you to punish him. I don't think she was lying, baby."

I frowned. "But why would Lazarus lie to me about it?"

"I don't know."

"There's one other thing we need to discuss," announced Sam.

Cursing, Butch cupped my neck. "You don't have to do this."

Sam spoke again. "We never mentioned this before because we didn't think it was significant, but there is a small symbol on the blog that's blabbing about our kind. Marco claims that it's some kind of insignia and it means something. He offered us a deal. If we let him live, he'll talk. But...he'll only talk to you."

"There's a very high chance he's just playing games," Jared warned me.

As I took in Jared's expression, I said, "But you don't think he is."

"He had every motivation to hurt you," Jared conceded. "But from all accounts, Marco isn't a messy killer. He covers his tracks. We can't link a single kill to him. If he was going to hurt you, it doesn't make sense that he'd do it in a way that put him under suspicion."

Though I was loathed to admit it even to myself, Jared made some good points. "I'll talk to Marco." Because whether he tried to kill me or not wasn't the issue here; it was whether or not the insignia truly meant anything.

Butch froze. "Imani."

"You can be there," I told him. "You'll know I'm safe. He can't reach me through the glass."

"Which is why he'll play with you," said Butch. "Even if he's telling the truth, he'll still play with you."

"I know. But what do we have to lose?"

"You don't have to do this."

"I do."

"You can take Fletcher along as well," said Sam. "He'll give us an idea of Marco's emotional state. I want to know whether he's pissed with you or as obsessed as he seems."

"It's probably a little bit of both," grumbled Butch.

Seeming in agreement with that, Sam and Jared headed for the door. Just as they were about to leave, she turned and said, "Oh, I almost forgot. Lazarus and Annalise have been asking to speak with you. Obviously, it would be via teleconference since Lazarus doesn't leave his castle and none of us are comfortable with you going there. Will you be up to speaking with them tomorrow after meeting with

Marco?"

I nodded. "Sure. I'd like to talk to them." I'd like to know whether Juliet was telling the truth.

"All right. Take some time to wind down and recover your strength. We'll see you tomorrow."

Once the pair was gone, I asked Butch, "Do you think Marco even knows anything about the insignia?"

His mouth twisted. "I think it's unlikely. But I also think we shouldn't talk about it or that fucker. Sam's right; you should wind down. After the rough time you've had, you need it."

"We both need it." Being with me during the transition had to have been hard for him.

He surprised me by running a bath; filling the bathroom with the scent of jasmine. As he slowly stripped me, his touch was caring and soothing, not sexual or invasive—dammit. His eyes glittered with possessiveness as they raked over me. My nipples tightened under that heated gaze, but the bastard ignored that and helped me into the tub. After shedding his own clothes, he slid in behind me.

Resting against him with a happy sigh, I caught sight of his toothbrush next to mine. It was only then it occurred to me that a lot of his stuff had found a place in my apartment. I kind of liked that. "So are you just planning to move your things in here, little by little, hoping I won't notice until suddenly *bam* you're all moved in?" Butch could be sneaky like that.

He nuzzled the crook of my neck. "Don't you want me here?"

"Well, sure. You're nice to have around—you're a good cook, you're pretty to look at, and you make baths and showers much more fun."

"But...?"

"There's no 'but.' I just thought you would have liked to stay in your own apartment until you were certain that this is working for you." I didn't want him making huge decisions like moving in here permanently unless he was one-hundred percent sure. I didn't want him to regret it.

His fingers traced my collarbone. "This isn't a complicated situation for me, Imani. I have no doubts whatsoever about you. I'm sure that this is what I want. Just because I'm not very good at relationships doesn't mean I'm scared of the commitment."

"Okay, I was just checking."

He spoke into my ear. "You know, sometimes I'd dream that you were with me. Then I'd wake up, and you weren't there. And I'd remember that I let you go. I hated that. I don't want to wake up and not find you right there again."

Swallowing, I shook my head. "I really had no idea you were feeling this way. I'm sorry that you were hurting. And I'm sorry I didn't see it. As your friend, I should have seen it."

"It was my own fault. You offered me you, and I didn't give you what you need."

Well he'd given me what I needed over the past few nights. "It just occurred to me that I haven't thanked you yet."

"For what?"

"Staying with me. Taking care of me during the transition."

He nipped my ear. "You don't have to thank me. You're mine. I'll always take care of you."

"Dude, you say some pretty nice things." It wasn't that he was attempting to be romantic, sensitive, and soppy. He was just being honest, and I loved that. "Did you even take a break while I was going through the transition?"

"Of course not."

"Not even for a change of clothes?"

"Jared packed me a bag and brought it to me." He kissed my hair. "It was hard to see you like that. Weak and in pain. You didn't even know who I was most of the time. When you did recognise me, you kept asking me to make the pain stop. But I couldn't, and I hated that. I couldn't even hold you tight because your skin was so sensitive. Then you turned into a cat in heat, and I was worried I'd hurt you. But *not* fucking you seemed to hurt you more."

I grimaced. "I wish you hadn't seen me like that."

"I've seen you in worse states than that."

My frown deepened. "Oh yeah? When?"

"Like the time you and your squad were totally shitfaced and stripped down to your underwear to go for a swim in the ocean. You then fell asleep on the sand with seaweed in your hair—but not before putting a shell over each nipple."

And, in my drunken state, I'd been convinced I looked like a mermaid. "You saw me?" Oh, the shame and horror.

"Who do you think carried you to your apartment?"

I blinked. "I thought I walked home but just didn't remember."

He snorted. "You couldn't have lifted your head, let alone walked. You did mumble a few things, though, while I was carrying you."

Something about his tone told me this was going to be embarrassing. "What did I say?"

"You started squirming, so I told you it was just me. You said that no one who's as much of an asshole as me should be 'so damn hot and so good with his hands.'"

Groaning, I closed my eyes. "Tell me you're kidding."

"I shit you not, baby," he chuckled.

"You just left the other girls sprawled all over the sand?"

"They aren't mine. You are." He kissed my neck. "Onto other things…You haven't told me how you're feeling about Lena's news. It can't have been nice to hear."

Total understatement. "It would be fair to say I've avoided even thinking much about the subject."

"Then think about it now. Work it out in your head."

"What do you want me to say? Am I worried? Yeah. Am I pissed? Yeah. Do I find it ironic that I was devastated at the thought of being human again when once upon a time it would have thrilled me? Yeah, I definitely do." I shrugged. "But there's no point in dwelling. As far as I'm concerned, I'm still a vampire. Just a vampire with an edge."

CHAPTER THIRTEEN

(Imani)

Waking up alone, I did a long, languid stretch. I could hear Butch moving around my apartment, and I smiled. He wasn't an early riser, but since I was a late riser he was often awake before me.

Slipping out of bed, I took inventory. The nausea had subsided and my head no longer hurt. Also, my body didn't feel so heavy tonight. In fact, I felt refreshed. Invigorated.

How awesome.

I pulled on a long t-shirt and headed straight for the bathroom. While I was standing in front of the mirror, checking my irises for signs of any changes, Butch came up behind me. I met his gaze in the mirror and smiled. "Hey."

"Hey, baby." His bare chest pressed against my back as he curled his arms around me.

I snuggled into his warm hold. "There's no change to my irises."

"Lena said your body's state was frozen again now."

"I know, but she also said there are all kinds of symbols in my DNA that she doesn't understand."

He nuzzled my neck. "You don't look so tired tonight. How do you feel?"

"Better."

"Still queasy?"

I shook my head. "Nope. I feel fine. Really."

"Good." He sucked on my pulse as his hand slid under my t-shirt and closed around my breast. "Because I want to fuck what belongs to me."

I was totally down with that. He whipped off my t-shirt one-handed, and I arched into the possessive hold on my breast, hooking my arms around his neck. It felt like months since he'd touched me like this—the sex we had during the transition didn't count as I barely remembered it—and I'd missed it. Missed him.

His fingers danced down my navel to my slick folds. He gently squeezed them together, teasing my clit. I gasped. Damn, that felt good. He did it again. And again. And again, driving me freaking insane. I moaned when he rubbed them from side to side. "Butch…"

"You have no idea how important you are to me." Raking his teeth over my pulse, he thrust a finger inside me and swirled it around. "Sometimes I wake up and can't quite believe you're there."

I swallowed hard at the emotion in his voice. "I'm here, and I'd really like to come." But he withdrew his finger, the bastard.

"I want in you." There was the sound of a zipper lowering, and then his cock bumped my folds. I tilted my hips back for him. "Good girl." He thrust hard, burying himself balls-deep inside me in one smooth stroke. My muscles clamped around him, and a growl rumbled up his chest.

The burn of his cock stretching and filling me was heavenly. I needed more. "Move."

One hand gripped my hip while the other moved up to span my throat. "All mine."

He rode me hard, fingers biting into my skin. Savage possession glittered in the dark eyes that met mine through the mirror. Every merciless slam of his cock built the friction until I could feel my climax creeping up on me.

He splayed one hand over my lower stomach. "I can feel me moving in and out of you. Owning you." The words made my body clench. "That's it, baby, squeeze me. Play with your clit, Imani, make yourself come."

"That's your job."

He flashed me a crooked, bad-boy grin and then took my hand. "Is that right?" He used my finger to work my clit; alternating between circling it, flicking it, and rubbing the side of it over and over. "I can feel you getting hotter. You ready to come for me, baby?"

"Yes."

He upped his pace, grunting into my neck. "I haven't tasted you for almost five nights." He licked my throat. "Not going without it any longer." His teeth sank down. My body tightened, and my climax slammed into me. He roughly jammed his cock deep and exploded with a growl.

"I seriously needed that," I panted as I leaned back against him.

His arms looped around me once more. "Your blood tastes different. Not in a bad way. It just has a slight fizz to it...like sparkling champagne." He kissed my neck. "I like you this way. All soft and relaxed with sex-drunk eyes."

I chuckled. "I'm more buzzed than relaxed. I'm also hungry."

"Then I'll feed you."

We both cleaned up and pulled on some clothes before heading to the kitchen.

"I need you to try something." He took an NST out of the refrigerator, opened it, and held it out to me.

I recoiled at the smell. "No thanks."

He resealed it and set it aside. "Hmm." Leaning toward me, he bit his lip hard enough to draw blood and then kissed me. "What about that?"

I licked my lips, tasting him, and smiled. "I'll never turn down your blood."

"So it's just human blood you have an aversion to," he mused. Both our cell phones beeped at the same time.

"That's probably a message from Fletcher telling us he's ready for our meeting with Marco."

Butch's smile faded. "Probably. You can change your mind, you know."

"I know, but I won't."

"I know you won't, you're too damn stubborn." He curled his arm around me and drew me against him. "First, you need to feed."

It was oh so very tempting but..."I fed from you for three nights straight during the transition."

"Then you went twenty-four hours without any blood or food, which I'm going to note is totally unnatural and worrying the shit out of me. In that time, I drank plenty of NSTs. I'm fine."

"You're sure?"

"Positive. Whatever you need, you'll have." He kissed me. "Feed."

I lapped at his pulse, and his arm contracted around me. I bit down and moaned as the taste of him filled my mouth. No blood or NST had ever tasted this good. When I pulled back, I sealed the bite closed and smiled up at him. "Thank you."

"You don't have to thank me." He patted my ass and disappeared. In the blink of an eye, he was back, cell phone in hand. "It *was* Fletcher. He's ready."

"Tell him we'll meet him at the entrance to the cells." As Butch typed the message, I followed him to the door. Just as his hand reached for the knob, a knock sounded. Keeping me behind him, he opened it wearing the scowl from hell.

Alora's smile was somewhat animated. "Hi, Butch. It's nice to see you." He grunted.

Maya cleared her throat. "We'd like to see Imani." She peered around him and grinned at me. "I expected you to look like shit. You look…well fucked."

Ava chuckled. "It works on you."

In a rush, Paige charged past Butch and clamped her arms around me. "I'm so sorry I was an unsupportive bitch. I was so worried about him letting you down that I didn't realise *I* was the one letting you down. And then you got hurt and…and…"

I patted her back gently. "Hey, don't cry."

"I'm not."

She was.

Jude looked at Butch. "And we're sorry we didn't even give you a shot."

Cassie nodded. "We were totally out of line, and we hope you'll give us the chance we didn't give you…even though we probably don't deserve it."

Without releasing me, Paige glanced at him over her shoulder. "You really took care of her during the transition." Which showed them just how serious about me he was. "Thank you for that."

Butch just stared at her. *Ooookay.*

"Your irises really are back to normal," marvelled Ava, shoving Paige aside. "Dude, this is some crazy shit."

"Yeah," I sighed.

"I'm so sorry we weren't there for you during the transition," said Alora. "We wanted to be, but…well, Butch was right to send us away. We totally messed up, and we hope you'll forgive us."

I stepped away from them and moved to Butch's side. "Honestly, girls, I'm glad you've come and I'm glad you're sorry. But I can't truly move past this unless you're *all* willing to give Butch the chance he deserves. He's important to me. I need you to accept that or there's no moving forward."

"We completely accept it," Jude assured me. "We knew he was important to you, we just didn't realise you were important to him." She looked at Butch. "We really are sorry we misjudged you." It was an authentic apology. It also pulled absolutely no reaction whatsoever from him. He could hold a grudge as well as Paige.

He took my hand. "We have to go, baby."

Cassie's brow furrowed. "What's going on?"

I sighed. "I have to talk with Marco. I'll explain everything, just not right now."

"Okay," said Paige. "Call me later."

Butch herded them out of the apartment and, my hand still in his, zoomed out of the building in vampire speed. He paused as we reached the mansion and turned to me. "Are you pissed at me for not graciously accepting their apologies?"

I shook my head. "Hell, no. They were totally in the wrong, and I don't blame you for being wary of them. Just note that I won't be so forgiving toward your squad either."

He kissed me. "They won't apologise, baby."

"Sure they will. It'll hurt their egos, but they'll do it." I tugged Butch inside the building, and we then headed beneath the mansion where the containment cells were located. Fletcher was waiting there, looking like a bag of nerves. I smiled at him reassuringly. "You'll be fine. Marco can't get to you."

Fletcher fanned his face. "There's nothing fine about being in the company of a complete sociopath." Wincing, he said to Butch, "No offense."

"Butch is *not* a sociopath," I ground out. "Marco, well, he's another matter. When you're around both guys at the same time, you'll see the difference."

"I've informed Jared that we're here," Butch told us. "He'll teleport in to collect us when we're done."

I nodded. "Let's get on with this, shall we?"

Fletcher straightened his shoulders and stayed at my side as we walked through the passages with Butch leading the way. I couldn't resist waving at Tait and Juliet as we passed their cells, though inside I was scowling. Finally, we reached Marco's containment cell. Butch and Fletcher stood against the back wall as I moved closer to the glass.

In a blink, Marco was off the mattress and beaming at me. "Hello, sweetheart." His smile shrunk as his gaze shifted to Butch. "Why are you here? I want some time with my Imani."

"If you want to talk to her, you'll deal with me being here," said Butch, his tone non-negotiable.

Marco glared at him. "Does she know you're just as cold and wacked as me? Or do you hide that part of yourself from her?"

Playing games already. "I thought you wanted to speak with *me*."

Switching his attention back to me, Marco studied my face. "The serum cured you?"

"No."

"But it changed you."

Obviously, but this wasn't a social visit and I needed to keep the conversation on track. Marco was trying to control it—typical. "You said the mark on the blog is an insignia."

"Getting down to business already?"

"Either you have something to tell me or you don't."

"I brought you into this life without your consent. How did that make you feel? Angry? Resentful? Depressed? Eager for revenge?"

I swallowed. "I just wanted to be human again. But I don't see how this has any—"

"The blogger and his friends want the same. They blend in with humans and exist in their world, but it isn't enough for them." A long pause. "Ever heard of The Order?"

Never but, for some reason, a chill crept up my spine. "No."

"For a long time, it was just a small group of vampires who got together and said, 'I hate what I am, you hate what you are, let's all be hateful together.' I actually forgot about them...until you mentioned the dragon shifter attack."

Frowning, I asked, "Why would you think that The Order and the dragon attack are connected?"

"My personal opinion is that the dragons who will invade this place are mercenaries. While we waited for Andres' agreement to meet with you, I looked into what enemies the Grand High Pair has. Our kind has settled since Sam and Jared took over; people fear and respect them enough to stay in line. So, I asked myself, who hated them enough to risk their wrath? Then I recalled the blog we've been monitoring that has The Order's insignia, and my gut told me to take another look at the association."

"And?"

"They've grown in numbers and strength. They no longer sit around, bemoaning their situation. They now have a mission."

This wasn't going to be good. "What's their mission?"

"To destroy us all."

Well, fuck.

"I was able to link them to several bombings that humans branded acts of terrorism. Ironically, the humans weren't wrong. The Order is, in effect, a large association of terrorists. But their targets are vampires. Get Sam and Jared to take a look at the terrorist attacks that occurred in the last two years. Many of them wiped out entire nests and buildings that belonged to vampires. I don't think that's a coincidence, considering that The Order has possession of human weapons of war."

"How did you find out about all this?"

His smile was mysterious. "I have my sources."

"None of this means that The Order is behind the upcoming dragon attack."

"If Sam and Jared had made enemies of a drove, Andres would have told you and worked with you to prevent a war; that's the kind of guy he is."

Okay, but... "Why hire dragons? Why not just bomb the island?"

"That would require them to get close. They're probably not brave enough for that, considering they hide behind bombs and guns. The result of a dragon shifter attack would be close to the result of a bomb. If they wipe out the most powerful of our kind, it will cause mayhem and panic."

"Why didn't you tell us all this sooner?"

"I wasn't given a chance," he pointed out, affronted. "The second we got back from our meeting with Andres, I was teleported away from you." His eyes glittered with fury as he added, "Then you were injected with the serum and I was wrongly imprisoned."

"Wrongly?"

My doubt strangely didn't anger him. In fact, he seemed hurt. "You know I didn't do it."

"If it wasn't you, who was it?"

"When I find out, I'll hurt them so badly they'll beg for death.

Believe that."

Unsure what to believe, I returned to the matter at hand. "The Order...where is it based?" He *had* to know, given all the information he possessed.

Marco smiled. "Come back tomorrow, and I'll tell you more."

Appearing at my side in a blink, Butch growled. "You get one conversation with her, asshole. Nothing more."

Smile widening, Marco said to me, "You'll come back, sweetheart. Do you want to know how I know that? It's because you're good. If you can help someone, you will. If someone relies on you, you'll do your best not to let them down. Right now, people are relying on you to get answers from me, aren't they?"

"This isn't a game, Marco, stop playing me."

His expression softened. "Playing you? I'm not doing that, sweetheart. But if I drag this out long enough for you all to realise I'm not the person you're looking for, I get to live and I get my freedom. I rather like living. The moment I'm no longer of any use to anyone here, *he'll* end me. And we both know it."

I couldn't deny that.

Marco turned his back on me and walked to the bed. "Tomorrow, Imani."

Barely holding back a frustrated growl, I spoke to Jared. *We're done here.*

In a matter of moments, he appeared and teleported us to the living area of his beach house, where Sam was waiting. I gave the couple a rundown of everything Marco said.

"Do we think Marco's spinning us some tales?" I asked, relaxing on the sofa. Butch was combing his fingers through my hair.

"I don't know," said Jared.

Sam took a sip of her NST. "I'll talk to Antonio, find out what he knows about The Order—if it even exists at all. This could be just a case of Marco trying to seem useful so we let him live."

"He wants Imani to visit him again," said Butch. "He'll drip feed us info so that he gets to see her."

"I'll talk to him again tomorrow. He might tell us where The Order is based." Not that I was particularly optimistic about that.

"What did you get from him, Fletch?" Sam asked.

Fletcher put his empty NST bottle on the coffee table. "Given everything he's done, I expected him to be hollow inside. He's not.

There's a lot going on in that dark mind. But even though his emotions are intense, they lack any real depth. He despises Butch, which I doubt comes as a surprise to anyone. He probably sees him as an interloper."

"He sees Imani as a possession," said Butch.

"He does want to own her, but it's more than that." Fletcher turned to me. "He has this nagging sense of boredom, but you stimulate him. Amuse him. Even soften him a bit. You're important to him. He cares for you about as much as he's capable of caring for someone; it's more like he's formed an attachment to you. What I know is that the bloke wouldn't cause you physical harm. He sees himself as your protector."

Well that blew a lot of theories out of the water.

Jared exhaled heavily. "We're missing something."

Totally. Hopefully Marco would give us the missing pieces of this shitty puzzle, but having that knowledge gave him power; I very much doubted he'd want to give that up.

"You look tired," Sam told me.

At dusk, I'd felt great. But my strength had waned as the night went on. The good news was... "I'm not as tired as I was last night." I'd take that as a win.

"If you want to postpone your conversation with Lazarus and Annalise, it's totally fine," she assured me.

Shit, I'd completely forgotten about that. "I want to talk to him." I had some questions for him, like had Juliet been telling the truth about Marco and had Lazarus lied to me all these years?

Sam, Jared, Butch, and I headed to the Grand High Pair's office, where Jared set up the teleconference call. Soon enough, the faces of Lazarus and Annalise were on one of the monitor screens.

"Imani, you cannot imagine how relieved I am to see you alive," said Lazarus.

Annalise nodded. "My beautiful girl, I am so sorry for what happened to you. It grieves me that you were harmed in such a way *and right under my roof.*"

I shrugged. "What's done is done."

"I see that the cure did not work." Lazarus' eyes narrowed. "Although your irises lost the amber glow. In what other ways have you changed? How is it that you survived the transition?"

"Your guess is as good as mine."

Annalise looked at Sam. "Have you questioned Marco, Tait, and Juliet? People came forward to say the three were nowhere near Imani during the concert."

"We all know that doesn't mean they weren't behind what happened to Imani," said Sam.

"Yes," sighed Lazarus. "But I'm unable to prove it. As much as I want vengeance for Imani, I cannot brand someone guilty unless I can be certain that they are. My gut tells me it was Tait, but if I punish her based on my gut and it turns out I was wrong, the person who is truly responsible would go unpunished. Imani would then not have the justice she deserves."

"You won't need to punish her, Lazarus," said Sam. "That's our show."

He stilled. "They, including Imani, are my vampires. The punishment is mine to deliver."

"Wrong. Come on, Lazarus, did you think I brought them here for tea, cakes, and a pop quiz?"

"I have witnessed via V-Tube your idea of interrogations. I do not want my vampires subjected to that—not when at least two of them are innocent."

"I'm not asking for your permission, Lazarus."

"I do not appreciate you taking over this situation."

Sam leaned forward. "Do you really think I give a flying fuck about what you appreciate? Whoever injected Imani did so believing the serum would kill her. I take an attack on my vampires very seriously. An attack on my friend? That's a mistake of epic proportions, so do not fuck with my patience."

Sinking back into her chair, she went on, "It's really not me you should be worried about. Butch is exponentially pissed, and there won't be any way of holding him back from slaughtering the person responsible for what happened to Imani. Not that I'll try to hold him back."

"No one could hold me back," Butch told him. "And I don't fucking like it that you don't seem as anxious to find out who hurt Imani as you should. Part of me wonders if you're just so curious to understand how Imani survived that it's overridden your concern. And part of me wonders if what you'd love to do most right now is take her to a lab and perform test after test until you finally find out why she survived what others didn't—and just what exactly she's become."

If Annalise's downcast expression was much to go by, Butch was right about the latter. And he clearly knew it, because a growl rumbled out of him that caused the siblings to tense. "She's a *person*, not a fucking lab rat. There'll be no testing her; she's been through enough."

"I wholeheartedly agree," Annalise assured him. "And so does Lazarus." Her brother didn't confirm that but nor did he deny it.

"It's hard to trust the word of someone who has potentially lied to her since the night he met her."

Lazarus blinked. "Excuse me?"

"Did Marco really abandon me, Lazarus?" I asked. "Or was that a lie?"

A heavy sigh left him. "He told you."

"No, Juliet did the talking. But *you* should have told me."

"I did not lie to hurt you, Imani. It was part of his punishment. He Turned you to keep you. He is not the first vampire in history to have done that to someone of course, but I was determined that he would be the last of my nest to do it. You're a good person, Imani. Compassionate. Forgiving. If you had forgiven Marco and the two of you had reconciled, what do you think that would have taught him and the others in my nest?"

Sam was the one who replied, "That it would all work out fine in the end."

"Yes. It would teach them that braving my punishment would be worth it because, in the end, all would be fine between them and the vampire they Turned. So I made you hate him. It stopped you from going back to him, and it was something he had to live with. He did not abandon you. People are interchangeable for him, but I think Marco sees you as a person in your own right. I believe something in you…spoke to him, if you will. But that was not a justifiable reason for him to do what he did, and for that he was punished."

Okay, I sort of understood that. There was no point in getting riled about it, because it hadn't been personal to me; the whole thing was much bigger than me and Marco. Lazarus had needed to set an example. "Did it work?"

"No one has since committed such an act," replied Lazarus. "I am sorry if you feel hurt that I lied to you. But it was the best for all concerned. And it has potentially saved a lot of humans from unwillingly being Turned."

That wasn't something I could or ever would be angry about.

CHAPTER FOURTEEN

(Butch)

I didn't think I'd ever gawked before, but Imani had a way of shocking the shit out of me. I wasn't in a great mood since she'd insisted on partaking in the training session. In my opinion, she needed more time to recover. But as she looked just as good as she claimed to feel, I didn't push her on it. I decided that I'd keep a close watch on her instead.

As the session went on, it became clear that her speed and strength weren't as good as before she was injected with the serum. Halfway through the session, I suggested that she take a break. Her response was, 'I can't afford to take breaks and go easy when there's a battle coming.'

She intended to be part of the battle? "You can't be serious."

"Why? I told you I feel better."

"That doesn't mean you *are* better."

"Stop fretting, I'm fine."

I advanced on her. "Tell me you honestly don't plan on being part of this battle."

"I could, but it would be a lie."

Her bored tone was pissing me off. "You're weaker now, Imani. You might feel good, baby, but you're not a full vampire anymore. Your reaction time isn't as fast. You can't rely on your speed and strength in the same ways that you could before. That means you need time to adjust to that and find ways to compensate for it." *Then* she'd be fit for battle. Now? Not a chance, and I couldn't risk her.

"I'm not denying that my strength and speed is more like that of a Sventé, but I may not need time to adjust to that because it's possible that the change isn't a permanent thing. I could just need more recovery time. Lena couldn't read my DNA properly, so we don't know anything for sure."

"Exactly. *We don't know.* That's not good enough."

She sighed. "Butch—"

"No, Imani, you shouldn't be part of this battle."

"Hey, do you remember that time when I asked what you thought? Yeah, me neither." She raised a hand when I went to speak. "I let you say your piece. Now you let me say mine. Yes, I'm not a full vampire anymore. Yes, that could mean a lot of things. You saw me hurt and in pain, and I understand that it was hard for you and has sent your protective streak into hyper-drive. But you've got to get a grip on it."

"If you think I'll watch you walk into certain danger, you're out of your mind."

She haughtily jutted out her chin. "I'm not asking for your permission or approval, Butch. I'm going."

She really *was* out of her mind. "You think Sam and Jared will allow it, knowing you're weaker now?"

"Let's ask them." She turned to the pair, who—along with the rest of our squads—were watching us in fascination. "What's your opinion on all this?"

Sam's mouth twisted. "I know what it's like to suddenly find yourself without your strengths; to have no real idea what's happening to you. When I was becoming a hybrid, my system messed up in all kinds of ways. It took me time to adjust to the transformation. You'll need that time as well. I'm going to make you a deal. We don't know how long it will be before the dragons come here. If you're in good shape when they come, you will be fighting along with your squad. If you're not fit for battle, you *will* stay behind for your safety and that of the people who rely on you to watch their back."

Imani rolled back her shoulders. "That's fair."

"What we need is a real test of strength to get an exact idea of how much progress you need to make," said Sam.

"Okay, so how do we do that?"

"You can spar with me."

Imani gaped. "You have to be kidding. I can't defeat you! You have Pagori strength and you're a Feeder! Hell, *none* of us could defeat you. Even Jared would find that hard."

Jared inclined his head at that, not at all offended.

"I wouldn't expect you to defeat me, Imani," said Sam. "This isn't us pitting ourselves against each other. I just want to get a good measure of your strength."

"Coach, no," I bit out. "You could hurt her. Not on purpose, but you could."

Sam scowled at me. "Like I don't know my own strength? Don't insult me, Butch."

"Let's just get this over with," said Imani.

My hand snapped out and circled her wrist. "No, not—"

She shook off my hold. "You should be happy. I'll no doubt have my ass kicked right here in front of everybody. They'll see just how much weaker I am than before, and you can rub it in."

That wasn't at all what I wanted. "Imani—"

"Fuck you, Butch. Fuck you sideways." She marched to the northern side of the arena and took position there.

Taking position on the southern side, Sam braced her feet shoulder-width apart. "No using our gifts."

"Not like it would do me much good against you anyway."

Radiating anger, Paige sidled up to me. "If she gets any injuries, I'm transferring them to you."

I wouldn't blame her. Tension riding me, I kept my eyes on the two females ready to spar. In that moment, I was proud of Imani. She didn't have an ounce of hope that she could take Sam on. But she wasn't backing down; wasn't simply accepting defeat. She would fight, even if it meant losing. Everyone in the arena saw that and would respect it.

For long minutes, nobody moved. The females just stared at each other, their gazes intense and alert. Anticipation sparked in the air, making the wait almost painful.

"One advantage you've got is that you don't look like a vampire," said Sam. "Oh, you have the pull of the Keja allure, but another vampire would dismiss the possibility of you being a Keja because your irises are normal. They might believe you're human or another preternatural of some kind. In any case, they won't expect a fight from you. *Use* that. Fake fear, give your opponent the image of a terrified human, and then surprise the fuck out of them by doing this." Sam's body blurred as she rushed to Imani, fist cocked.

Imani blocked the punch with one arm and used her free hand to deliver a hard palm heel strike to Sam's chest, sending the Feeder back a few feet.

Sam smiled. "Good. I half-expected you to move too early to overcompensate for your decrease in strength, but you didn't move until you absolutely had to. Keep doing that."

The females went at each other with a serious of punches, kicks, and dirty moves that Jared had taught them. Imani held her own. Oh, she hit the floor a few times—even crashed into the wall at one point. But she bounced back up every time. She also put Sam on her ass twice.

Sam's breath left her lungs as she took a hard kick to the solar plexus. Imani followed that up with a punch that split Sam's lip. The Feeder actually smiled. "Very good. I have to say I'm impressed."

Imani didn't respond. Just stared at Sam, her gaze unblinking.

"It's not easy to switch off to everything but your opponent. Butch pissed you off, but you didn't fight in anger. That's—"

"Hold up." Jared moved forward, concern on his features. "Sam, your lip isn't healing."

I frowned. Any vampire would heal pretty quickly from a small wound. As a hybrid, Sam healed exceptionally fast. Yet, Jared was right; the cut wasn't healing.

I looked at Imani. She was still staring at Sam, seeming oblivious to everything else. No, not staring at Sam. Staring at her mouth. A mouth that was bleeding freely.

"Imani?" I called out. She didn't respond. I headed straight to her. "Imani, what are you doing?" She was doing *something*. She was also ignoring me. I shook her a little. "Baby, stop."

She double-blinked. And I could have sworn the rims of her pupils flashed silver for a second. Then she scowled as she seemed to finally *see* me. "What are you doing? Let go."

"You called my blood."

Imani frowned at Sam's words. "What?"

"You called my blood." Sam wasn't pissed, she was fascinated.

"No, I didn't."

"I could feel a weird force pulling at it. As soon as you looked away, my lip healed."

Paling, Imani shook her head. I understood. She'd had enough weird shit going on around her. She didn't need more.

"Consciously or not, you called my blood to you," Sam insisted.

"No." Imani took a few steps back. "I can't call blood."

I reached for her, but she backed away even further. "Baby—"

In a blink, she was gone.

Fuck.

(Imani)

Hard to drown your sorrows when you were part-human.

The only way a vampire could get drunk was by feeding from intoxicated humans. But since the blood of the humans waltzing around the bar didn't appeal to me, I was sober as a judge.

Still, I wasn't ready to go home yet. I needed space. Space to accept that, whether I wanted to believe it or not, I'd called someone's blood to me. Space to accept that I was now back in that place where I didn't 'fit.'

That was what bothered me most about this being part-human business. Being different reminded me too much of the years I'd struggled to be accepted by my own damn family. I was the kind of person who'd always liked what I didn't understand. Mysteries, puzzles, and things that were 'different' had always fascinated me. But it was a whole other matter when *you* were the one who was different; when you didn't understand yourself.

As for Butch...what a shithead. A hypocritical shithead. In my position, he would never have sat at home like a good little boy while others went to battle. No freaking way. There was being protective, and there was being an interfering asshole who completely dismissed any input I had on my *own* decisions.

Well, both he and Sam had warned me that he'd fuck up a lot. I'd hoped they were exaggerating.

Something else ticking me off. From what Sam and Jared had learned, Marco was telling the truth about The Order. That meant The Hollow was facing a bunch of terrorists with the extinction of vampirekind in mind. It also meant I'd have to talk to him again. Jared had chosen to delay it until tomorrow night to send Marco the message that he wasn't running the show. It was a good idea and—

"You okay?"

My upper lip curled. *Dean.* Just what I needed. I didn't even bother to look at him.

He slipped onto the stool beside mine. "Seriously, are you okay? You have bruises on your face. Since when do vampires bruise?"

Since they became a little human, apparently.

"I came to see you when you were hurt. Richardson wouldn't let me in."

I was about to point out that, overcome with bloodlust, I would have drained Dean dry. However, given my new aversion to human blood, I probably wouldn't have touched him.

"You're still pissed at me, huh."

He expected anything different? "You broke my trust, Dean."

"It wasn't like that."

I did look at him then. "You let another vampire drink from you, even though you'd sworn you wouldn't. You broke your promise and, in doing so, broke my trust."

"I guess I didn't think it would bother you that much," he mumbled.

God, Butch was right; he really was a prick. "Just go."

"Wait, I just want to say—"

"I'm not interested in anything you have to say. I don't even want an apology. I just want you to leave." But the bastard actually went to take my hand. "*Don't* touch me."

A familiar scent swirled around me just as a hand possessively slid around my neck. "You okay, baby?"

Um, no. *Duh.*

"You need to back the fuck off, human," he rumbled.

Dean swallowed nervously. "This has nothing to do with you," he stated, but his voice was shaky.

"There is no 'this'—there's only you being a prick. Try not to be one all your life."

I didn't have the patience for either male right now. I shot off the stool and went to pass Butch, but he pulled me to him. I would have struggled, but his mouth moved to my ear and he said, "Don't, baby." If it had been a demand or an order, I could have ignored that. But it was a coaxing plea. It took me off-guard and made me freeze when I should have moved away.

"Imani, you know he's not going to stay with you," snapped Dean. "He's just using you."

"Not very bright, are you?" said Butch.

Dean snickered. "At least I'm not the rebound guy."

In a nanosecond, Butch went from holding me to lifting Dean up by his throat. The human was kicking his legs like crazy and struggling to get free.

I sighed. "Butch, put him down."

Instead, Butch pulled him close so they were nose-to-nose. "Hear me loud and clear, little human, because I won't repeat myself. You and Imani are done. Over. Accept it and move on, because I don't give up what belongs to me. And I sure as shit won't give up Imani." He flung Dean away, making the human stumble and crash into the bar.

While Butch was distracted, I went to leave. I didn't get far. Four steps later, he appeared in front of me. I hissed, *"Move."*

His hands cupped my neck. "I fucked up again, I know. I'm sorry."

By his tone, he seriously thought that was good enough. "Out of my way."

"Imani."

"When you're ready to make a real apology, I'll listen. Until then…" I hurried to my apartment in vampire speed. I'd just unlocked the door when I sensed Butch behind me. I whirled on him. "Did you not hear me just now?"

He backed me inside the apartment. "You know I have no respect for boundaries, and we clearly need to talk."

I put my hands on my hips. "You'd better have something *real* good to say, Richardson, because the last thing I want to do tonight is punch you in the dick…but it *is* on my schedule."

"Like I said, I fucked up. I can't apologise for freaking out about you going into battle. It would be a lie, and that would insult both of us. But I am sorry that you're hurting right now. I didn't want that."

As apologies went, it wasn't the best I'd ever heard. But it was honest. "I'm a member of the legion, Butch. That means I'm going to be in dangerous situations again and again. You accepted that before. Why can't you accept it now?" I might be partly human, but I was as strong and fast as a Sventé. Both Jude and Ava were Sventés.

For a moment, he said nothing. Just stood there, his expression almost tortured. "I didn't keep you safe." His words made me blink.

"I'm a living shield, Imani, but I didn't keep you safe. You got hurt *right in front of me*."

I mentally kicked myself. I should have known that, protective as he was, he'd find some way to blame himself. "It all happened so fast, there was nothing you could have done."

"The reason I didn't freak out about you being on assignments in the past was that I was there with you; I was confident I could protect you." A cynical, self-mocking smile surfaced on his face. "At the castle, I didn't. Intellectually, I know it's not my fault that you were hurt, and I know it's pointless to feel guilty about it. I also know that I can't lock you away where you'll be safe, and that you'd be miserable if I tried."

"So why get so wound up about this?"

"You don't get it, Imani. A year. I was without you for almost a year. Just when I thought I had you back, I felt you slipping away. You don't know how many times your heartrate slowed down during the transition. You don't know how many times you passed out, so weak I didn't think you'd wake up."

His eyes glittered with an emotion I would never have associated with Butch. Fear. "It scared you."

"Hell yes, it scared me."

While that softened the blow of what he'd done, it didn't make it okay. He had to understand that or he'd do it over and over. "That isn't an excuse. I don't expect you to always agree with my choices, but I expect you to respect my right to make them. Dictating to me, talking down to me like I don't know myself, was not at all cool, Butch. If I had behaved that way toward you, if I'd showed you that kind of disrespect, you'd be just as pissed as I am now."

He raked a hand through his hair. "I'm not good at this." He looked so lost.

"Yeah, I already figured that out." Although I was still mad, I knew I'd have to back down a little. Sam had told me he'd need the room to make mistakes; she'd warned me he'd be a difficult partner. I'd taken the risk, and that meant I had to make some allowances. "I understand that you want me safe. I'm glad that you care. But that doesn't mean I'll always bow to your wishes. That's not how it works."

He moved to me and brushed his thumb along my cheekbone. "I do respect you. I'm sorry if I made you feel like I didn't."

I gave a curt nod. "Okay."

"I hate it when we argue."

We'd only had two very minor arguments before now. "It's going to happen sometimes. You're an alpha, which makes you pushy and domineering. Neither of those things are much fun for me, even though I know you interfere because you're trying to smooth the way for me and make my life better. I'm stubborn and independent, which means I'll keep pushing back."

He rubbed his nose against mine. "I warned you that I'm not good for people."

Not liking that comment at all, I said, "That's bullshit. We both have strong personalities so we'll clash from time to time. That doesn't mean you're not good for me, or vice versa. Being dominant and decisive isn't bad. You're also very protective and supportive, which I appreciate. Tonight, though, you were *too* protective and *too* big, bad alpha."

He sighed. "Okay. I'll work on it. But we're good now?"

"We're good."

His arms locked around me and he pressed a gentle, apologetic kiss on my mouth. "Seeing those bruises on your face makes me want to punch something. Sam wouldn't have hit you that hard if she'd known you'd bruise. Baby, about what you did to her—"

"Let's not talk about it. It doesn't matter."

"Imani, you called blood to you. That kind of matters."

"I don't want to talk about it right now."

He rubbed my back. "Can't say I blame you for being freaked out." He pressed a gentle kiss to my temple. "Okay, I'll drop it."

I released a heavy breath. "I need a shower."

"Come on." He led me to the bathroom.

"I can shower myself."

"Of course you can. But I want to take care of you. Don't fight me on it. I need it."

Sighing, I allowed him to take care of me—massaging my head, shoulders, and arms until all my tension had left me and I was close to boneless.

As he dabbed me dry with a towel, I asked, "What were your other two relationships like?"

He paused. "You sure you want to hear about my past?"

"I want to understand what makes you think you're not good for people." That dumb idea had to have come from somewhere.

His hands resumed drying me off. "There was a girl I dated in high school. Back then, I was thinking with my dick more than anything else, so I didn't see that she was trying to lead me around by it. Kylie didn't want me to enlist, but I'd made up my mind. She said she'd wait for me. She wrote to me a lot while I was away, always included all kinds of soppy declarations. When I got back, it was to find that she'd moved in with another guy."

I gaped. "She was living with someone else?"

"In the letters, she hadn't given me even a hint of this. She'd been seeing him since a month after I left. She hadn't told me, because she'd wanted to enjoy my shock; she'd wanted to punish me for leaving her."

I rubbed his chest. "Butch, that wasn't your fault or—"

"This is just the background, baby. That wasn't one of the relationships I was talking about." He sighed. "I didn't like that she'd played me or that she'd cheated, but after being in a fucking war zone...the whole thing just seemed trivial. And considering she was a little wacked, I was glad to see the back of her. So instead of losing my shit, I walked away. I wasn't interested in a girl who played games. But Kylie didn't like that."

I'd bet she didn't.

"Maybe she'd expected me to fight for her or something. I know her parents were divorced and they spent most of her life in and out of court, fighting for custody and changes to the court agreement. Maybe that had messed her up. All I know is, she then decided to make my life hell."

"I hate her already." I kissed his chest. "Tell me the rest."

"Any time I was with a girl for more than a night, Kylie would try to chase them away. Most of the time, it worked. If it didn't, Kylie would step up her game."

Following him into the bedroom, I asked, "Chase them away how?"

Dropping his towel, he pulled on a pair of pants. "She'd start with telling them lies about me; she'd say things like I was a drug addict or a serial cheater. Other times she'd claim I was actually *her* boyfriend, and even the father of her unborn—and of course fictional—child."

"Oh. My. God." I slipped on a vest and shorts as I added, "What a total bitch."

"It didn't even matter to her that she was still living with that guy, who either didn't know what she was doing or just didn't care. It didn't matter that she was also sleeping with other guys. No, she'd decided my life was gonna be hell because I left her."

"Sounds like this wasn't about you at all. You said her parents were divorced, so one of them must have left home. That had to have hurt. Then they'd spent all those years fighting over her. Maybe she liked that kind of attention and thought that was what love was. But when you left her just like one of her parents did, you didn't fight for her. I mean, she told lies about you—I'll bet that was one of the court tactics her parents used."

He shrugged. "Only Kylie knows why she behaved that way."

"You said she stepped up her game if the lies didn't work. What did she do to the girls?"

"Sometimes she'd spread false rumours about them to piss them off. Other times she'd turn up at their houses with bruises and claim I hurt her, trying to scare them."

Grimacing, I said, "That's…there aren't words."

"Sooner or later, even the ones who were wise to her games would leave because they'd had enough of her shit and just wanted it all to end." And he didn't sound in the least bit judgemental. "One girl, Tori, she was different. She saw right through Kylie, she said she knew it wasn't my fault and she'd stick by me and make Kylie realise she was wasting her time."

This was obviously one of the relationships he'd mentioned. "Kylie didn't stop with her games, did she?"

He shook his head. "I tried to protect Tori from her as best I could; tried to shield her from Kylie's shit—even got the police involved, which didn't help because Kylie's dad was a cop; they tend to stick together. I went to her parents, told them what was happening. They were no help. They coddled her. No one could convince them that their only child was anything but perfect. It was hard, and it sucked. But Tori swore she wasn't going anywhere; that she wouldn't let Kylie drive her away."

"But she left," I said softly.

"She said she would have stayed if I'd just opened up to her more; if I paid her more attention and—"

"Bullshit," I snapped. "She was blaming you for her leaving, because she didn't want to lose face and admit she couldn't take it."

He didn't seem convinced of that. "After my second deployment, I moved to the next town over. I met someone. It got serious. All was good. Helena wanted me to put a ring on her finger. I wasn't ready for that, but I took her to meet my parents."

"Kylie saw you."

He nodded and then pulled on a T-shirt. "She flipped out. Totally lost it. It wasn't jealousy or a show of possessiveness. She didn't want me. She just didn't want me to be happy."

"What did she do?"

"My parents chased her off that night. She started showing up at my house and Helena's place of work, ranting the same old shit she'd said to all the girls that came before Helena. Helena was no lightweight, and she saw Kylie for what she was. Each time Kylie did something, she made Helena more determined to stick it out as a 'fuck you.'"

"But she didn't stay, did she?" The bitch.

"No. Like I said, she wanted a ring. She felt it was the least she deserved, considering the shit that she had to put up with from Kylie. Maybe she was right. But the thing is, baby, every girl that came before her had walked away. Every one of them. Hell, even my own mother had left me. To me, marriage is forever. I wasn't going to bind myself to someone unless I was certain they weren't going anywhere."

"Helena walked out because you didn't propose?"

"She left me for a guy she worked with who had been her 'confidante' throughout all the trouble with Kylie." Butch snorted. "She said he was sensitive, made her smile, and cared enough to be open with her. The oh-so-perfect guy dumped her a month later. She came back, but I sent her away. The next time I was in a war zone, I was Turned into a vampire. I never looked back."

I moved to him. "Now I get it. All of it." I grazed his jaw with my nails, knowing he liked it. "Butch, they didn't walk away because you weren't good enough for them to want to stick around or because you couldn't make them happy. They blamed you because they didn't want to admit to you or themselves that they were letting Kylie win after swearing that they wouldn't." He had to see that...but he was shaking his head.

"With you, I'm happy. No one could do anything to make me walk away." His hands settled on my hips. "If they had been this happy, they'd have stuck it out with me."

Oh, he was too adorable...in his own weird way. "If they weren't this happy, you aren't at fault for that. And to be fair, Kylie made things nearly impossible for you."

"I'm not going to lay the blame at Kylie's feet. I was never good at relationships. You know me, baby. I'm not a master of communication. I'm not patient or gentle. I don't have a great sense of humour, and I'm probably the least compassionate person you'll ever meet. Hell, I find it easier to kill than I do to talk about what I'm feeling. I don't blame them for leaving."

He honestly didn't, and that just pissed me off. "That's a load of crap. You know that, right? The first night you announced your intentions to me, you said you don't know how to make people happy. You make me happy."

His expression called me a liar. "Baby..."

"It's true. Sometimes it's simple things, like when you cook my favourite meals or run me a bath without being asked. Then there are big things, like taking care of me during the transition and making my safety your priority. You're always there when I need you. Oh, and you give first class orgasms. Just sayin'."

His mouth curved into that lopsided smile I loved. "You happy enough to stick around?"

"Totally."

He kissed me, savoured me, until I melted into him. Tapping my ass, he said, "Come on." He led me to the living area, where we settled on the sofa. "Here." He grabbed my Kindle from the table and handed it to me. "I'm going to watch the game. You're going to stay with me and just relax."

So—tired and eager to read a book that had recently been released—that was what I did. Until I received a text message from Fletcher. I gasped. "Ryder's awake."

Butch's eyes shot to me. "About fucking time."

I jabbed him with my elbow. "It wasn't Ryder's fault he was in a freaking coma. According to Fletcher, he's a little weak right now but he'll be fine by tomorrow."

"At which point he'll mind-swipe Marco, Tait, and Juliet and tell us who the fuck hurt you."

That was the hope. "I think—" I paused as a knock came at the door.

Sighing, Butch headed straight for it and swung it open, revealing David, Max, Salem, and Chico.

"Hey." David smiled as they walked in, like it was their regular hangout. When Butch just looked at them blankly, David added, "It's your turn to be host."

"You forgot," guessed Chico, pulling out his cell phone. "No worries. I'll order pizza."

"Don't forget chicken wings, potato wedges, and onion rings," said Max.

Soon enough, my living area was packed with Butch's squad members. I ended up sitting on his lap to make room on the sofa. Others settled on the floor or hauled in the breakfast bar stools. As I watched them interact, I quickly realised that this was a guy apology of sorts. It was a shit one, in my opinion, but I supposed if *one* alpha had trouble apologising, a whole bunch of them at one time were bound to be shit at it.

I drowned out all the noise, concentrating on my book. Though I did pause to eat two slices of pizza and a few onion rings.

Once the game was over, David—who was sitting beside me and Butch—gave my leg a little shove. "How've you been, Imani?"

I smiled. "Good. I'd feel a whole lot better if everyone here who'd been utter dicks to Butch would actually make a real apology. This version of one is totally crap and it ain't gonna fly with me."

David's mouth twitched into a smile while Salem grunted, seemingly in agreement. The others all looked at each other, rolling back their shoulders and cricking their neck.

Chico cleared his throat. "Imani's right, Butch. We were dicks."

I waved my hand, encouraging him to continue because, yeah, that wasn't good enough.

"We should have had your back but we didn't," added Chico.

"And you're sorry," I prompted.

A muscle in Chico's cheek ticked. "And we're sorry."

Half-placated, I looked at the others with an expectant brow. "You're going to make Chico do all the work?"

Reuben straightened. "I was out of line, asking you to leave the arena. Totally out of line. I won't insult you by trying to make excuses. All I can say is that I swear I'll always have your back in the future."

"We took our protectiveness of the girls a little too far," Harvey admitted. At my snort, he added, "*Way* too far. That's not an excuse, though, I know."

Denny nodded. "Judging you like that wasn't fair, and it won't happen again."

The image of self-recrimination, Damien spoke. "I was a total ass, and I had no right to say the shit I said."

"I won't lie and say I think my concerns were unfounded," said Stuart. "They weren't. But it still wasn't my place to voice any of them. And I truly am sorry for not giving you the benefit of the doubt."

"We won't blame you if words aren't enough for you," said Max. "We've got to show you we mean it, and we will."

I looked up at Butch, who surprisingly seemed to be stifling an amused smile. "What do you think? Shall we give *them* the benefit of the doubt, even though they didn't do the same for you?"

His amused smile broke free. "I guess we could."

"Yeah. They're not too bad at grovelling, are they?"

Affronted, Max objected, "We don't grovel."

David snorted. "It was impressive. Maybe not as impressive as Imani's behaviour in the arena, though."

Oh, how males moved on from emotional moments so quickly.

"I gotta say, Imani," began Damien with a grin, "when you called Sam's blood, I was totally envious. That would be a cool ability."

"I thought you might lose your gift," said Stuart, swirling his NST. "I wasn't expecting you to develop another."

"I don't think I did develop another," I told him.

Chico frowned. "We all saw what you did."

"But it's not a gift. It's just…something weird." Something I didn't like.

Harvey smiled. "Whatever it is, it's awesome."

"How did you do it?" asked Denny, fascinated. "How did you call the blood?"

"I didn't mean to. When Sam started to bleed, I recognised the scent, and suddenly the taste was in my mouth…like a sensory memory."

Butch curled my hair around his fist. "You fed from her during the transition."

Well that explained it. "I couldn't stop looking at the blood. But I didn't have an urge to leap on her."

Reuben bit into his pizza. "Why do you think you can suddenly do it?"

I shrugged one shoulder. "Your guess is as good as mine."

Butch gave my hair a playful tug. "Lena said the serum could cause side effects. Maybe this is a side effect."

Chico put down his beer-flavoured NST. "See if you can do it now."

I blinked. "What?"

"I'll cut my arm. You call the blood."

I jerked back. "Hell, no! I don't want to call people's blood to me."

"But you will, Imani; you might not *mean* to do it, but you will." Butch's voice was gentle. "And you'll keep doing it unless you learn to control it. So start learning."

It was hard not to growl. "This is *so* not the definition of winding down."

Butch kissed my temple. "You need to learn how to control this, baby. You know it's important."

I sighed. "Tomorrow, okay. We'll go to the arena tomorrow and I'll practice. Let me have the rest of tonight to relax." That wasn't too much to ask.

"Tomorrow," he agreed.

CHAPTER FIFTEEN

(Imani)

I'd kind of hoped Butch would forget about my agreement to practice calling blood, since the idea of watching Chico cut himself seriously didn't appeal to me. But when we woke at dusk, Butch was quick to remind me of our little agreement. And since Sam and Jared thought the whole thing was a good idea, I had no support from their corner.

As such, no sooner was I dressed and well fed than Butch was ushering me to the arena. I ensured he knew I was there under sufferance, but that didn't appear to bother him. Apparently his squad hadn't forgotten about the agreement either, because they were already waiting at the arena with Sam, Jared, and my squad.

I walked to Jude. "I'm surprised you're okay with this." She didn't look at all reluctant to stand there while her mate wounded himself repeatedly. But then, Jude did have a fondness for knives.

"You won't be training with Chico. You'll be training with me."

I stiffened. He did *not* just say that. Slowly, I turned to face Butch. "You're not serious."

"What's the problem?"

"Call me weird, but I don't want to watch you hurt yourself."

"This is necessary. You know it."

Paige put a supportive hand on my shoulder. "You can do this, sweetie. He's right; it's necessary that you get a grip on this."

I rounded on her. "You're *siding* with him? Well, thanks, Judas."

"Stop talking to Paige so we can get started," interjected Butch. "*Now*, Imani."

Rubbed the wrong way by that order, I gritted out with a false smile, "Sense the danger of continuing with that tone."

"You're just trying to start an argument so you can stalk out of here in a huff. Did you think I wouldn't see right through it? Do I look stupid to you?"

"Do I have to answer that?"

Growling low in his throat, he turned to the others. "Everyone move."

They all backed away, giving us plenty of space as we faced each other like two cowboys having a showdown.

"Concentrate," said Butch. "Sense what triggers the call. Then you'll know how to block it." In a blink, he whipped off his shirt, snatched a knife from his waistband, and then sliced his chest.

Taken off-guard by the speed in which he'd acted, I did nothing more than wince at the sight of his injury. I had a strong stomach, but one thing made me cringe—the sound of a knife cutting into flesh. It was like nails on a chalkboard for me.

"You're not concentrating," growled Butch.

Yeah, well, the wound had closed before I had the chance to act anyway. In any case… "I didn't feel a pull toward the blood."

"I'll make the cut deeper this time." He sliced his chest again.

Cringing, I balled my hands up into fists. "You need to use a different weapon. I hate knives."

"Hey," whined Jude, offended on behalf of sharp implements everywhere.

When the wound healed, Butch took a tissue from Reuben and wiped away the excess blood—the scent of it was in the air, teasing every single vampire in the arena. "Again."

"There's no point; nothing's happening."

"Because you're not concentrating. You're overthinking it—obsessing about the wound."

Yes, I was. "I'm not doing this. I can't stand here while you slice yourself over and over."

"Then call the blood and get this over with. I'm not stopping until you do. Think about what you could do with this, Imani. It might not be an ability, but you can damn well use this in a duel. It can be a good thing. But it can be a bad thing if you're accidentally calling the blood of people you care about. They could weaken or, worse, bleed out."

God, he was so right. How annoying.

"Is that what you want?"

"Of course not," I snapped.

"Then focus. Ready?" He didn't wait for me to answer, just carved a deep line into his upper chest, a little beneath his collarbone.

My back teeth locked at the sound and sight, but I didn't let myself think about who the chest belonged to or how fucking weird this was. I just concentrated on the blood, took the scent deep into my lungs, thought about how good it would taste, how thirsty I was starting to feel, and how—

"Well, shit." Paige's awed words pulled me from my thoughts. That was when I realised Butch's blood had dripped all the way down to his waist.

"That was good," praised Butch as he took a clean tissue from Reuben and wiped his chest clean. He looked at Sam. "Did you notice it?"

She nodded, face grim.

I frowned. "Notice what?"

"When you're calling blood, the rim of your eyes have the slightest silver glimmer to them," replied Butch. "It happened last night, but it disappeared so fast that I wondered if I'd imagined it." He moved closer to me. "I think it's because you drank Sam's blood. I think it caused some changes."

I shook my head, confused. "Vamps drink from each other all the time; it doesn't change them."

"That's because vampires *can't* change; their bodies are frozen. But during the transition, your body wasn't. You were changing, and you had the blood of Sam, Jared, Antonio, and me running through you. That's a powerful combination. It's probably what kept you alive. It hadn't occurred to me that Sam's blood would cause any changes within you."

"I'm different because of the serum. I'm not a hybrid."

"No, you're not a hybrid. Your system evolved into something that is stuck somewhere between human and vampire. But Sam's blood triggered some changes."

I didn't see how calling on blood was in any way related to Sam.

"Look at the facts," said Butch. "Your blood tastes different. You can call blood to you. And sometimes the rim of your eyes briefly glow silver...or mercury."

Jared stepped forward. "You said her blood tastes different."

Butch nodded. "There's a slight fizz to it."

"Sam's blood has a sherbet-quality to it," said Jared.

Butch looked at Sam. "You call on energy, in a sense."

She shook her head. "I *feed* on it."

"Since becoming a hybrid, you haven't had to suck in energy to use it," Butch pointed out. "It comes to you. You call it without trying."

Her brows lifted. "Never really thought of it like that."

Paige sidled up to me. "But Imani isn't calling energy."

"Of course not," said Butch. "She's not a Feeder, so her ability isn't energy-based."

"My gift isn't blood-based," I said.

He arched a brow. "Isn't it? You can sever blood-bonds."

I sighed. "They're psychic constructions."

"Constructions that are born from blood. Can you sever other psychic links?"

"No, only blood-bonds."

"So, your gift is blood-based."

Shit, he was right.

"I agree with Butch," Jared told me. "Sam's blood caused the changes."

Sam winced. "Sorry, Imani."

I forced a smile. "At least now I have an explanation."

"Whatever gave you the ability to call blood, it's a fucking cool ability, Imani—I don't care what you say." Harvey wasn't the only one who looked impressed.

Denny turned to Butch. "How does it feel when she calls it?"

Butch rubbed at his nape. "It's hard to explain."

"Come on, dude, try," said Damien.

Sighing, Butch said, "It was almost like a heavy weight was tugging at my veins, pulling at my blood...like a magnet. I could feel my heartbeat in my head, could hear it pounding." He curled an arm around my shoulders. "What was the trigger for the call?"

"There wasn't one. I just concentrated on nothing but the blood."

"I know this is gonna piss you off...but you need to do it again."

I froze. "Butch—"

"Doing it one time isn't enough. We keep practicing until this is under your control. It needs to be second nature for you. Okay?"

"What-motherfucking-ever."

"So charming," chuckled Paige.

We practiced for hours. Jared and several members from the squads took part, eager to know what it felt like. I did pretty well. I focused and persevered, pushing past my discomfort at the knife. I *had* to or I'd be calling people's blood accidentally. In a battle, that would be bad. And I fully intended to be part of the upcoming battle, whether Butch liked it or not.

After lunch, we all had a regular training session with Sam and Jared in the rainforest, during which Sam and Butch practiced extending their shields. I was exhausted by the end of the session, and I tried hard to conceal that I'd tired much sooner and easier than the others. Tried and failed, because Butch and Paige saw it clearly enough. Thankfully, neither rubbed salt in the wound.

When Butch and I returned to our apartment, we showered and changed. Dinner was a pretty quiet affair, and I knew it was because he was trying to think up ways to stop me from going to visit Marco. I couldn't really blame him for that. I didn't want to waste minutes of my life with the dick either, particularly since he could be the person who tried to kill—

"You're not eating."

I blinked. "I was in deep thought."

His perceptive eyes narrowed. "You were thinking about Marco. He's the only person who makes you look that pissed." Butch put down his fork. "You don't have to see him. No one would judge you for backing out."

"Trying to talk me out of it?"

"Hell, yes. Going to see him is pointless, baby. He won't tell you anything."

I reached over and threaded my fingers through his. "I understand why you don't want me to see Marco and give him another chance to play games, but it has to be done. Like it or not, he's our only real hope of finding the answers we're looking for."

"And he's loving that," said Butch. "He's loving the power it gives him."

"I know, but—"

"And he's loving that it gains him access to you. He's not going to give up that power easily."

"You're right. You're absolutely right. But I have to try."

With a heavy exhale, Butch leaned back in his seat. He kept a firm grip on my hand. "Ryder will be scanning his mind tomorrow night. Why not wait and see what he finds in there?"

"Because the poor guy's just woken from a coma. Take it from someone who has a psychic hand—traversing through a person's head is not at all easy. It's also pretty uncomfortable. While he's tired and unbalanced, it'll be hard enough for Ryder to scan three minds. He'll need time to recover before he can do a thorough scan of Marco's mind, which means there'll be a delay in getting the information we need. We can't afford delays."

Butch looked away, clearly intent on brooding. It was almost cute.

I squeezed his hand. "Look, I know this is hard for you. I don't like it either. But you'd do the same in my position."

His jaw hardened and I thought he'd argue again. Instead, he sighed. "Fine."

Apparently he was learning the need to respect my choices. Progress. "It's not—" The rhythmic tapping of knuckles on the door made me smile. There was only one person I knew who knocked like that. "It's Fletcher."

Still sullen and broody, Butch grunted. Whatever.

Putting down my fork, I hurried to the door and opened it. Fletcher and Norm both pranced inside, beaming. They did those air-kissing things. Noticing Butch, they each waved at him. He tipped his chin at them.

Fletcher leaned close as he asked me quietly. "What's he sulking about?"

But Butch heard him. "I do not sulk."

"Of course not," Fletcher assured him. "No one would ever imply otherwise."

I blinked as Norm thrust a bag at me. "What's this?"

"I saw it and immediately thought of you," Norm told me with a wink.

It had to be raunchy underwear. He liked to pick things like that up for me and the girls. With a smile, I delved into the bag and pulled out something black and soft…and my stomach sank. *Fuck.*

Instantly sensing my mood shift, Butch blurred to my side. "You okay, baby?"

No, I wasn't. "I was wearing this vest in my vision." That meant the battle could happen at any point from this night onwards.

Butch cursed. "Call Sam."

After assuring a distressed Norm that he hadn't done anything wrong, I called Sam's cell phone. Like Butch, she cursed...only she did it better and with more creativity.

"We still don't know when the attack's coming," began Sam, "but we've ran out of time to really prepare for it."

"No, we've trained harder than we ever have before."

"But we don't know whether that will be enough against a drove of fire-breathing creatures. Imani, I don't mean to pressure you, but we really need you to get something out of Marco."

"I'll get him to talk." I wasn't yet sure how, but I would.

"Jared will be waiting at the entrance of the cells in ten minutes."

"We'll be there." Ending the call, I turned to Butch. "Now I really, really have to do this."

He curled a stray lock of hair around my ear. "I know. I just wish this wasn't on your shoulders. It isn't fair to you."

Better my shoulders than his. But I didn't say that aloud, because it would probably piss him off.

As Sam had promised, Jared was waiting near the entrance when we arrived. He gave me a grim smile that said that, like Butch, he didn't expect this meeting to achieve anything. Presumably Jared was eager to get this over with, because he teleported us straight outside Marco's containment cell. Both males then backed up, moving to stand against the wall behind me.

Marco shot off the mattress and walked to the glass with a wide smile. "Sweetheart, you didn't come to see me last night. That wasn't nice."

"I wasn't sure you'd have anything helpful to say."

"And I suppose Sam and Jared wanted to take some time to check out what I told you."

To be fair... "It's not beneath you to waste our time to prolong your life."

"No, it isn't. But everything I told you was the truth."

"So it would seem." I took one step toward the glass. "You said you'd tell me more if I came back. Here I am."

"I said I'd tell you more if you came back last night. You didn't."

I gritted my teeth. "We don't have time for this, Marco. Or do you want this war to take place?"

He thought about it for a moment. "Nah. Wars are messy. People die."

"I didn't think you'd care if people die."

"I care if you die."

Recalling that Fletcher said Marco considered himself my protector, I spoke, "You can see I'm partly human now. That makes me vulnerable. I might not have asked for this life, but I don't want it to end. Still, I'm part of the legion now. You know what that means. If there's a war, I *will* be fighting in it—vulnerable or not."

The amber tint to his irises flared.

"So help me avoid a war and tell me where The Order is based."

"You're not stupid, Imani. Where do you think they'll be?"

"How the hell would I know?"

"Ask yourself this question: if you were a group of vampires who tried to blend with humans, despised your kind and conspired to destroy them all, where would you stay?"

Well, when he put it like that... "Somewhere away from vampires. Neutral ground."

His eyes brightened. "Very good."

"There has to be hundreds of spots all over the globe that are free of vampires."

"Yes, but why are those spots free of us?"

"Most have already been claimed by other species of preternatural. They won't share their territory with vampires." Especially shifters and demons.

"So then, where will The Order be based?"

"In a place that's totally unclaimed."

"Good girl. In one of those places, you'll find The Order."

That still left dozens of possible locations. "That's as much as you're willing to tell me?"

"I don't want you to die, Imani. It really is as simple as that. They have weapons that could wipe out entire towns. These people would sooner die in a blast than die at the hands of the things they loathe. I don't want you near them."

"And you still want to seem useful to us so that you get to live."

"Of course."

Jared sidled up to me, eyes on Marco. "I'll make you a deal. I have a vampire who can sweep minds. If he finds that you didn't inject Imani with the serum, we will free you and allow you to live."

"If...?" prompted Marco.

"*If* you tell us where The Order is based."

Marco's gaze briefly slid to me. "She'll die if she goes there."

"What makes you think any of us intend to go there?" asked Jared. "If it's true and that place is rigged, it wouldn't be smart of us to invade it. Where is it based?"

"You're not taking me seriously enough," snapped Marco.

"Wrong. If you think I'd be reckless with the life of Imani or any other member of my legion, you're very much mistaken. So, do we have a deal?"

After long moments, Marco told Jared, "If you agree to free me once your vampire verifies my innocence, I'll give you the name of someone who knows where The Order is based; someone who will make you see why the last place Imani should be is there. He'll make you understand."

Jared's lips pursed. "Deal."

"Joel Sanders."

I frowned. "Who is Joel Sanders?"

"One of my sources. He knows plenty about The Order. Find Joel, and then follow the rabbit trail." Marco's gaze moved to Butch. "You keep her safe." Then Marco returned to the mattress. He was done.

The instant Sam took a seat, she slapped a file on the conference table. "All right, this is what we know about Joel Sanders. He's a Keja who's part of a very small nest in Colorado. He's committed pretty much every computer crime there is; earns his money by hacking into company computers and selling the information to rival businesses." She took a photo from the file and handed it to Max, who took a look before passing it on.

"Could he be the blogger we're looking for?" asked David. "I mean, if he's so good with technology—"

Sam gave a quick shake of the head. "Joel's gift is simple yet very substantial: he cannot be held captive. The bloke literally can't be kept any place he does not want to be."

That *was* pretty substantial.

A pacing Luther halted. "Would that extend to any kind of restraint? Could he escape from the grip of your whip?"

Sam shrugged. "I'm hoping he won't try to escape. I have no issue with him; I just have some questions. But I won't leave until I have my answers."

The photo of Joel Sanders reached me just as Jared said, "In the meantime, Mona and Cedric will find out just how many preternatural-free zones there are in the world. By the time we're back from paying Joel a visit, we should have that information. But I'm hoping that Joel will have already given us an exact location."

Marco had seemed sure that Joel knew—

Stumbling, Luther breathed, "Jared."

Sam was at his side in a blink. "Luther, what's wrong?"

He didn't answer; just stood there, eyes closed. Having watched my squad have a vision through him, I knew exactly what it looked like when someone experienced one. It would seem that Luther was having one now.

Finally, he blinked. He gripped Jared's arm, his gaze desperate. "We do not have long before they come."

"Dragons?" asked Sam.

Luther's eyes moved to her. "Yes. At least forty of them. They will come from the south."

"Do you know when?"

"A few nights, at most."

"They'll come at night?" Jared asked. At Luther's nod, he added, "I figured they'd come in the day in the hope of taking us off-guard."

That would have made more sense.

"Your only hope of preventing this is to destroy The Order before they have a chance to hire the mercenaries," said Luther.

Sam told us, "Go top yourselves up with NSTs and then meet me and Jared outside the mansion in ten minutes. Then we'll pay Joel a little visit."

When Butch and I entered the apartment, he went straight to the fridge and pulled out two NSTs. As he drank them, I said, "Luther's vision wasn't great, but I noticed he seemed relieved to have finally had one. Maybe now he'll stop blaming himself for not helping us prevent all the shit that's happened so far. He's forgetting how much he's helped The Hollow over the years. Even allowing people to have their own visions has helped."

Something suddenly occurred to me. "You never told me about the vision you had through Luther."

Butch's eyes were wary. "No, I didn't." And he didn't seem inclined to share it.

"You know about mine."

His lips pressed together. "You don't need to hear about it, baby."

It was a warning. "I don't like the way you said that."

"It's not something you'd want to know."

"I don't expect you to tell me every little thing. But I can sense that this isn't little. Tell me." Instead, he drank the last of his second NST. "Butch—"

"In my vision, I was in bed with a woman."

My lungs seemed to constrict with shock and hurt. Despite that my throat was painfully tight, I asked, "Do I know her?"

A muscle in his cheek ticked. "Yes."

"Who was it?" I was torturing myself, really, but I had to know.

"Marla."

"Marla?"

He slowly prowled toward me. "Not a lot happened in the vision. I was in bed, she was lying next to me—naked and asleep. And I felt…empty."

Empty? Well that made me feel a teensy bit better.

"I didn't understand why I'd have a vision like that. I didn't understand why the fuck that would be important enough for me to need to foresee it. But when I met her, it all became clear."

Well at least one of us understood.

He seemed hesitant to continue, but finally he added, "She first came onto me the night you broke up with Dean. And I realised then that my vision was a warning that the decision I made that night would be pivotal. I could take Marla up on her offer and carry on as I was; having meaningless one-night stands, taking no risks. Or I could get my fucking head straight and go after what I really wanted—you, even if that meant a relationship."

"You're saying you didn't sleep with her?"

"I didn't sleep with her—not that night, not any of the many nights she came onto me."

The ache in my chest faded. So Marla was right; he *had* rejected her because of me. Huh. I was bitchy enough to feel satisfied about that. In my defence, she was a heifer who broke my Kindle!

He curled my ponytail around his fist. "Not once, not even when we first started, have I ever felt empty lying next to you." Tugging me close, he kissed me. "Why are you so stiff? I didn't touch her, baby."

"Sorry, it's just…the image in my head of you guys in bed together isn't pleasant." But it was my own fault that it was there.

"That was why I told you that you didn't need or want to hear about the vision."

"Still, I'd rather know. For me, no truth can be worse than a lie." Not wanting him to regret telling me, I made a conscious effort to relax against him as I kissed him. "So I appreciate that you were honest."

"You're not gonna stew on this? We aren't going to end up arguing over something that didn't even happen?" There was a cautious note to his voice that was often present when we even came close to arguing. Every time we had the smallest dispute, I'd see the worry in his eyes. It was almost as if he was just waiting for the moment when I declared that I'd had enough and I was leaving.

Rubbing my nose against his, I said, "You have to trust me not to hurt you."

"I don't trust *me* not to hurt *you*. I won't mean to do it, Imani. I never mean to."

"We're gonna fight, Butch. It would be unhealthy if we didn't because it would mean that either we were trying *too* hard to keep each other happy or all the passion was gone."

He frowned, not understanding. "But I *want* you to be happy."

"And I want you to be happy, but not to the extent that I neglect my own wants and needs. The same should go for you. There has to be a balance." I slid my arms around his neck. "There's no right or wrong way to have a relationship. We're still trying to find *our* way. Even when we find it, we'll still piss each other off, and we may even hurt each other. But we'll work it out and we'll move past it." I kissed him. "I'm not going anywhere. I'm not like them." Not like the others who walked away.

"I know." He didn't even need to ask who I was referring to.

"But you expect me to leave you."

"I don't *expect* you to leave. I've just never had anything that was important enough for me to care if I lost it. Not good at dealing with that yet."

"Okay. But let me reiterate, I'm not going anywhere."

His eyes bore into mine, searching. He nodded, apparently satisfied with whatever he found there. "Now you need to feed. Then I'll drink a few more NSTs, and we'll leave."

And hopefully our talk with Joel would lead us in the right direction, or I'd seriously lose my shit.

CHAPTER SIXTEEN

(Butch)

Outside the grubby apartment building wherein Joel Sanders lived, Jared instructed Denny, Stuart, and Damien to scope out the place. There was a chance, though it was slim, that Marco had led us into a trap, the dick. We needed to be prepared for that. So Denny reduced his body to liquid, Stuart burst into molecules, and Damien went astral walking.

"If the guy makes good money out of what he does," began Imani, "you'd think he'd live in a better place than this." Her nose wrinkled at the stench of mould and cigarettes.

"He could afford it," I conceded. "But then his neighbours would wonder where he got his money from. People who live in places like this don't ask those kind of questions."

She tipped her head. "Fair point."

In a matter of minutes, the puddle of goo returned and reformed into Denny. "It's not a nest of vampires," he told us. "The place scents more strongly of human than vampire."

"Any guards inside?" asked Sam.

"None at all."

Damien's head snapped up, and he took a long breath.

"Good to have you back," Chico told Damien.

"Anyone guarding the perimeter?" said Jared.

"No," replied Damien. "There are some humans round the back dealing drugs, but that's all."

We waited in silence for Stuart to reappear. It didn't take long. In a blink, the cluster of molecules were once again Stuart. "No vampires are lingering in the woods behind the building," he said. "Was the interior clear?"

Denny nodded.

"Well it would seem that Marco hasn't led us to our deaths," mused Sam.

"That doesn't mean he hasn't sent us on a wild goose chase," Jared pointed out.

Personally, I didn't think Marco had done so. Not this time. He wouldn't want Imani to be angry with him; he'd want to impress her with his knowledge. He wanted to be in her good books. Setting us up wouldn't achieve that.

"The place might seem safe enough," said Sam. "But I won't take any chances. I don't trust Marco as far as I can throw the wanker. That means I want a number of people monitoring the exterior of the building, keeping an eye out for trouble." She fell into a pensive silence. "Reuben, weaken Chico's gift just enough for his darts to make their target dizzy."

Neither male protested as Reuben did as ordered, though they both looked confused.

"This bloke can't be held captive, which means there's a good chance I can't restrain him. That's why Jared and I will need Imani, Chico, and Max to come inside with us—if he makes a run for it, use your gifts to distract him and slow him down. There are ways to pin him in place that don't involve restraints."

Sam was right. If Max took away the guy's senses, Imani played with his blood-bond, and Chico shot him with darts that caused dizziness, Sanders wouldn't get far. "Coach—"

"I know, I know, you want to be with Imani. As I'm currently feeling uneasy and she tired herself out earlier, I'm good with that. The rest of you guard the perimeter and telepath Jared if there's a problem."

With that, Jared teleported Sam, Max, Chico, Imani, and I right outside Joel Sander's apartment.

I half-expected Sam to kick the door open, but she actually knocked. Maybe she wanted to seem friendly and nonthreatening. But there was really no way that a visit from the Grand High Pair wouldn't unnerve someone.

I could hear whistling as footsteps approached. The door opened, revealing a tall, skinny Keja that I recognised from the photo that Sam provided.

Her smile was wide but a little forced. "Hello Mr. Sanders."

His startled eyes darted around, taking in Jared and the vampires at the pair's back. Then he tried to slam the door shut. Like that would work. Sam just pushed it open, allowing us all to enter. He was heading for the window of the living area when he abruptly fell to his knees, cradling his head and groaning through his teeth. I knew exactly how much that hurt, since Imani had once played on my blood-bond like it was a damn guitar string to show that her gift could be effective in a fight.

To his credit, Sanders tried crawling toward the window. Chico's darts embedded themselves in his back, making him collapse on the floor mere seconds later.

We all gathered around the fallen Keja, whose mouth was open in a silent cry of pain. Apparently Max had taken away his ability to speak.

After plucking the darts from his back, Sam rolled him over with a frustrated sigh. "That wasn't the best move, was it?" She gave a subtle signal to both Imani and Max. Like that, Joel sagged in relief.

Jared tilted his head. "Now why would you run?"

Sanders licked his lips nervously. "If the Grand High Pair comes looking for you, it can't be good."

"That would normally be true," allowed Jared. "In this case, we simply have a few questions for you."

"Questions?" he echoed, doubtful.

"About The Order," added Sam. "What can you tell us about it, Joel?"

His eyes darted from Sam to Jared. "Seriously? You're only here for intel on The Order?"

"Seriously," she assured him. "You don't look very comfortable down there. Let's fix that."

Jared and I heaved up the male and plonked him on the old, swamp-green sofa. With the exception of Sam and Jared, we all stepped back; not wanting to loom over the Keja and make him feel even more intimidated than he already did.

Sam smiled. "Better?" At his shaky nod, her smile widened. "Good. Now talk."

Sanders cleared his throat. "In sum, The Order is an association of vampires who hate what they are. They want our species to be completely extinct."

Sam nodded. "How big is this association?"

"Last time I hacked into their database, there were hundreds."

"Database?" Jared repeated. "How long ago was the last time you hacked into it?"

"About a week ago. One of Lazarus' assassins wanted an update on the group." *Marco.*

"If you've rifled through their database," began Jared, "I'm guessing then that you know plenty. That's good. The Order is proving itself to be a bigger threat than expected. We need to take them out before things go tits up."

Sanders spoke. "I take it you know about their plan to destroy The Hollow, huh? I told Marco about it; he said he'd pass on the info."

"He did, though he took his time about it," grumbled Sam. "I'm hoping you can help us with a few things. There's a blogger who's leaking facts about vampirekind. His gift is technology based, which means we can't electronically track him."

"Oh, that guy?" Waving a dismissive hand, Sanders snorted. "He's just a lowly member."

Sam pounced on that. "So there's a hierarchy?"

"The main guy, the leader, is like their Messiah. They all serve him. There isn't anything they wouldn't do for him. Suicide missions. Assassinations. Bombings. You name it, they've done it over the years if the content of their computer system is to be believed."

Biting out a string of harsh expletives, Sam exchanged a look of outrage with Jared.

Staring at her, Sanders double-blinked, looking mesmerised. "Your irises really are mercury."

She snapped her fingers. "Focus, Joel. Do they have a specific date in mind for the attack they plan on The Hollow?"

"If they do, it's not on their computer."

Jared slowly took a step toward Sanders. "We need to know where they're based. Marco left out that part. We've narrowed it down to a short list of locations. But scouting each of those locations will take up precious time."

Sanders didn't miss a beat. "The place they meet is in Lost Springs in Converse County, Wyoming. It's an underground bunker beneath a ranch."

Satisfaction lit Jared's eyes. "A bunker?"

"But you really don't want to go there," Sanders hurried to add, looking panicked. "The whole place is wired to blow in the event of an invasion. They have all kinds of scary shit, ready for war."

Clearly frustrated, Sam said, "We need to get to them somehow. Do they live at the ranch?"

"Some do. Not many."

"Can you get us the names of all the members and their addresses?" Jared asked him.

"Sure. I can print out a list for you to take with you."

Jared nodded. "You do that. Highlight the blogger's name so we know exactly which one he is."

I understood why. Sam and Jared would need to punish him separately and via V-Tube as an example of what would happen to those who betrayed our kind by leaking information.

"And I want a big, fat asterisk next to the name of the bloke who runs it all," Sam told Sanders, and he wasted no time in doing their bidding.

When we were all finally back at The Hollow, we had a short meeting in the conference room, where Sam and Jared informed the rest of the squads what Sanders had told us.

Harvey made a noise in the back of his throat. "We're fucked. I thought that once we found out where they were, we could pounce on them all and stop our battle with the dragons before it started. But we can't invade the ranch—we'd find ourselves bombed."

Sam nodded. "It would be sheer stupidity to try it. They would set off explosions that would not only kill us, but maybe even lead to human casualties. I'm not so desperate to get to those bastards that I'd send us all on a suicide mission."

"So we can't get to them," growled Reuben.

"That's not strictly true," said Jared. "Joel Sanders gave us the names and addresses of the members. We can pick them off a few at a time, show them what it feels like to be hunted. We'd start with the guy who formed The Order, Beau Irons, only there was no address for him. We'll have Mona and Cedric look into it."

"But they'll realise pretty quickly that they're being targeted," said David. "The others will then hide. We won't be able to get to them."

"Yes," allowed Sam. "But you know from past experiences how we reach people we can't physically get to."

"We get them to come to us," said David.

"Exactly. One of the things that ticks me off most about all this is that I don't know when the attack is going to happen. If Luther's estimation is correct, we have at least two more nights before they arrive. I don't want to rely on that. I say we take control of this. I say we taunt The Order into striking while we're ready and waiting."

Ava tucked her hands in the pockets of her jeans. "I can't believe The Hollow's going to be attacked again."

"It won't be," said Sam.

Ava blinked. "Say what?"

"We know what direction the drove will come from," Sam pointed out. "There's another off-the-map island in that direction. We'll wait for them there."

"And they'll crash into Butch's shield when they do." Ava rubbed her hands together. "We'll take the war to them."

"It's our best chance of keeping The Hollow and its residents safe." Sam rose to her feet. "Get a good day's sleep, people. At dusk, the legion will be sent out in threes to pick off as many members of The Order as they can. The rest of us will go to the neighbouring island and familiarise ourselves with it." She looked at me and Imani. "Before you two go and wind down, let's find out who tried to kill Imani, shall we?"

"Ryder's done with the suspects?" I asked.

"He should be by now," replied Sam. "Jared and I just need to have a quick chat with Antonio. Then we'll meet you at the entrance of the containment cells."

"Who gets to kill the fucker responsible?" Paige's tone said she'd be happy to do it.

Hell, no. "Who do you think?" She smartly didn't fight me for the pleasure. In my eyes, she'd redeemed herself just a little by tackling—literally—a female Pagori for bragging that she'd had me before Imani and could easily have me again. Paige and the rest of Imani's squad had also fiercely defended me against anyone who had doubts about my commitment to Imani.

"Ooh, can we watch?" begged Ava, eyes wide with excitement.

Smiling, Sam snorted. "No. Go play with Salem."

Tugging on my hand, Imani got to her feet. "Come on. I'm ready." And eager, going by the gleam in her eyes, to finally have the truth.

Leaving the conference room, we took the elevator to the ground floor of the building. Then we descended the spiral staircase that led to the cells, where we found a pale Ryder sitting on the bottom step.

"Hey, you okay?" Imani asked him.

Strain in every line of his face, Ryder forced a smile for her. "I will be once I've had some sleep. Man, I'm wiped after that. I hope I don't look as bad as I feel."

I decided not to tell him that, yeah, I was pretty sure he did. "You done with them?"

Ryder puffed out a breath. "Yes."

"So you managed to get into Juliet's mind?"

"Yes, Salem used his gift to put her unconscious," said Ryder. "It stopped her from hurting me, but it also meant it took a while to scan her thoughts. It's harder to read the minds of unconscious people. You can't ask them to hold an image in their mind to lead you to the info you're looking for."

At our 'I don't get it' expressions, he went on, "Minds aren't easy to navigate. There aren't separate compartments for memories, thoughts, personal details, etc. A mind is more like a road map. You have to get on the right road if you want to find what you're looking for. A mental snapshot of a person or event is like a red cross on a map. It shows me which road to go down."

"So, who was it?" I pressed, impatient. "Who hurt Imani?"

Ryder sighed. "None of them."

I stared at him in disbelief. "You're fucking kidding me," I rumbled.

His expression said that he wished he was. "Tait hates Imani enough to kill her, but she fears Marco too much to attempt it. Juliet…she doesn't care enough about Imani's existence to be bothered whether she lives or dies. And Marco, well…let's just say he wouldn't do it."

"You mean he's too obsessed with her."

Ryder's mouth twisted. "Pretty much, yeah."

Pacing, Imani bit her lower lip. "Do any of them know who did it?"

"Juliet thinks it was Tait, and Tait thinks it was Juliet. Marco believes he knows who it is, but he guarded that thought from me."

I frowned. "Guarded it?"

Ryder nodded. "It was smart how he did it. He visualised a brick wall between me and the answer. That blocked the road on my map."

Just then, Sam and Jared appeared at our side. "You look like crap," Sam told Ryder, concerned.

"You're not going to like what I have to say," he warned them.

After Ryder repeated what he'd told us, Sam grumbled, "I'm not surprised Marco hid his suspicions. He believes Imani belongs to him, and he thinks he's her protector. Since her life actually matters to him, he isn't going to give up the opportunity to get vengeance on whoever harmed her." She looked at me. "In his place, neither would you."

She was right about that. "I can't believe we have to fucking free them," I growled. "Marco still has every reason to die."

Jared nodded. "But I made him a deal. I won't go back on my word, even though I wish I could." He cast Imani an apologetic look.

My girl quickly assured him, "I wouldn't expect you to. And to be fair, Marco has already been punished for what he did."

Fair? Fuck fair. He didn't deserve to breathe. But I couldn't ask Jared to break his promise. It would make us both bastards. So, minutes later, we had to free the two smug-looking bunnies and escort them to Marco's cell.

Ignoring the gasped greetings of his bunnies, he studied our expressions from behind the glass. "Joel gave you the information you needed."

"Yes," said Jared.

"Have you come to free me?"

"I gave you my word, didn't I?"

Marco smiled, probably because Jared sounded pissed about it.

Having unlocked the cell, Sam told him, "Ian will teleport you all home." The male was currently standing with the bunnies, appearing no happier about their freedom than I was.

Rolling back his shoulders, Marco left the cell. His consorts flung themselves at him, kissing his cheeks and petting his chest, telling them how they'd missed him and never once believed he could be guilty blah, blah, fucking blah. Their words cut off as Imani spoke.

"Who injected me with the serum?"

Marco turned to face her. "What makes you think I know who it was?"

She arched a brow. "Don't you?"

"In my opinion, it can only be one of two people. I'll find out which one."

When he and his consorts moved to Ian, Imani demanded, "What two people, Marco?"

His face softened with what looked like sympathy. "Good people can do bad things sometimes—not just because they have the potential to do bad things like everyone else, but because they've found a way to justify it to themselves. Like someone who steals from their sibling, telling themselves it was okay because their sibling owed them in some sense."

She growled. "What are you getting at?"

"You're smart, Imani. You'll work it out. But don't worry—by then, they'll be dead."

At Jared's nod, Ian teleported the three vampires out of The Hollow.

I rubbed Imani's back, trying to ease the tension from her body. "He wouldn't have told you, baby. He wants to be the one to punish them. He might not even know anything—he could be just trying to fuck with your head."

"I know," she sighed. "But it's not his right to punish whoever it was."

"In his warped mind, it is," said Jared. "With any luck, we'll get to them before he does."

She released a calming breath. "Right now, it isn't the priority. We have The Order to destroy and dragon shifters to fight."

Sam patted her arm. "Go home, get some rest. Things are going to be hectic at dusk when we get ready for the invasion."

Nodding, Imani leaned into me as I slid my arm around her shoulders and began to guide her out of the mansion.

(Imani)

The whole thing was a little like an adrenalin crash. I'd gone down to those cells with anticipation flooding every part of me, thinking I'd finally get my answers; finally get my chance at vengeance. Or, more specifically, I'd stand back while Butch got it on my behalf. I didn't mind giving him that, because I knew how much he still blamed himself for my being hurt. I thought that if he could get vengeance for me, it might make all that unfounded guilt fizzle away.

When Ryder revealed the three were innocent, the anticipation pouring through me came to an abrupt halt. Then the emotion left me completely. At first, I hadn't felt anything. Not anger, not a sense of injustice, nothing.

Maybe it was the shock, or maybe I just hadn't known how to feel. But by the time Marco was leaving his cell, I'd felt my mad coming on. And the bastard hadn't even shared the names of the people he suspected, like he hadn't owed me that at the very least.

Closing the apartment door behind us, Butch pulled me against him and pressed a light kiss to my mouth. "I'm sorry you don't have your answers, baby."

I curled my arms loosely around his neck. "You don't have to bottle up your anger, you know." That was what he was doing in an effort to not feed my own.

"I don't want to spend the rest of tonight pissed and stewing on things outside of our control."

"Me neither. And I don't want to spend it thinking about what's coming, or about how bad things are going to get. I just want time with you." He could make me forget.

"I have no issue with that at all." Sliding his hands in my hair, he kissed me. Hard. Deep. Exactly how I hoped he intended to fuck me in, say, the next two minutes. Still kissing me, he backed me into the bedroom while his skilled hands roamed and teased. Abruptly, he released me and stepped back; his gaze expectant. Knowing what he wanted, I slowly stripped until I was completely naked.

He pulled off his shirt, but he didn't shed the rest of his clothes. Instead, he circled me. Like a predator circling its prey and admiring the sight. Pausing behind me, he kissed my shoulder. "Perfect. Mine." With a nip to my earlobe, he walked to stand in front of me. "On your knees."

My eyes flew to his hands as they tackled his fly. His cock sprang out—long, thick, and full.

"Now, Imani." His authoritative tone made my stomach clench. I dropped to my knees, and his dark eyes gleamed with satisfaction.

He tapped my cheek with his cock as his hand fisted in my hair. "Open up, baby. Good girl." His grip on my hair held me still as he fed me inch after inch of his cock. His thrusts were sure, bold, and dominant. The thumb of his free hand traced the curves of my mouth. "Fucking beautiful."

Sucking harder, I swirled my tongue around him. He growled. So I did it again. Tightening his hold on my hair, he fucked my mouth. Hard. Rough. Inwardly, I smiled. I wanted him to lose control, to let go.

"Swallow it, Imani." That was the only warning he gave me before he thrust deep and came with a low growl, eyes holding tight to mine.

I'd no sooner let him slip from my mouth than he scooped me up, kissed my forehead, and flung me on the bed. Then his mouth was on me, licking between my folds and stabbing his tongue inside me. He was as good with his mouth as he was with his hands, so I didn't last long. My back arched as bliss crashed over me, leaving me a shuddering mess.

He crawled onto the bed and draped himself over me, eyes once again glittering with satisfaction. I thought he'd kiss me. Instead, he licked his mouth clean. "Tastes too good to share."

(Butch)

I wasn't kidding. If I didn't know any better, I'd think she had the preternatural ability to addict people to the taste and feel of her. But I knew it was just Imani; it was just the affect she had on me. I'd been addicted since the very first night, and I'd craved her from that night onwards. If she had any idea how obsessed I was with her, she'd probably freak.

Slipping one finger inside her, I groaned against her nipple. "Nice and slick for me." I drew the taut bud into my roof, sucking and biting as I fucked her with my finger.

"Inside me," she breathed.

Withdrawing my finger, I cupped her ass, tilted her hips just right, and thrust hard. *Fuck*. Her tight muscles squeezed and contracted around my dick, and a groan slid through my teeth. She was almost too hot. "So fucking good, baby."

Humming in agreement, she licked my throat.

I rolled onto my back. "Take what you need, Imani." She didn't hesitate; she slammed herself up and down on my cock, nails digging into my chest. I met each of her downward thrusts with a punch of my hips, slamming deep in her body. Watching her take my cock inside her, watching her pretty breasts bounce and her eyes glaze over…it was fucking amazing. *She* was fucking amazing. No one else would ever compare to her.

Knifing up, I wrapped her hair around my fist and yanked her face to mine so I could look right into her eyes when she came. "Fuck me, Imani." She started riding me again, moaning against my mouth. I slid my free hand between us and found her clit, pressing down with my thumb. Her pace became faster, frantic, and her muscles began to flutter around me. "That's it; fuck me harder, make us both come."

Moaning louder, she frantically impaled herself until finally her body clamped down on my cock. I rolled her onto her back and pounded into her as she came hard, biting into my shoulder…and then I fucking exploded.

As she lay beneath me, shaking with aftershocks, I said, "Promise me now while my cock and my come is inside you that if we do ever Bind, you won't sever our bond." It worried me that she had that 'out.' I could be a total asshole at times. I was pushy and dominant and messed the fuck up. Being with me couldn't be easy. "Promise me that whatever happens, we ride it out. When I fuck up, you tell me how to fix it and I will. No walking out on me."

Her head tilted. "I'm such a freaking idiot."

That wasn't the response I'd been expecting.

"I should have guessed this would play on your mind. Everyone else walked out on you, including your birth mother. Life has taught you that whenever things get rough, people disappear…and it's made you believe that you weren't enough for them to stay. Which is, of course, a load of bullshit. They left because they were fickle, had no staying power, and were such assholes that they would allow you to believe you weren't good enough."

I swallowed. "Imani—"

She lightly pressed her hands to my face. "Unless what we have withers away and dies, which I don't see happening, I'm here for good. I promise."

Releasing a breath I didn't realise I'd been holding, I gave a crisp nod.

"You believe me?"

"I know you wouldn't say something you don't mean. And I know that if you *did*, it would be easy to tell, since you can't lie for—"

"I can *so* lie."

"No, baby, you can't," I chuckled. "And I love that about you." I always knew where I stood with her. There was never any need for guessing games.

"You love me?" The question was quiet, almost shy.

"I thought you'd have figured that out by now."

She play-punched my shoulder. "No girl ever assumes a guy loves her. She has to hear those words to believe it."

I held her gaze, never wanting her to doubt what I said next. "I love you, Imani. Didn't think I'd ever say those words to anyone. Didn't think I had it in me. Not sure I'll be good at expressing it, but there it is. I want us to Bind someday, when you're ready. Why do you look so surprised by that? I told you in the beginning that I want everything that you are."

"I know. I suppose I just didn't expect that you'd offer the same in return." She smiled. "I'll take this moment to note that you're a lot better at sharing and being open with me now." She lifted her head and kissed me. "And I'm glad you love me, because I love you. You'll struggle to believe that, I know. And even when you do believe it, you'll have dumb moments where you panic that because I'm mad at you, I don't feel that way anymore." She shook her head. "I've said it before, and I'll keep saying it until you believe it: I'm here for good."

"I know you are, because you don't have the option of leaving me."

She burst out laughing. "See, you make me happy."

At first, I'd found that hard to believe. But now I saw it clearly. Saw that I'd somehow lived up to my promise. I was now the one who made her smile and laugh. I swore to myself that I'd keep on doing it.

CHAPTER SEVENTEEN

(Butch)

The island where the battle would take place wasn't much different from The Hollow; there was the white sandy beach, the thick, vine-covered trees, the waterfalls, the light sea breeze, and the sounds of tropical birds and other exotic wildlife.

We spent hours learning every inch of the island, searching for the best places to lay in wait. Meanwhile, other members of the legion were picking off the vampires that belonged to The Order. A squad had also captured the blogger, Marvin, and placed him in a containment cell. Sam and Jared intended to deal with him at a later date.

One thing that was aggravating everyone was that Mona and Cedric couldn't find an address for the founder of The Order. In fact, there was no record of Beau Irons ever existing, even as a human. I was more pissed—and, quite frankly, panicking like fuck—about the fact that Imani would be part of the battle.

In Sam's professional opinion, Imani was fit for battle. In my personal opinion, my girl was *barely* fit for it. So when I came close to objecting, Sam reminded me that she couldn't make that decision based on her personal feelings on the matter and, as such, neither could I. Maybe, but I'd still objected, even knowing that Imani would be pissed at me. I'd rather she was pissed than dead.

Instead of yelling at me as I'd expected, Imani had leaned into me and said, "Thanks for caring so much, but the last thing I intend to do is die and leave you. Trust me to keep my word." With that, she'd walked away, determination in every step. And I'd had no choice but to accept that there would be no talking her out of it.

As we came to a halt on the beach, having completed our tour of the island, Chico turned to Sam and Jared. "So, what's the plan for tomorrow night?"

Standing solidly, Jared replied, "One squad will remain at The Hollow to be ready if any dragons manage to get past us. The rest of the legion will be lying in wait on the island. That's a lot of vamps, I know, but forty dragon shifters can cause a lot of damage and mayhem."

"They'll all be huge, strong, powerful, and covered in thick scales that act as seriously good armour—they can also bloody fly," said Sam. "Hopefully my shield will stay in place because we can't afford to let them pass this island and reach The Hollow."

"When they realise the Grand High Pair are here," began Max, "I don't think they'll bother trying to pass. You two are their main targets—as long as they end you both, they've completed their mission."

"You could be right," said Jared. "If they *do* pass, every squad will be teleported back to The Hollow and we'll continue the fight there."

Making strong eye contact with each of us, Sam slowly paced. "Whatever our location, the plan of attack will be the same: as you already know, our aim is to *get them on the ground*. That's the priority. While they're flying, they have an advantage."

Brow wrinkled, Chico said, "I'm seriously doubting my darts are going to get through their scales."

"That is an issue," said Sam. "But Lazarus told us that it's hard for these shifters to maintain their dragon form if they're weak. If any are shot down and return to their human form, kill them."

"Remember that they don't just breathe heat, smoke, and fire," Jared warned. "They can breathe air so cold it encases whatever their breath touches in ice."

Denny rocked on his heels. "I have a feeling this will be the hardest battle we've ever fought."

A small smile graced Sam's mouth. "Are you sorry you wanted some action?"

"I will be if I become encased in ice."

Harvey frowned at Denny. "If you're encased in ice, you probably won't think or feel shit."

Denny snorted. "Whatever."

"I doubt it'll be easy to target them," said Jared. "They probably fly pretty fast. We'll have to—" He stopped as Sebastian appeared at his side with a blonde Pagori female who couldn't have been much more than five foot tall. I instinctively moved closer to Imani. Unsurprisingly, Paige did the same.

Sam smiled at the newcomers. "Sebastian, I take it Keeley's made up her mind."

"Keeley?" echoed David, brow raised.

"Well, I knew that fire-breathing creatures were going to be a big problem," said Sam. "And they say fight fire with fire, right? But that ain't gonna work here. What we need is someone who can put *out* the fire. Those within the legion who can create or call on water will have to do our best to calm the flames, but there aren't enough of us for that. So Mona and Cedric checked the register for any vampires with gifts that can help. Sebastian then tracked down Keeley for us."

"You can create water?" Imani asked.

Sam's smile widened. "She can do something even better. She can create rainstorms."

It was hard to imagine that a little thing like her had that kind of power. "Storms powerful enough to put out a bushfire? Because it's a big possibility that the dragon attack will have the same effect."

Keeley's voice was strong and confident as she replied, "I can create rain so heavy, it'll feel more like rocks hitting your flesh." Impressive. So impressive that all the females smiled.

"You must have some kind of limitation," insisted Max.

"The rainstorms never last long," Keeley reluctantly admitted. "It's pretty tiring to keep them going."

"*But* if Reuben amplifies her gift, we won't have to worry about that," Sam pointed out.

"Are you combat trained?" Chico asked her.

Keeley lifted her chin. "Enough to hold my own."

"Does that mean you're joining the battle?" Sam asked her. "If I didn't need to concentrate on keeping up my shield, I could feed on the small amount of energy leaking from you and have your gift for a while. I've created a storm before, though it wasn't a rainstorm. But I can't concentrate on creating, sustaining, and containing a rainstorm when I have to focus on my shield."

Keeley was silent for a moment. "I'll join the battle."

"You'll have protection at all times," Jared assured her.

I had one concern. "You can keep the storm under control?"

She nodded curtly.

"What happens if you're hurt?" I asked. "Will it go out of control?" That would be seriously bad and possibly make a shit situation even worse.

"If I'm hurt or killed, it will quickly die off."

Fair enough.

"When do you think the dragon shifters will come?" Sebastian asked Sam and Jared.

"As soon as The Order realises its members are being hunted," Jared replied. "It will be the only way they can stop us from going after them."

Ava kicked at the sand. "How will we know when they've figured it out?"

"When the squads can no longer find the members they've been assigned to kill," said Salem. "It will mean they're in hiding."

"According to the register," began Jared, "one of the vamps at the top of the list is a telepath. He'll have psychically warned the others before he died. They'll be angry, scared, and they'll feel forced to move forward with their plans and kill all of us before we kill the rest of them. I'd say we have twenty-four hours at most before the dragons arrive."

Sam nodded her agreement. "All of you go have a long rest and tank yourselves up on NSTs. Or, in Imani's case, have a little munch on Butch. Meet us outside the mansion at dusk."

(Imani)

Later on, I was snuggled into Butch's side while he lay in bed, his fingers brushing through my hair. Deliciously sated, I was on the verge of falling asleep when he spoke.

"It's at times like this, when there's a battle coming, that I wish we were officially mated."

Instantly awake, I blinked. "What?"

"If I hadn't messed up a year ago, we'd have been together long enough for you to feel secure and so sure of my commitment to you that you'd have agreed to Bind with me by now."

I knew that part of the reason he was worrying so much was that Jared had ordered Butch to personally guard Sam throughout the battle. Vampirekind knew plenty about Sam's abilities, and The Order will have passed on that knowledge to the dragons. That meant that as soon as an energy shield covered the island and trapped them, they would know that the shield was hers. They would do their best to get to her. Butch's shield would keep her safe while she concentrated on maintaining her own shield.

His strategic mind would understand and agree with Jared's decision. But the rest of Butch was no doubt balking at the thought of parting from me during the battle. I'd promised him I'd stay close enough for him to see me at all times—not just to placate him, but because I didn't want him distracted, wondering where I was. He still wasn't happy about it.

"I know that's not a reason to Bind with someone, but we both know that's not why I want to Bind with you. It's just a plus." He tapped my lower lip. "But you're not quite there yet, baby." There was no judgement in his tone.

"It's just that—"

"You need a little time to be sure I'm not going anywhere. I don't blame you for it. I understand."

"That's not what I was going to say. It's not that I doubt *you*. I trust you and I—"

"You don't have to justify it, Imani, I'm not trying to pressure you. I walked away from you once before, so of course you'll want to be sure it isn't going to happen again."

"That's not it. If you'd let me speak, I could explain," I said a little haughtily.

Lips twitching, he swept out a hand, inviting me to continue. Smart ass.

"Like I said, I don't doubt you. I just find the thought of Binding a little...worrying."

He blinked. "Worrying?"

"I'm not a full vampire anymore. I'm physically weaker than I was before. I bruise and I don't heal as quickly. It's why you and Paige are panicking about me being part of the battle. There's really no such thing as immortality—anyone can die. And now that I'm a little vulnerable, I could die a lot easier. If I was mated to you and that happened to me, you'd die too."

Eyes narrowed, jaw hard, he arched a brow. "Let's get something straight. You are not rejecting the idea of Binding with me out of some misguided idea that it will protect me. No fucking way."

"Butch—"

"If you want to make this about protecting me, let's look at it another way. If we were officially mated, I'd be able to feel you through the connection; I'd know where you were, that you were alive, and I could help boost your strength. It would keep me sane in battle, which would mean I wasn't distracted worrying about you."

"Yeah, but—"

"And if we were mated, I'd fight harder, faster, and dirtier to keep you safe. And you would do the same, wouldn't you?"

"Of course."

His mouth curved smugly. "So your worries are pointless, baby."

"It's easy for you to say. If you thought mating with me would make me vulnerable, you would be just as hesitant as I am."

"Yeah, I would," he admitted instantly, not at all repentant. "And what would you say to me?"

That there was no way I'd let him refuse to Bind with me out of some stupid idea that it would help protect me. I'd be prepared to take the chance. I sighed, "Point taken."

"Good." He kissed me, his tongue licking into my mouth as his hand slid into my hair. "I hope you're done fighting me on this. I want us to Bind. You're it for me. There never has and never will be anyone who's as important to me as you are. I know what it's like to be without you. I know how much better my life is with you in it. Got no intention of letting you go again. As far as I'm concerned, you're already mine. Binding would just solidify that."

"Yeah?"

"Yeah." He lifted my hand. "I want to look at this finger and see a Binding knot that says you belong to me. I want a matching knot on my finger. Can't say you're getting a good deal here, but I'm not kidding, baby, I'm not letting you go again. Not ever."

"Why would you think I'm not getting a good deal?"

"I'm a realist, Imani."

Not when it came to himself, thanks to his past. "If you want, I can hunt Kylie and smack the bitch down."

He chuckled, dragging me on top of him. "I'm not sure she's even alive. If she is, she'll be in her seventies by now. Anyway, she probably messed up her own life. But the gesture is appreciated."

"I don't think you realise that I'm completely serious."

"What I think"—he flipped us so that I was beneath him—"is that we should forget about her." He sucked at my pulse, making my inner muscles spasm. "And you should lie there like a good girl while I pound you into the mattress."

"So romantic."

"Ain't it though?"

CHAPTER EIGHTEEN

(Imani)

I'd spent years of my vampiric existence in hiding, so I was no stranger to it. But I'd never liked it. Never liked that feeling of not facing danger head-on. I supposed it went against a vampire's predatory nature to hide. The only reason I wasn't mentally bristling now was that this time I wasn't running from the danger that was coming. I was simply tricking it.

Concealed among vine-covered trees with Butch and David on either side of me, I waited impatiently for the dragon shifters to arrive. We knew they were close because a certain member of the legion was able to sense when danger was approaching—he could even estimate how long it was before that danger arrived.

It seemed like hours ago that Jared had telepathically sent out a five minute warning, but it couldn't have been longer than a few minutes.

Where were the fuckers?

I didn't realise I'd said that aloud until Butch looked at me. "They'll be here soon," he whispered into my ear. "Remember, don't go far. Be vigilant. I need you to stay alive for me."

I kept my voice just as low. "I need the same from you, so watch your ass."

His mouth kicked up in one corner. "I'd rather watch yours. It's hotter than mine."

I just snorted, not fooled by that smile. He was still brooding about having to leave my side during the battle. The fact that both David and Paige had sworn they would flank me throughout the entire fight only barely mollified him.

The majority of the legion was spread across the perimeter of the island. Sam, Jared, and our squads were in the centre, because that was where Butch's shield needed to be. We wanted the dragons to fall smack bam in the middle of the island so that the legion could box them in the moment that Sam's shield went over us.

She'd enlarged her shield many times in training, and I had every faith that she could do it here and now. As she'd once said herself, this *had* to work. We'd all be on Shit Street if it didn't.

David's impatient sigh seemed like a boom in the quiet of the night. The forest was unnaturally silent—no doubt Alora had 'spoken' to the wildlife and told them to keep quiet so that they didn't make noise that would alert the dragons. She had probably also recruited the predators to join the battle. Good.

Since I didn't have a gift that would help me bring the bastards down, my job was to take out the fallen. But I had no idea if my gift would help me with that. It was possible that they didn't have blood-bonds. If that was the case, I'd have to rely on combat moves. I was good at combat—Jared wouldn't have accepted anything less. But since the shifters could be just as competent at it, there was no saying that taking them out would be easy.

I rolled back my shoulders, trying to shake off the dread that snaked through me. It didn't work. Tension and anticipation thickened the air until it was almost tangible. This waiting around shit headed into a whole new level of frustrating.

Discretely, I took in Butch's scent on a long inhale. It was comforting. Reminded me of his strength; that he would be fine in this battle. The natural scents of the forest usually had the same calming effect on me, but not tonight. Not when so much depended on the outcome of the war.

Among all those scents was something else: the smell of ozone. Rain would be coming soon. It would seem that Keeley was preparing to unleash the storm. I could see a grey cloud beginning to form. Hopefully she was as in control of her power as her confident nature suggested. We were going to need her in a big way, especially since it—

They're coming, Jared warned.

A shot of adrenalin pumped through me, and I squeezed Butch's hand. This was it.

"If we hadn't been watching out for them, we would never have known they were on their way," whispered Butch.

As I stared up ahead, I understood what he meant. They were all dark and moving so silently it was eerie. Now I got why they had chosen to come at night—they could better conceal themselves in the dark.

They were flying directly toward the island, and they were *huge*. Fierce. Seriously scary looking with long curled horns and massive bat-like wings. And they were here to kill us.

Butch took a single step out of the trees, ready to do his part. As David and I moved with him, he cast us both a 'stay back' scowl. We just stared at him.

Conscious that there was no time to argue, Butch planted his feet wide apart and raised his hands. I couldn't see his shield. I couldn't even sense it, since it didn't buzz with energy like Sam's did. But I knew that if I reached out, I'd feel it—hard and totally impenetrable.

His face was a mask of concentration as he enlarged the shield. Able to see the creatures and the formation they were traveling in, he would know just how far and high he'd need to extend the shield to prevent any from passing. If he was struggling at all, it didn't show in his expression.

More adrenalin flooded my system as the dragons neared. Had they been moving at a slower pace, they might have scented us—we were positioned all over the island, after all. But the creatures were flying at such an admirable speed that they didn't have a moment to sense us.

The five in the front slammed into the shield, causing it to glimmer much like sunlight reflecting off glass. I winced at their ear-splitting, harpy-like sounds of shock and pain. They might have bounced backwards if the others—moving too fast to avoid a collision—hadn't crashed into them. Only the dragons at the rear managed to halt in time. Unfortunately, none fell to the ground. *Shit*.

Before they could even *think* to act, a buzzing silvery-blue shield blanketed the island. With a roar of challenge, vampires came at the dragons from every angle.

Butch gave me a quick kiss. "Stay alive." He darted to Sam's side just before our squads formed a wide protective circle around him and the Grand High Pair.

Chaos then reigned.

Jared's lightning bolts illuminated the sky, showing flashes of red-hot arrows, balls of ice, and ripples of psychic energy whooshing through the air toward the dragons. The creatures screeched and roared as they retaliated from above, breathing streams of fire; the responding agonised cries of my kind made my stomach roll.

Two things became swiftly clear: they were much faster than we'd expected, and they weren't going to go down easy. Flying around the island, they attacked with fire and ice, swiped people with their spiked tails, smacked them aside with their punctured wings, or grabbed them with their claws and then tossed them at other vampires. They also breathed clouds of smoke to impair our vision, making it harder for us to defend ourselves.

Basically, they were total bastards.

Beside me, David sent out a series of fatal psionic blasts. He bared his teeth in a feral smile when his aim rang true and one of the creatures fell mere feet in front of us, shifting into his human shape as death took him.

Hearing a roar of hatred and, if I wasn't mistaken, grief, I looked up to see another dragon doing an actual nose-dive as it headed right for David.

"David, above you!" I warned.

His head snapped back, but the creature didn't get any closer as Harvey swept out his arm and telekinetically sent it careening *hard* into a tree. The impact snapped the thick tree, which almost crushed me and Paige as it collapsed with a thud.

Harvey winced. "My bad."

Growling, the dragon quickly righted itself. But instead of taking to the air, it stumbled and shifted to his human form. Eyes flaming with hatred, he lunged for David. But I'd already leaped toward the shifter. Intercepting the move, I jammed my elbow into his throat and thrust a psychic hand into his mind.

And there it was. A blood-bond.

I pulled it hard, almost sending him to his knees with a cry of utter agony. But it didn't break; probably because it was different from vampiric bonds—perhaps a link that had formed as a result of a blood oath. I settled for tugging on it as I went at him with a series of dirty moves that should be illegal even in the world of vampires.

Weak though he was, he held his own—even got a few real good shots in, causing my lip to split and nearly cracking one of my ribs. Gritting my teeth against the pain that pulsed through my abdomen, I whipped out my leg, kicking his knee hard enough to knock his balance and make him fall to his knees. Then I was on him, hands gripping his head while my psychic hand stretched his bond. In a move that was one of Ava's favourites, I snapped his neck.

I might have perversely smiled in victory if a stream of fire hadn't blown in my direction. I jumped back, watching as it scorched the ground mere feet away from me. Although I'd evaded the fire, the boiling heat still caught my skin. Blisters formed on my face as it burned and prickled.

"Shit, Imani, come here." Paige gently placed her hand over my seared flesh. As she took away my wound, it looked as though something was rippling under her skin, moving from the hand on my face all the way up to her elbow. The process didn't weaken her because injuries were weapons for her to use.

Touching my healed cheek, I said, "I really wish I had your gift." Or maybe a water-based gift since, at this point, fire was spreading like…well, wildfire. The rain coming from the spooky dark cloud hovering above helped, but it wasn't enough. I sure hoped Keeley's storm picked up fast.

As the fight went on, more and more dragons fell—many of whom had been heading right for Sam. Not only were dragon shifters seriously strong in their human form, injured or not, but they would fight to the bitter end. It would have been admirable if they weren't trying to kill us.

The more mercenaries that died, the more the remaining ones tried to escape by charging at Sam's shield or trying to damage it with fire. Of course, the intelligent creatures swiftly realised that the only way to fight the shield was to kill Sam.

That was when they came at her even harder than before. But Sam and Jared had known that would happen. And since coming at Sam meant facing our squads, the creatures were basically just flying to their deaths.

When one came much too close, I sent a telepathic warning to Jared. He lifted his hand, and currents of electricity streamed from his fingers and crashed into the creature's skull. The shifter was dead and back in his human form before he even hit the ground.

"Can I just say thank God for Keeley!" shouted Paige, but I barely heard her over the hissing of fire, the snarls of a jaguar, the screams of pain, the pounding of heavy rain on the ground, and the cries of fury that rang throughout the air.

Keeley's rain was coming harder and faster, incredibly managing to calm the flames. Wiping rain out of my eyes, I cast a quick look over my shoulder, wanting to get a brief glimpse of Butch. His hand was gripping Sam's upper arm, supporting her weight. It seemed that keeping the massive shield intact was taking its toll on her.

Ava's infuriated cry made me whip around. A dragon had snatched her from the ground, its claws digging into her shoulders. "Salem!" I shouted, but his psychic energy was already rippling in the air toward the dragon; it hit the creature right in the skull—like that, it was dead and shifting mid-air. Which was great and all, but it meant that *Ava was falling too.*

Yellowy-green ooze shot out of Denny's fingers and formed a net that thankfully caught Ava. I didn't have time to enjoy my relief as dragons rushed at us from several directions. The mass attack took me by surprise, thanks to all the smoke billowing around us and messing with my vision. But I was ready when the charging shifters fell to the ground, either dead or too weak to shift.

With a snarl, a short blond lunged my way. I was just about to attack when something barrelled into my side and rolled me onto my back. Now I had a heavy motherfucking asshole straddling me, fingers digging into my throat. I shoved my psychic hand into his mind, found his blood-bond, and played it like it was a banjo string.

Crying out, he released me and cradled his head. I knifed up and punched him in the jaw. He rocked backwards, almost falling off me. Almost. The bastard was too freaking big and heavy. Eyes glittering at me, he struck me right in the temple. *Motherfucker.*

Glaring at him through the spots filling my vision, I blocked the next punch and tried to shove him back. No success. Then Paige was there, slapping her palm on his head. There was a rippling from her elbow to her hand as she transferred an injury to him—an injury that would be three times worse for him.

His skin began to blister, peel, and smoke, making him scream in total agony. I took advantage of the moment and punched him in the dick. His breath exploded out of him, and he slumped to the side.

"Bastard!" I wheezed as I got to my feet, rubbing at my throat. A blast of psychic energy whizzed past my ear and crashed into his head. Like that, he was dead.

Twisting, I gave David a nod of thanks and looked around, unable to see much through all the smoke. Keeley's rainstorm was fighting the fire—the heavy raindrops would probably leave bruises on me, now that I was partly human—but the dragons just kept creating more damage and breathing more smoke.

"You're tiring!"

Paige's accusing words made me snap my gaze to hers. Yes, I was tiring. Hell, even my psychic hand was tiring. Like Butch had predicted, I still wasn't yet accustomed to not having my old level of strength and speed. I'd overexerted myself, forgetting my new limits. And her protective instincts no doubt told her to get me out of the way.

Suspecting she might try to follow those instincts, I lifted my chin. "I'll be—" A blast of cold rushed our way and a dragon literally rocketed out of the thick smoke. Butch blurred to my side and slammed up his shield, blocking the blast and making the creature do a sharp turn to avoid the shield.

"Sam agrees that I need to be with you right now!" Butch told me, which meant they'd also noticed I was tiring.

Paige scrubbed at her eyes. "The smoke needs to go!"

But it couldn't. It was trapped inside Sam's shield, just like everything and everyone else. Thankfully, the smoke did our internal organs no harm, though it was uncomfortable to inhale. My eyes, on the other hand, didn't do so well against it; they stung and itched like crazy.

"I just spoke to Jared!" shouted Butch. "He said—"

A large wing snapped out and sent Butch, Paige, and I zooming backwards, soaring what felt like miles through the air. The breath whooshed out of me as I crashed into something hard—most likely a tree. Groaning and coughing, I got to my feet, utterly pissed. These winged bastards needed to die. I blinked rapidly as I glanced around, searching for Butch and Paige. I couldn't see them through the smoke.

But I could smell Butch.

More specifically, I could smell his blood. A *lot* of it. The scent wafted over me, reached something *inside* me. I didn't let myself think of how good it would taste; didn't give in to the pull of the scent. Instead, I blocked it, just as I'd practiced with him in training.

"Butch! Paige!" I shouted as I followed the scent of his blood. But there was little chance that they'd hear me over all the roaring, snarling, screeching, and screaming.

Not allowing myself to panic, I called out their names over and over. Just as Butch's scent became stronger, something long and spiked shot out of the smoke and swung at me—a fucking barbed tail! Cursing, I ducked. But one of the spikes grazed my scalp and it hurt like a bitch. Quick as I could, I rolled toward Butch's scent, pushed to my feet and—

Motherfucker! The spiked tail darted out of the smoke and struck my chest, stabbing me hard just as it sent me flying several feet away. My head hit the ground with a crack that reverberated around my skull, and I almost blacked out.

Ears ringing, I blinked to clear the stars from my vision. I was gonna kill that bastard when I could see it. God, my chest *hurt*. I grit my teeth against the streaks of burning pain as, for the third freaking time, I awkwardly got to my feet. I needed to get to Butch, needed to ignore the pain and just hope I didn't heal too slowly or—

A strong arm looped around me and began dragging me backwards. I would have struggled like crazy, except the unexpected scent made me freeze in surprise. "Marco, what the fuck are you doing here?" He kept dragging me away. I twisted in his grip. "Let me go!"

"No, we need to get you out of here!" he growled into my ear.

"Let go of me, you bastard! I need to—"

Everyone brace yourfuckingselves!

Before I could wonder at the panic in Jared's warning, I felt the buzz of Sam's energy leave the air. Her shield winked out. *Oh, shit.*

As the smoke began to clear, I watched as three dragons shot high into the air. Or, at least, they tried. One screeched as it was hit by a telekinetic blast that sent it crashing somewhere. The second shook as sparks of high-voltage electricity assailed every inch of its huge body. The third halted as a silvery-blue energy whip lashed out of the smoke and wrapped tight around its throat, yanking it back down.

They weren't the only ones that tried to flee. They might have succeeded, but the problem for them was that since Sam no longer had to concentrate on keeping her shield in place, she could use her gift in other ways—ways that were causing the dragons to hit the ground.

"Hurry before he comes for her!" Marco shouted to a vampire on his right. That was when I saw a large, swirling portal. I'd be damned if I let Marco take me anywhere.

I kicked and punched at him, but all the struggling in the world didn't make him release me. "Put me down, you fucking bastard!" I thrust my psychic hand into his mind, but it was tired and half-numb; flicking his blood-bond to his Sire did nothing more than make him wince.

"Imani, enough! We're leaving *now*!"

"I'm not going anywhere!" I was about to telepathically call out to Jared when Marco sharply turned me in his arms, making my head spin. I'd sustained too many head injuries tonight.

"I'm not here to hurt you. I told him to keep you safe, and he didn't!"

I realised he was talking about Butch. "He's hurt, I need to—"

"What we need is to get you to safety!" Ignoring my struggles, Marco carried me toward the portal—a portal that abruptly closed as the vampire controlling it hit the ground with a thud.

"Let. Her. Go."

Stilling in surprise at the familiar male voice, I looked over Marco's shoulder. It wasn't so hard to see now that the rain was putting out the fire and Sam had taken down her shield, allowing a lot of the smoke to clear. And there was Lazarus with a small group gathered behind him. I blinked. "What are you doing here?"

"We teleported to you so we could partake in the battle," he replied. "My vampires are joining it as we speak. Marco, release her."

Marco's arms slowly slipped from around me and he turned to face Lazarus. No, he positioned himself *between* me and Lazarus. Like a protective barrier. Marco's vampires flanked me, glaring at those that stood with Lazarus.

The Master Vampire held out his hand, a sense of urgency in his manner. "Now come along, Imani. You should not be part of this. Not when you are half-human."

I would have pointed out that I actually wasn't half-human, but this whole scenario felt distinctly wrong. "Marco, what's going on?"

He didn't take his eyes from Lazarus as he responded. "I told you, Imani. Good people do bad things sometimes."

Realisation quickly dawned. And it hurt almost as bad as the burning pain in my chest. "Lazarus is one of the people you suspect injected me with the serum?"

"No, sweetheart, it wasn't Lazarus. But he ordered it done."

No way. "I don't have time for games, Marco." Butch was lying somewhere, wounded. *Jared, find Butch and Paige. I think he's hurt bad but I can't get to him—I'm watching Marco and Lazarus have some kind of standoff.*

"I knew it had to be one of two people," Marco went on. "Him or Eleanor."

I frowned. "Eleanor?" And then I saw her, standing slightly behind Lazarus. There was a seriousness in her expression that took me by surprise. She was usually always so animated and jolly.

"They both want the same thing so badly that they'll do absolutely anything to get it. It was Eleanor's mate who told me the truth...though he took some *persuading*."

Eleanor gasped, eyes widening in horror.

I might have told Marco to just shut the fuck up because I wasn't in the mood for games, but something occurred to me as I looked at Lazarus, whose expression was carefully blank. "You should be denying this. He's accusing you of trying to kill me." Yet, Lazarus hadn't said a word.

"Lazarus didn't want to kill you," Marco said. "Oh, he'd known you could die, which is exactly why he's going to suffer for what he did to you. But he didn't want you dead."

Confused, I shook my head. I didn't get what was happening. I didn't get why the air pulsed with some kind of strange energy, or why I thought I could hear bullets being fired. I *thought* I could but wasn't sure, because distant sounds seemed weirdly muted, distorted, and crackly.

Marco cocked his head at Lazarus. "You theorised that a vampire was more likely to get through the transition if they could feed on powerful vampires during that time, didn't you? You knew that if Imani was injected, she'd be taken straight to The Hollow where the Grand High Pair and other powerful vampires would give her blood."

Lazarus hissed. "You're suggesting I was using Imani as a guinea pig?" The outrage in his voice sounded very genuine...but the emotion was absent from his eyes.

"It worked, didn't it? She got through it because she had access to very potent blood. Congratulations. You were right. But I won't let you take her."

Take me?

Lazarus looked at me, a fanatical gleam in his eyes that made my stomach churn. "Imani, you have the power to save all those who suffered the same fate as you."

"What?" Was he high? Maybe *I* was high, because this was all fucking weird.

"Within you lies the answer to the cure for vampirism. Your blood has the answer."

"I'm not cured," I clipped, anger building inside me as it began to penetrate that, hey, he'd totally betrayed me. And I wanted to smash his face in. "There is no cure."

"Wrong, Imani. You are partly transformed. With your blood, we can find a true cure. Then all of us who had this life forced upon us can once again be human."

He said it with so much yearning and desperation that I almost felt bad for him. I had been in his position. I'd had everything ripped away from me, and for a long time I'd thought of nothing but getting back what I'd lost. I knew what it was to despise what you were, knew what it was like to long for all the things you once had and took for granted in—

I gaped as the truth slapped me hard across the face. "*You're* Beau Irons." I wanted him to deny it. He didn't. He smiled.

"Well done, sweetheart," said Marco. "It took me a while to figure that out. By the time I knew, he was already planning to take you while everyone was distracted in battle."

And if Lazarus was Beau Irons... "All these vampires you've brought with you...They're part of The Order, aren't they?" Which meant they were fighting *against* The Hollow's vampires, not alongside them. *Shit.*

Lazarus' smile turned a little creepy. "Yes. And you will join us, Imani. You will leave with us."

Marco slowly shook his head. "I can't have that."

"This is not about what *you* want," Lazarus told him.

Staring at the vampire who'd once taken care of me, who I'd trusted with my life, I swallowed. "I can't believe you'd do this to me. To *anyone.*"

"It's really nothing personal," Marco told me, his eyes still locked on the Master vampire. "He's so intent on being human again, so focused on the end goal, that he can't see anything or anyone else."

Lazarus again held out his hand. "Come with me, Imani. You were brought into a life you did not want. You deserve to have back what was so callously taken from you. I can give you that."

"There is no cure, Lazarus." Marco shook his head. "You'll never find one, because vampirism isn't an illness. It's just another state of being."

Lazarus went on as if Marco hadn't spoken. "You once told me that you would give anything to be cured. Now we can work together to make that happen."

Maybe I'd felt that way in the early nights, when I'd been filled with hopelessness and confusion and found it very difficult to adjust. But now? Now that would mean giving up the one thing I wanted more than anything. In which case... "Fuck. You." I distantly noted that a whirl of energy had built behind me, and I knew the portal had re-opened.

His jaw hardened. "You want this as much as I do."

He was wrong. "What I want is very simple. I want to be with Butch."

"If you are thinking that he or anyone else from the legion will save you, prepare to be disappointed. Their gifts will not get them passed my force-field, and my vampires will prevent them from trying."

Well that explained the weird energy I could feel in the air.

"Imani, come with us." Eleanor's voice was soft, desperate. "Please?"

I snarled at who I'd considered a friend. I supposed I should have expected her betrayal—people with perfect teeth couldn't be trusted. "Fuck. You. Too." She made the slightest move toward me, so I reached into her mind and flicked her blood-bond to her Sire—the warning wouldn't have hurt her because my psychic hand was weak as all shit, but it made her halt with a hiss. "You weren't Turned against your will. You wanted this life."

"Because I was stupid," said Eleanor, bitterness in every syllable. "Ignorant. Blind. Too scared to grow old, too frightened of death. I made a mistake, and I'm tired of paying for it. I want to be human again. Your blood can give me back my life."

"You see, Imani, this is about more than just you," said Lazarus. "It's about more than just me. Your blood can help so many people."

"You expect me to go with you? Seriously?" He *was* high.

"I understand that you feel I have betrayed you and that you are hurting. But you are a good person, Imani. You will quickly come to see the wisdom behind what I have done; you will understand that this was necessary."

Oh he was fucking special. I felt my upper lip curl. "You don't even see it, do you?" I hit him with a truth that I knew would be like a bullet to the chest. "You're just like Marco and the vampire who Turned you."

Every muscle in his body seemed to tense. "That is not true."

"You did this to me without my consent. You didn't think of the impact it would have on my life. You didn't care about the pain it would put me through. You were only thinking about what *you* want. So yes, Lazarus, you've become what you loathe. And I wouldn't go anywhere with you even if I wanted to. What I want is to stay with Butch."

"I cannot allow that, Imani." Lazarus made a hand gesture to the vampires at his side, and their eyes zeroed in on me as they went to move. Marco reached back and shoved me hard, knocking me off my feet and right into the fucking portal.

CHAPTER NINETEEN

(Butch)

"Butch, this is going to really hurt." Jared yanked the spike out of my chest. I grunted through my teeth because, yeah, it hurt like a motherfucker—especially since my skin had started to heal around the spike.

One of the damn dragons had brought his tail down hard on my chest. I wasn't sure whether the spike came off by accident or not, but it had pinned me to the fucking ground. I'd been stuck there as the shield fell, the dragons tried to flee, and the smoke cleared.

Jared had teleported to me with Paige seconds ago, and she was now healing my gaping wound. I'd lost a lot of blood and I was woozy as hell, but I didn't care. Didn't care about anything except one thing. "Where's Imani?"

Jaw hard, Jared sighed. "I don't know. Well, I have a general idea of where she is, but—"

"What does that mean?" I growled, unease slithering through me. "And why can I hear bullets being fired? What the hell is happening?"

"About ten seconds ago—which was roughly a minute after a small army of vampires appeared and started attacking us—Imani sent me a message to tell me to find you, but she didn't respond to my reply."

Healed, I jumped to my feet. Jared and Paige did the same. "Go to Imani," I urged impatiently.

"Tried that."

"And?"

"And something bounced me right back to where I teleported from."

"*What the fuck?*"

"She told me you were hurt and that she was watching Lazarus and Marco having a standoff," Jared explained. "I'm thinking that one of them is here to hurt her and the other is here to protect her."

I suddenly recalled Marco's words...*Good people do bad things sometimes.* I cursed. "Lazarus came for her. He's who we should have had locked up." And I was going to kill him, and I was going to enjoy watching him suffer. I drew in a slow, steady breath, needing to keep calm and think.

Jared nodded. "That would be my guess. The vampires who've arrived all have guns and little badges that have a familiar insignia. That tells me that they and Lazarus are part of The Order. It wouldn't surprise me if the bastard is Beau Irons."

"The armed vamps have formed some kind of wall," began Paige, "so Imani must be somewhere behind it, right?"

"I'd say so," replied Jared. "Sam's on the front line with the rest of the two squads. Whenever anyone gets close, The Order starts firing to pin them in place."

Like the night hadn't been hard enough until that point. "Why can't you teleport to Imani?"

"There's some kind of force-field around her that's repelling psychic energy," replied Jared. "It's obviously a vampiric gift. It's like your shield in that it deflects whatever power comes at it. But the force-field isn't solid."

"So we could walk through it, but not get through it using any kind of preternatural force," I mused.

"Yes," said Jared. "That's why my telepathic messages aren't getting through to her."

"If she managed to get a message to you, the force-field doesn't contain psychic energy and prevent it from escaping; it only deflects it," I reasoned. "That means if we get through it, we can use our gifts once we're inside it. We just can't use them to *get* inside."

Jared swore as more bullets rang through the air. "Getting to her will be hard while we have a wall of vampires in the way. It wouldn't be so bad if they weren't standing inside the force-field. Our gifts can't touch them, but theirs can hit us. With gifts *and* guns, they're doubly armed."

Paige's mouth had a cruel curve to it. "Which will make them double the fun to kill."

Jared smiled. "There's always a bright side." He teleported us to Sam and the two squads, who were all taking cover behind trees that approximately ten feet away from The Order.

It was an impressive wall of defence; their arsenal of bullets, grenades, fire balls, and flaming arrows did its job well. I frowned at Sam. "You're not fighting."

Her scowl cut to me, her mercury irises glowing as she grumbled, "I have to take a break while my system recharges."

"She used up most of her energy on maintaining the shield and then attacking the dragons," said Jared, a supportive hand on her back.

Max turned to me. "We've attacked that force-field in every way we can think of. Nothing is getting through that fucker, and nothing is taking it down."

"I can get through it," I said, my voice so carefully controlled that I doubted anyone would sense the turmoil racking my entire system. "I'll use my shield to protect me while I make a run for it."

Max's brows lifted. "That could work. They won't be expecting someone to charge their way. It will take them off-guard."

Sam spoke. "You would have to lower your shield to get inside, Butch. The force-field would repel it."

I nodded. "I'll slam it back up once I'm through. I can do this, Coach. I'm damn fast. By the time they see me coming, I'll already be inside."

Paige put her hand on my arm, her eyes swirling with a soul-eating anxiety I could relate to. "Take me with you. You can extend your shield around both of us; you do it for David all the time."

"You're not as fast as me, Paige, and we both know it." It was an insensitive comment but it was true. "I need to move quickly, I can't afford to go slower just so someone else can keep up."

"He's right," sighed Max, which made Paige snarl at him.

"I'll tell Damien to distract those bastards," said Jared. I guessed he'd telepathically order Damien to run at them in his astral form, since it was a technique we had used before. "When I say go, run."

"Make sure you bring Imani back safe, you get me?" Paige fairly growled.

Jared turned to me. "All right, *go!*"

Pulling my shield around me, I bolted at vampire momentum out of the trees and toward the wall of vampires. As I came up against the buzz of energy that had to be the force-field, I dropped my shield, ran straight through it, and instantly slammed it back up to knock down the vampire in front of me.

In a millisecond my brain absorbed the situation; Marco and Lazarus facing one another, vampires gathered either side of them...and Imani in mid-air, falling into a portal.

Fuck.

Heart in my throat, I lowered my shield, reached out, grabbed her wrist, and yanked her to safety before slamming my shield back up to protect us both. Taking her inside me with every one of my senses, I shoved back the fear that had come close to choking me. The sour taste of it still sat on my tongue.

"Don't shoot!" Lazarus yelled at his vampires, but his eyes were locked on me as I held Imani close, keeping my back to the portal. Everyone had frozen in place, most likely shocked by my sudden arrival.

Almost everyone. Marco threw me a glare over his shoulder. "Where the fuck have you been? Didn't I tell you to keep her safe?"

Yeah, and I didn't fucking like that *he'd* been the one to rush to her rescue. Or that he seemed to think we were some kind of team. But my anger wasn't focused on him right then. Keeping my arm tight around Imani, her back pressed against my front, I glowered at Lazarus. "It was you. You did this to Imani, and you caused this war tonight." Caused the pain and the deaths. "You're Beau Irons."

Lazarus sniffed and flicked his hand, dismissive. "You cannot understand our cause, so I will not bother explaining it to you."

"I understand that you betrayed Imani and used her as a lab rat," I spat. "I understand that she didn't do a single thing to deserve any of what you've done. And I understand that I won't be happy until you're a pile of ashes at my feet."

"A pile of ashes?" echoed Imani, a bloodthirsty smile in her voice. "That sounds awesome." It did.

"Take her through the portal!" Marco told me.

I blinked. "Are you fucking insane?"

"It will take you both to The Hollow. Get her away from here."

Call me strange, but I wasn't going to trust a word that asshole said.

"No, Imani, you must come with us," said Lazarus. "You hold all the answers."

"He thinks I'm half-human and he can use my blood to create a cure," she explained to me. "In other words, he's warped."

I whispered into her ear, "Who created the force-field?"

"Lazarus," she quietly replied.

"We need it down, baby."

"I know, but my gift has been overused tonight."

"You don't need your psychic hand for this."

Lazarus again spoke to Imani. "If you agree to come with us, I will tell my vampires to stand down. We will leave here, and all those left alive can return to The Hollow."

I snickered. He couldn't honestly expect us to believe that. "You want them all dead. You want our whole race dead."

"I want a cure more."

"But not enough to perform any tests on yourself, right?" I needed to keep him talking; to distract him while Imani worked. "You have all these vampires willing to die for you and your cause. But you've never been willing to do that for them."

He held his arms out wide. "Without me alive and leading them, there would be no one to ensure the survival and success of our cause."

Noticing Eleanor, I snarled. "*You* betrayed her too."

She licked her lips, her eyes sad. "I didn't know that Lazarus planned to use her like this."

"I could not tell you, Eleanor, because I could not risk that you would try to stop me," Lazarus told her. "But now that you see it worked, you can understand." He turned back to me. "I knew Imani would survive it."

"You didn't *know* anything," Marco said through gritted teeth. "*You risked her life.*"

Lazarus tilted his head. "You really do care for her, don't you, Marco? I thought so, but I was never entirely sure. You are very manipulative, after all. But I see it now."

Marco's fists clenched. "She's good."

"She is," Lazarus agreed. "She's good through and through. But that did not stop you from taking her human life from her, did it? As I see it, you are in no position to judge me."

"Yeah? Well I…" Trailing off, Marco grimaced. "Your nose is bleeding."

Eleanor stepped forward to take a look. "There's blood coming out of your ears too."

The vein in Lazarus' temple pulsed and more blood flowed from his nose. His gaze darted around before coming to rest on me. "Whatever you are doing, stop!"

"That's not me calling your blood," I told him. "That's Imani. You didn't make her half-human, Lazarus. Not even close."

He shook his head in denial.

"Look at her irises. She didn't partly heal. She just evolved, and her abilities evolved right along with her." I didn't bother explaining it any further—no way would I feed his hungry scientific mind.

Blood trickled out of the corners of his mouth. "Stop, Imani." But she didn't. "Do not make me kill you."

I growled. "As if I'd let that happen. You wouldn't see your lab rat dead anyway—not after all you've done to get this far."

He winced, putting a hand to his head. More blood gushed out of his nose. "Shoot her, but do not shoot to kill," he told his vampires.

"No!" screamed Eleanor. But no one listened. Bullets zoomed our way...and each one crashed into my shield and fell to the ground.

Marco smirked at Lazarus. "Didn't you know that was his gift? Or did you just forget?"

Sneering at him, Lazarus opened his mouth to speak. Instead, he let out a cry of agony as his face reddened and the veins in his head looked close to popping. The force-field flickered.

My heart jumped in my chest. "Keep going, baby."

It flickered again. And again. And again. Then it fell. I smiled.

Four things abruptly happened at once.

I heard vampires crying out as energy balls, lightning bolts, lethal darts, a jaguar, and psychic attacks slammed into them.

Marco lunged at Lazarus, moving too fast for Eleanor or the males flanking the Master Vampire to act.

Marco's vampires launched themselves at Lazarus' group, snatching the guns and crushing the weapons before attacking the group.

Imani's knees buckled a moment before she passed out in my arms.

Cursing, I scooped her up and held her tight as mayhem ensued for a second time that night. She was pale, even for a vampire. And I knew she'd be seriously pissed when she woke up to realise that she'd lost consciousness.

Paige rushed to us and slapped a hand on my shield. "Drop it."

I did. "There's nothing to heal. She just exhausted herself."

Slipping two hands underneath Imani, she said, "I've got her; get to Lazarus before he has someone teleport his ass out of here."

Shaking my head, I tightened my grip on Imani. I badly wanted to get my hands on that motherfucker but... "Lazarus won't be the only one here convinced that she can help create a cure. Others might try to take her."

"They'd have to get through us," announced Ava as she and the rest of her squad—including Maya in her jaguar form—appeared.

At Paige's signal, the females all formed a protective circle around us. "Go, we'll protect her. You're needed over there."

She was right. Only a few vampires were left standing—one of whom could be the teleporter—and Lazarus was slicing at Marco with a glimmering blade that seemed to be sucking the life-force out of him. *Fuck.*

"Listen to me a sec," said Paige. Her next words tumbled out of her in a rush. "I know you want to beat the fuck out of Lazarus but don't make this into a fight. Marco's his vampire, so the moment he kills him their blood-bond will break and Lazarus will be in so much agony he'll be vulnerable. He'll have someone teleport him away before anyone can leap on that vulnerability. Your attack has to be quick and fatal. You'll have sheer milliseconds to make that happen. You're the fastest of all of us; you can do this."

Again, she was right. My grip flexed on Imani. "I'm trusting you with her."

Paige inclined her head. "Go!"

Relinquishing Imani, I turned...just in time to watch Marco drop to his knees, speared by a long spiral blade. He was laughing.

Pulling out the blade, Lazarus huffed at him. "Only you would laugh as you lay on death's door."

Well, the guy didn't feel pain and he was mostly insane, so...

"I did what I came here to do. I saved Imani from you." Marco shot to his feet and blurred to my side.

I instinctively brought up my shield, but what I saw in his eyes told me this wasn't an attack. I lowered the shield, certain I could take the fucker if he was playing me.

"He needs to suffer." Marco slapped something into my hand. "An eye for an eye, right?" Curling my fist around the object, I nodded. He looked at an unconscious Imani. "Take care, sweetheart." His legs failed him again, and he collapsed on his back, but he wasn't yet dead.

"Butch!"

I knew what Paige's warning meant; knew that Lazarus was about to leave before Marco could burst into ashes. Shield back up, I dived at Lazarus and his two vampires, knocking them so hard with my shield that they all toppled over. Then I dropped the shield, bent over Lazarus, and stabbed him in the throat with the object that Marco had given me.

His vampires lunged for me, but I'd already instinctively pulled my shield once again.

I backed away, giving Lazarus the room to stand. It didn't matter now if he teleported away. The damage was done. Marco knew that, which was probably why he was again laughing; the sound was weak now.

Hand to his throat, Lazarus swayed. "What have you done?"

I held up the syringe. "As Marco said, an eye for an eye." And I was cruel enough to carry through with this plan.

A tremor ran through Lazarus. "No," he breathed. Eyes beginning to glaze over, he turned to his vampires. "Kill me. Kill—" A sudden force pulled him backwards at least ten feet…and right into Harvey's waiting arms.

Surrounded by my squad and with Jared at her side, Sam looked at Lazarus in disgust. "Yeah, that's not gonna happen. You're going to suffer exactly the way you deserve. You're going to suffer the way all those other vampires suffered before you. But not in the name of science, in the name of vengeance."

Marco smiled at her. "I might actually like you now." His head slowly turned to face Imani as I took her from Paige and brushed a kiss over her forehead. "You're a lucky bastard, you know," he said, his voice fading fast. "You kept her safe, in the end. Keep doing that." He burst into ashes.

Lazarus instantly doubled over in pain, which made grim satisfaction settle deep in my gut. If that made me sick, whatever. He'd hurt Imani, he'd started this war, and he was the cause of too many deaths. He'd had this coming for a long time.

"She all right?" Sam asked me, though her eyes were on Imani.

I nodded. "Calling Lazarus' blood when she was already tired sapped her of what energy she had left." But she'd done it, confident that I wouldn't let anything happen to her while she was vulnerable.

"So we have Imani to thank for the force-field falling?" asked Jared.

Again, I nodded. "Battle over?"

Sam took a cleansing breath. "Battle's over, The Order's no longer an issue, Lazarus is in custody…and I seriously want Imani's ability to call blood."

Jared rolled his eyes. "Does that surprise anyone here?"

Everyone shook their heads, smiling. Sam just snorted.

CHAPTER TWENTY

(Butch)

One hand braced against the tiled wall, I fisted the other in Imani's hair as she sucked my cock like it was covered in cream or something. She knew exactly how to use her tongue, knew exactly what I liked and how I liked it. And she gave it to me every time.

The hot spray of the shower pounded on my skin as she hummed and moaned around me, bobbing her head up and down while raking her nails down the backs of my thighs. And when she swallowed around my cock, taking me even deeper, I felt my balls tighten. "Stop."

She did, smiling as I pulled out of her mouth. She looked damn pleased with herself.

"Up." I helped her stand, hoisted her up, and pressed her against the wall. She locked her legs around my waist, arching into me. "Ready?" I knew the answer to that, because I could smell how ready she was; knew that if I slid my finger between her folds, I'd find her dripping wet.

At her nod, I dropped her hard on my cock. She gasped, head falling back against the wall as her slick muscles squeezed me so hard I was surprised I didn't see spots. She was so tight it should have hurt, so hot it should have burned. But nothing felt better than being balls-deep in Imani.

"Eyes," I growled. They opened as I pinned her hands above her head, wanting to look at the Binding knot on her third finger while I fucked in and out of her. It was something I often did. "Don't make a sound until I say you can." Not because I didn't love hearing her little moans and gasps, but because having no outlet always made her wind tighter.

Her eyes narrowed, even though I knew she loved the challenge. "Just fuck me already."

I pulled back and thrust hard, shoving my cock as deep inside her as it could go; groaning as her body pulsed and contracted around me. Her mouth fell open, but she didn't make a sound. "Good girl." I hammered in and out of her, brutal. Relentless. Giving no reprieve. Taking everything. "Made for me." She was. No one would ever make me think differently. I craved her, needed her; I knew I always would.

Tilting her hips a little, I thrust harder. She inhaled sharply. I shook my head. "Not a sound." Eyes blazing with frustration, she tightened her muscles around me. If that was supposed to be some kind of punishment, it didn't work. "Do that again." She did.

Growling against her mouth, I gave her lower lip a sharp nip, sipping at the few drops of blood that seeped to the surface. "Did you know that I get hard every time I look at that knot on your finger? It says you're mine, you belong to me. You always did, Imani. Always did." I gripped her hip with one hand, slamming her down on my cock each time I thrust upwards. "Let me hear you."

A loud moan tore out of her throat. "I'm gonna come."

"I know. I can feel you getting tighter and hotter." Her dazed eyes flicked to my throat. "You thirsty, baby? Give me what I want, and then you can feed from me." I slid a hand between us and found her clit with my thumb. "Say it. Baby, *say it*."

"I love you," she breathed.

"Good girl. Take what you need." Groaning as her teeth sank down hard, I thrust deeper and faster. Her body clamped around my cock, contracting and milking me and taking me over the edge. I exploded with a growled, "Love you, baby."

Shaking and panting against my mouth, she smiled. "I like feeling you come through our bond."

"Same here." I kissed her hard, deep, taking her taste inside me. Since Binding a month ago, I'd become more possessive and protective than before—something neither of us would have thought possible. Surprisingly, it didn't wear on her and she didn't give me shit over it. In fact, she mostly just smiled about it. She got me, and she let me be. Until I pushed too hard, of course, which was really only fair.

"What does the bond feel like? I've felt you run your psychic fingers over it."

"It hums with some kind of energy. Feels light and crisp, but also very strong." Her hands lightly pressed to my face. "Let me just say that you never have to worry I'll ever pluck on it like a banjo string. I'd never use our bond to hurt you."

"I know. Just like I know you'd never sever it."

(Imani)

I smiled. Deep down, I'd worried that he wasn't fully secure in our mating for the reason that I was able to cut the bond. After all, his past had left him believing that people didn't stick around for long. I was concerned that worries would always lurk deep inside him, even when it made no sense. "Never," I confirmed.

Our Binding ceremony had been a huge celebration during which his squad played pranks and my squad got so shit-faced there was another catfight. Sam joined the fight this time, to Jared's utter dismay.

Dean, aka The Prick, had left The Hollow a few weeks before the ceremony, which Butch had decided to view as a Binding gift from Dean to us. It would have been nice if Butch's exes had left with him, but my luck didn't stretch that far. To be fair, though, Jen's warning appeared to have made a difference, because it had been a while since his ex-one-nightstands had tried flirting with him.

In addition to the Binding, a lot had happened since the battle. Firstly, each and every member of The Order had been totally destroyed, including Marvin who Sam and Jared executed via V-Tube as an example to our kind that leaking information was an extremely bad idea. Considering his death hadn't been quick or easy, I was assuming the message was clearly received.

Lazarus, too, had suffered an agonising death. He hadn't even gotten halfway through the transition before he'd started to weaken and age dramatically while going pretty much out of his mind. Not that I'd seen any of this for myself. But Butch had visited him several times and found a dark joy in watching him suffer the way I had suffered. In fact, my squad—including Keeley, who had recently joined—had also paid the bastard the occasional visit.

Annalise, who claimed she had no idea that her brother led The Order, was devastated by his death and also by the discovery that he was responsible for what happened to me. She had taken over from Lazarus as the leader of the nest and destroyed his lab. She'd also gotten the codes for The Order's compound so that we could get inside the place without setting off any bombs. The place had long since been reduced to a pile of rubble.

It had been weird to hear that Marco had died in his efforts to save me from Lazarus. Butch, being seriously possessive, had worried that I'd be sad about my Sire's death. On the contrary, I'd found some kind of closure in it, though I was confused by his self-sacrifice. I had to wonder if he'd gotten tired of this life and saw that as a way to go out with a bang—a way that might also redeem him for taking my human life.

Butch agreed but, in his opinion, nothing would make up for that, just as nothing would excuse what Lazarus had done. There had been a lot of casualties from the battle, and a ceremony had been held to commemorate the members of the legion who had all died doing what they loved. If it wasn't for Paige, there would have been many more deaths.

Sam had wondered if dragon shifters might, given their general dislike of vampires, use the deaths of all the mercenaries as an excuse to start a war between the species. Andres had assured us, however, that there would be no retaliation. So far, there hadn't been.

In fact, things were once again pretty quiet. But no one was complaining about it this time, not wanting to tempt fate. Our training sessions were the only action we got. During those sessions, my strength and speed had improved to the extent that they were very close to what they had been prior to the transition. My fangs had seemingly gone for good though, along with the amber tint to my irises.

Slipping out of me, Butch set me on my feet and tapped my ass. "If you're still going to the movie night thing, you better hurry."

"Why do you always call them movie night *things*?"

"Because they're not really movie nights." He turned off the spray, stepped out of the stall and grabbed us both a towel. "They're just an excuse for all you girls to get together and get smashed with Fletcher and Norm."

I wrapped a towel around me. "That's so not true."

"And you're such a shit liar. Tell me there'll be no drinking."

"There'll be a *little* drinking." I'd learned that I could still get drunk providing I fed from an inebriated vampire, which was usually Paige.

"We both know that you'll get shitfaced and I'll end up having to come for you."

I huffed. "You're wrong."

(Butch)

For some reason, whenever I found the girls drunk, it was almost always the same: they'd all kicked their heels off, they were all convinced they weren't drunk, and they were all acting weird.

One would be dancing on her own, one would be eating, one would be asleep, one would be laughing for the sake of laughing, one would be cursing her ex, one would be crying about nothing while others comforted her, and one would be sprawled on the floor, singing to herself totally off-key.

Tonight was no exception.

Salem and Chico appeared at Fletcher's apartment just as I arrived. A singing Ava was so plastered that her mate had to carry her home by a fistful of her shirt. Chico just threw a struggling Jude over his shoulder while she threatened him with dismemberment.

Lifting my chin at Fletcher and Norm, who were snuggling on the sofa, I crouched beside Imani. How she'd fallen asleep on the coffee table, I didn't know, but my girl could sleep anywhere. "Wake up, baby." Taking her hand, I traced her Binding knot. "Come on, open those pretty eyes for me."

Her lids slowly flickered open, and she gave me a dazzling smile that hit me right in the chest. "Hey, whatcha doin' here?"

"Why do you think I'm here, baby? I've come to get you." Just like I'd known I'd have to. She was lucky she was cute when she was hammered.

"Wanna know a secret?" She lowered her voice. "I like that you call me 'baby.'"

I smiled. "Yeah?"

"Totally yeah."

"Good. Ready to come home?"

She pouted. "S'early."

It was actually *way* past dawn. "Time to go." I scooped her up. "Say goodnight to everyone." She did, though she was still pouting. I carried her home in vampire speed, lay her on the bed, and gently began to strip her.

Without even opening her eyes, she said, "Dude, you're seriously hot. You know that, right?"

I chuckled. "You might have said it once or twice before."

Her eyes fluttered open. "You make me happy. You know that too, right? Like, super-duper happy."

I had to smile. "Yeah, I know." I still had no idea how I was doing it, though. "And you make me happy, so all is good." I pulled the covers over her. "You need sleep."

"But the night is young." Her nose wrinkled. "I'm hungry. Let's make beef noodles."

I might have said yes if she wasn't half-asleep. "Okay, baby, I'll do that."

"You're the shit, Richardson. *The shit.*" Then she passed out. She was gonna have a bitch of a headache at dusk. "It's a good thing I love you, Imani Prince. More than anything."

EPILOGUE

(Jared)

Keeping my arm tight around a swaying Sam to support her weight as we neared our home, I said, "Maybe you should pass on movie night things in future." It was always the same: she got smashed, lost track of time—or simply didn't give a shit what time it was—and I was forced to go find her.

Her aquamarine eyes narrowed and cut to me. "They're not movie night *things*."

"Well they're not movie nights." They were excuses to get blind drunk without mates and boyfriends hovering around. "Our squad agrees."

She almost tripped over nothing. Quickly righting herself, the picture of dignity, she cleared her throat. "I'm all right."

I sighed. When I'd reached Fletcher's apartment and saw the drunken state she was in, I'd offered to carry her but she'd point blank refused. This wasn't an uncommon occurrence. She was as stubborn when she was hammered as she was when she was sober. "Let me just carry you, it'll be easier."

She straightened, affronted. "I got this." But she didn't have it at all.

I sighed again. "You're going to fall, and it'll be your own fault for drinking alcohol like it's going out of fashion."

"I'm not rat-arsed. Just a bit on the tipsy side."

I snorted. "Sure, baby."

She stumbled again. Throwing out one arm, she declared, "Seriously, I'm all right."

It would be annoying if it wasn't so amusing. I guided her up the wooden steps to the wrap around porch of our beach house. "Let's just get you inside." I'd planned to put her to bed and strip her, but she shed her clothes one item at a time as she unsteadily made her way to the bedroom.

Sinking into the mattress, totally and deliciously naked, she lifted a brow. "You're not naked. Why are you not naked?"

Slipping off my jacket, I took a moment to drink her in. I knew every inch of that body, knew every sensitive zone and every ticklish spot. Sam might say she wasn't ticklish, but she was talking shit. The truth was that she just didn't relax and let her guard down that much for many people.

She examined her Binding knot. "Have you noticed how often Butch traces Imani's knot, as if reminding himself that it's there? It's sort of sweet. I didn't think he had it in him."

I smiled down at her. "You're taking credit for him going after Imani, aren't you?"

She blinked, the image of innocence even when she was decadently spread out before me. "Why would I do that?"

"Maybe because you urged Marla to proposition him the night Imani split up with Dean." My tone dared her to deny it.

She exhaled heavily. "I wanted him to see just how much it was *Imani* that he wanted. And it worked, didn't it? He did us all proud and bucked the fuck up."

I crawled on the bed, leaning over her and bracing my hands either side of her head. "It was nice of Dean to leave The Hollow. Or, should I say, it was nice of you to kick him out."

She slid her hands under my shirt and up my chest. "I didn't kick him out. I just strongly suggested that he bugger off and let them live their lives in peace."

"Just like you strongly suggested after he cheated on Imani that he shouldn't try to win her back."

"Well—"

"And just like you strongly suggested to every single one of Butch's exes that they back off."

She huffed. "I want to secure the happiness of my squad members. Is that so bloody awful?"

"Not awful." Smiling, I kissed her. "Your matchmaking skills failed with Paige and Stuart."

She frowned, appearing offended. "I had no hand in them getting together. I wasn't surprised when it went wrong; they don't suit each other at all. Paige needs someone a lot different than him."

I arched a brow. "And I suppose you know exactly who she needs, don't you?"

"As it happens, yeah."

"And I suppose you're going to meddle, aren't you?"

"Well it's fun and it works."

Giving her my weight, I nipped her lip. "I can think of a better kind of fun."

Her eyes gleamed. "Yeah? Do tell."

"It involves your legs hooked over my shoulders, my cock deep inside you, and my teeth in your skin."

She pursed her lips. "The plan has potential. Is there more?"

"A lot more." I licked at her throat. "I like sex with Drunk Sam. Drunk Sam lets me do things that Sober Sam refuses to believe ever happened." Things that always made her blush the next evening. Not a lot made my mate blush.

"Then maybe you should hurry and take advantage of Drunk Sam."

"Maybe I should." I kissed her hard, deep, long. Taking my time, eating at her mouth the same way I intended to eat other parts of her. She could still, even after years of being mated, get me hard with just a look. She never ceased to surprise me. She kept me on my toes. And she still meant more to me than anything else. The woman fucking owned me. But since she belonged to me just as much as I belonged to her, I was good with that. "Love you, baby."

"And I love you. But you're not naked. This is a problem."

I chuckled. "I'll rectify that, shall I? Then I can get inside you and make you scream for me."

She rolled her eyes. "Must we always have this conversation? I don't scream."

Oh, she did. And she was loud. "I'll enjoy proving you wrong and making you scream my name." I always did.

"You're still not naked!"

"I'm shy."

She growled, "Pain in my arse."

"By dawn, that's exactly what you'll have after I'm done with you." A pause. "Just don't tell Sober Sam about it."

I laughed. "I really fucking love you." Then I set about making her scream.

FRACTURED

ACKNOWLEDGMENTS

I need to say a massive thank you to my family for just being them. They're amazing people and always so supportive. I honestly couldn't do it without them.

Also, huge thanks to my Beta reader, Andrea Ashby – she's a total rock star and I loved her.

Last but definitely not last, a big thank you to all my readers. Every one of you is absolutely awesome. It's great to be able to say that I have the best fan base *ever*.

If for any reason you would like to contact me, whether it's about the book or you're considering self-publishing and have any questions, please feel free to e-mail me at suzanne_e_wright@live.co.uk.

Take care,

Suzanne Wright

TITLES BY SUZANNE WRIGHT

The Deep in Your Veins Series

Here Be Sexist Vampires
The Bite That Binds
Taste of Torment
Consumed
Fractured

The Phoenix Pack Series

Feral Sins
Wicked Cravings
Carnal Secrets
Dark Instincts
Savage Urges

The Mercury Pack Series
Spiral of Need
Force of Temptation (coming soon)

The Dark in You Series
Burn
Blaze (coming soon)

Standalones
From Rags

SUZANNE WRIGHT

ABOUT THE AUTHOR

Suzanne Wright lives in England with her husband and her two children. When she's not spending time with her family, she's writing, reading, or doing her version of housework – sweeping the house with a look.

Website: www.suzannewright.co.uk
Blog: www.suzannewrightsblog.blogspot.co.uk
Twitter: twitter.com/suz_wright
Facebook: www.facebook.com/suzannewrightfanpage

Printed in Great Britain
by Amazon